T.A.G. HUNGERFORD'S PREVIOUS WORKS

Novels
The Ridge And The River
Sowers Of The Wind
Riverslake
Shake The Golden Bough

Short Stories
Wong Chu And The Queen's Letterbox
Stories From Suburban Road
Knockabout With A Slouch hat
Red Rover All Over

Travel
A Million Square (with Richard Woldendorp)
Fremantle, Landscapes And People (with Roger Garwood)

Anthologies
Australia Writes (editor, short stories)
Australian Signpost (editor)

Children's Book
Swagbelly Birdsnatcher And The Prince Of Siam

Stage Play
The Day It All Ended

Radio Plays
Help Me Cut Up A Cat
Looking After Bert

Hungerford

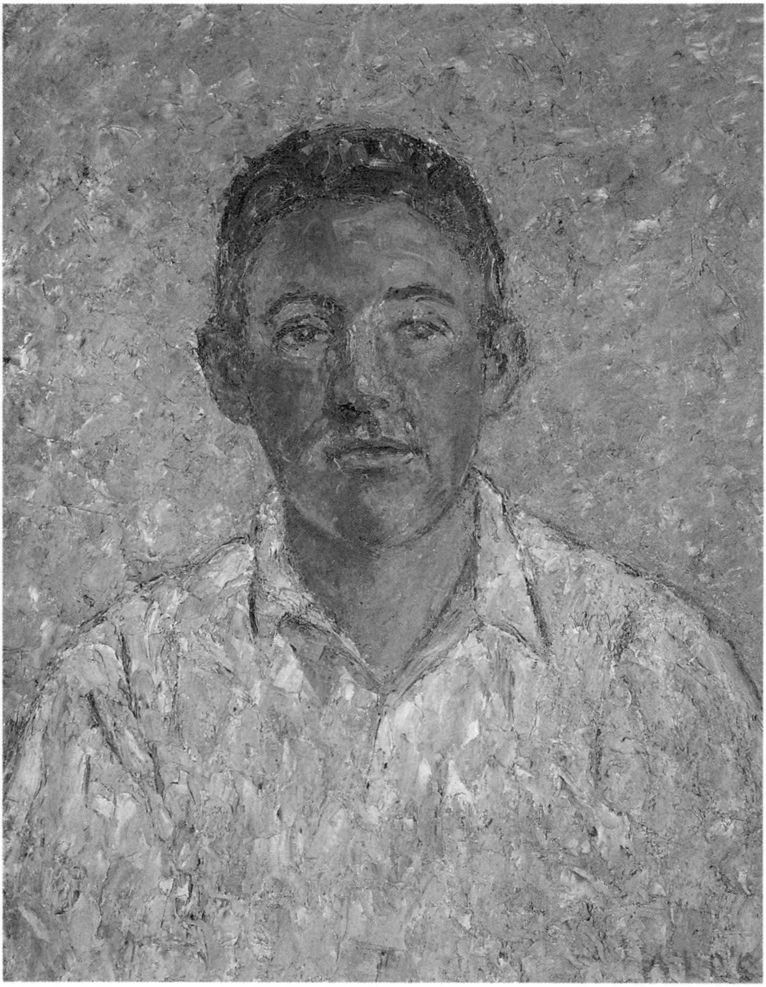

Kathleen O'Connor 1876?-1968 *Portrait of Tom Hungerford.*
oil on wood panel 69 x 54.8 cm.
National Library of Australia.

Hungerford

SHORT FICTION BY T.A.G. HUNGERFORD
SELECTED AND INTRODUCED BY PETER COWAN

FREMANTLE ARTS CENTRE PRESS

First published 1989 by
FREMANTLE ARTS CENTRE PRESS
1 Finnerty Street (PO Box 891), Fremantle
Western Australia 6160.

Designed by Jenny Longbon and John Douglass.
Production Manager Helen Idle.

Typeset in 10½/11½ pt Century by Caxtons, Perth, Western Australia, and printed on 90 gsm Bookprint Ultra White by Lamb Printers, Perth, Western Australia.

National Library of Australia
Cataloguing-in-publication data

Hungerford, T.A.G. (Thomas Arthur Guy), 1915 - .
Hungerford: select stories of T.A.G. Hungerford.

ISBN 0 949206 50 4.

I. Cowan, Peter, 1914 - . II Title.

A823'.3

CONTENTS

Introduction *by Peter Cowan* 1

Visit To The Lutts 13
The Wedding 17
- And Gertie Dances In The Moonlight 22
Lesson By Firelight 27
Happy Summer Days 32
'Going Back', Say The Wheels 40
The Woomera 47
It Always Takes Two 57
The Letter 66
Last Entry In Red 80
The Willow Of Bream Creek 90
The National Game 104
The Only One Who Forgot 122
Sowers Of The Wind *(Extract)* 135
The Magnolia Tree 144
Looking After Bert 152
Wong Chu And The Queen's Letterbox 168
No More Than You Can Afford 175
The Old Waterfront, Macau 198
Green Grown The Rushes 202
O, Moon Of Mullamulla 221
Balcony Of Dreams 245

ACKNOWLEDGEMENTS

The creative writing programme of Fremantle Arts Centre Press is assisted by the Australian Council, the Australian Government's arts funding and advisory body.

Fremantle Arts Centre Press receives financial assistance from the Western Australian Department for the Arts.

Acknowledgement is due to the following publications and publishers for first publication of the stories included in this selection: Angus and Robertson - *Sowers Of The Wind*, 1954; *As You Were* (Australian War Memorial) - 'Last Entry In Red', 1950, 'The Letter', 1949; The *Bulletin* - '- And Gertie Dances In The Moonlight', 1943, '"Going Back", Say The Wheels, 1944, 'Happy Summer Days', 1944, 'It Always Takes Two', 1945, 'Lesson By Firelight', 1944, 'The National Game', 1951, 'The Wedding', 1942, 'The Willow Of Bream Creek', 1950, 'The Woomera', 1944, 'Visit To The Lutts', 1942; *Meanjin* - 'The Magnolia Tree', 1956; *New Country* (edited by Bruce Bennett, Fremantle Arts Centre Press) - 'O, Moon Of Mullamulla', 1976; *Portrait* (edited by B.R. Coffey and Wendy Jenkins, Fremantle Arts Centre Press) - 'Balcony Of Dreams', 1986; *Southerly* - 'The Only One Who Forgot', 1951; *Westerly* - 'Green Grow The Rushes', 1976, 'Looking After Bert', published under the title 'The Budgerigar', 1965, 'No More Than You Can Afford', 1971, 'The Old Waterfront, Macau', 1972, 'Wong Chu And The Queen's Letterbox', 1968.

INTRODUCTION

T.A.G. Hungerford has been writing since the nineteen-forties, perhaps a long time for any writer, but in Australia an achievement in itself. He has combined his writing with a varied career — journalism, work in government publicity and information, travelling, a period in the Army and Occupation Force in Japan. If writing had provided any real standard of living in Australia in the early years of his career, Hungerford might have chosen no other work. It may be ironic that his writing has been enriched by, indeed found its basis in those other occupations.

A comparison of T.A.G. Hungerford and Seaforth Mackenzie may appear more tempting than realistic. Yet there are at least similarities. Both were born in Western Australia, and did a good deal of their writing in times that were difficult and restrictive for writers in Australia — in Mackenzie's case all his work was done under such conditions. Both wrote four novels, and for considerable periods were working and writing outside the State. Hungerford is continuing with this form, but his published novels are not concerned with Western Australia, and Mackenzie's last two novels, and his most mature, were not to do with his home State. Both used autobiographical material freely and successfully. Each produced an outstanding novel of Australia's concern with the Second World War, arguably the best two Australian novels to reflect that conflict. Both turned to the then oddly neglected issue of the opening of Australia to refugees at the time of the war and the immediate period afterwards, and produced outstanding novels from this beginning of change for Australia. Both were writers with a fondness for words which produced at its best rich and evocative description — and both could at times be entangled in this very richness. It might be argued both were essentially novelists, less at ease with the short story. Mackenzie confessed he found the short story form difficult, though he would have liked to pursue it. His love of description of place, of personality, of motive, belonged to the novel, he was never able to give his material the significant compression and emphasis demanded by the short story.

Hungerford in his introduction to his first collection of short stories, *Wong Chu And The Queen's Letterbox* (1977), long after he began writing, expressed his belief 'that of all the different forms of creative writing, they (short stories) are the most demanding, the most engrossing, the most rewarding and the most difficult to bring off properly'. Unlike Mackenzie he pursued the short story to achieve his own command of the form.

T.A.G. Hungerford noted that he began writing stories at about eight years of age, and that 'off and on' he has been writing them ever since. His first published stories appear to have been in the *Bulletin* in early 1942. By this time he was in the army, though his first stories give no indication of this. 'Visit to the Lutts', in March 1942, began 'Things were different in those days ...' and developed the narrator's remembrance of boyhood, and of an earlier time, a time and place closely described. 'The Wedding', which followed in the same year, was concerned with the same background, and some of the same people, with, it would seem, the same narrator — 'I was only little then, but I remember it like it was only yesterday ... If I close my eyes I can see every smallest detail'.

The stories were not concerned with the narrator as a man, or as in some way marked by that past, but with memories of childhood, a childhood where if there were shadows they were hardly seen, fused into time, a time the narrator has been reluctant to leave; indeed in strong nostalgic memory has never left, never forgotten. The writer is not concerned with the narrator of the present time, a figure almost of shadow, his concern lies with a realistic and meticulous capturing of place and people — people as they seemed to the child.

This kind of story was not uncommon in Australian fiction and was to develop its detractors who claimed it as offering a romantic view, a falsification, or simplification. In some hands that was true enough, but it was not an objection to deter Hungerford from persisting with certain aspects of this kind of writing. In fact, of course, such a concern for the past could be realistic, remembrance obviously a selective process, and what was unpleasant or ugly ignored or softened. Hungerford was to write a good deal about the past, much of it the past of his own youth and childhood, and was to remain strongly affected by an earlier time and place. Some of his stories are reminiscent of a kind of world described by Mark Twain, yet without the shadows that lay about Huckleberry Finn, and the Swan River was not the Mississippi. Nor was his a representation of the world of the younger person of the early Hemingway stories, haunted by experience of adult life glimpsed too soon. 'It was always summer' in the early world seen by Hungerford. Harshness, killing, and death were to be factors of his later writing of adulthood, but they had diminished place, or no place at all, in this earlier time. In July 1943, again in the *Bulletin*, Hungerford's story ' — And Gertie Dances In The Moonlight' sees a shift in time to the present and in background to the north, to country just out of Darwin, to men in the army. The setting of the country is detailed, but with less description of landscape and people, more concern for the men and their present movement. It is a movement which in fact does not lead anywhere, movement from place to place in a land they do not actually, or lastingly, touch. The story is in one sense a factual account of army life, in another, and essentially, a questioning, a doubt about 'things' undefined; about perhaps real purpose. It does not specifically question what they are doing, or war, or what men have done in a past that stretches even beyond this deserted and seemingly untouched land. Hungerford's narrator, seen as an adult in the present, does not look back to the past, or to childhood, but perhaps sums up his musing in the comment 'we forget so easily'. Forget because there seems no focus for memory — such as indeed the past might provide — and this land where they find themselves seems so indifferent and beyond time.

'Lesson By Firelight', a year later, holds the same echoes and preoccupations. It has the same setting and again an adult narrator, but one less isolated in his telling of the story, part of a group. Briefly, as he listens to the discussion with an Aborigine about the Aboriginal names for the things about them, he reflects on the school teacher who 'taught me another language years ago'. This would seem a factual reference, since Hungerford has referred to a teacher who gave him his first interest in and love of words. He was perhaps lucky in this, in an era when teaching was as likely to produce an indifference or plain aversion to books and language. But the story does not revert to the past, and again there is the sense of the men dwarfed by the land, in some sense isolated, perhaps by the very transcience of their daily tasks and movement. In the end the narrator thinks back to the known, to Sydney, 'light and music, noise and a girl to dance with', to set against this unknown landscape.

'"Going Back", Say the Wheels', in 1944, suggests again the sense of transience, the meeting and parting, of wartime, and the fact that it was not only in war 'the circle of security' was very small, outside it always 'pain and death'. Like most of the war stories there appeared here to be a strong element of personal experience, confirmed in Hungerford's use of the same title, and the same incident, in his book *A Knockabout With A Slouch Hat*, more than forty years later, where the story is changed from its original form to personal narration.

These stories had been relatively short, but with 'Happy Summer Days', in 1944, Hungerford begins to develop a longer form, which he was to prefer, and which the *Bulletin* was obviously willing to accomodate. The setting of the men isolated in army life remains, but the story uses a different, more obvious, focus on the past. Here there is no first person narrator, but a character, Brook, who becomes aware of a long distant past when looking at the inscription in a book sent to the men as one of a batch for recreation. The main portion of the story concerns the people conjured up in Brook's imagination by the inscription, the present time with which the story briefly opens and closes is a frame for this longer, distant story. Yet in the end Brook is aware of his own past, 'his childhood had come flooding over him, calm and serene; and now, of all things, tears burned in his eyes'. As in the first two stories, the writer recreates an earlier time, a small town in a past era. There is the world of the child, and the adult, again an adult world not understood by the children. The story has deeper echoes, though the frame perhaps obtrudes and has to be accepted.

The longer form became characteristic of Hungerford's use of the short story, enabling a greater use of description and narrative, sometimes perhaps over-indulgent, but which is so often saved by an awareness and sensitivity that lifts the story beyond narrative, or merely descriptive writing, however evocative. Where these combine his stories achieve their greatest power and effect.

The stories that follow in the *Bulletin* explore many of the earlier devices, but develop them. 'The Woomera' takes the interest and awareness of the Aborigine seen in previous stories to an expression of concern, and at times anger, at what is happening to the Aborigines, in this story focussed on a young boy at an army camp hospital where there are Aboriginal patients because there were 'no civilian hospitals for hundreds of miles'. But where there were missions, 'people who had stripped the boy of his code and given him in return something half understood and a troubled memory of something his people had believed in since time began ...'. The lack of understanding rather than any racial ill will is clearly shown. *Capricornia* had been published in 1938, *The Timeless Land* in 1941, but it could hardly be said that consideration of the position of the Aborigine, let alone an attempt at understanding, was a feature of Australian writing of the period. In this, and a story like the later 'The Only One Who Forgot', one of his best stories, Hungerford's strong independence and sensitivity is clear. His clarity of view was not to be affected by time or fashion, as the much later 'O Moon Of Mullamulla', returning to another aspect of the same theme, shows with some irony.

The actuality of war, the fighting and killing, found its way into only one of these early stories. The character depicted in 'It Always Takes Two', in 1945, was a man who had seen much combat. 'Death, or fate, whichever you preferred to call it, had chased him halfway round the world, from the Middle East to New Guinea; but now he knew that it was he who did all the chasing, and that fate just sat in its pre-destined place and waited for him to come'. Now, in the hills beyond, in this place in which he finds himself, he feels the confrontation will come. He thinks, not with hate, or the propoganda of war, of another man, 'his opposite number', not known, or properly understood, waiting, somewhere in these hills, like himself caught up in something beyond him.

The story suggests the later novel T.A.G. Hungerford was to write, *The Ridge And The River*. And it suggests something of the classic theme of the Western, in fiction or film, a theme to occur in other of Hungerford's stories whether of war or civilian life, as for instance 'The Remora', the individual caught in a situation he can no longer control, a struggle to survive, to be better than the next man in some test of combat — war, gunfighting, fistfighting — and a welcome of the time when in inevitable defeat he has no longer to contend, it is all passed on to another who sees himself as victor, but takes in turn the burden of challenge and survival. 'It Always Takes Two' carries also the sense that has haunted some of the other stories, that though in this case the man is saved by one of his companions, nothing has changed, and life or death, 'people would soon forget, and in the long run it wouldn't make much difference to the course of history'.

'The Willow Of Bream Creek', published exactly five years later, in February 1950, is a sudden return to the manner and theme of the first two *Bulletin* stories. It is something of a surprise, as if the concerns of the other stories and their development had been discarded. Indeed it has the flavour of a nineties story, a form fostered by the *Bulletin* before the turn of the century, and in which the magazine had never lost interest. A long story, with a great deal of circumstantial detail, it uses the pattern of some of the earlier stories, a narrator becoming aware of the darker undertones of an adult world, but perhaps the very accumulation of detail lessens the impact of the awareness, and the reader is left only with the suggestion that youth is not simply an idyll.

During this period after the war Hungerford had been with the occupation forces in Japan, and on leaving the army he did not immediately return to live in Western Australia, staying for a time in Sydney. In 1948 he contributed to the Australian War Memorial publication *As You Were*, the successor to *Stand Easy* of 1945, a collection of stories, articles, and illustrations from the different areas of war, and published yearly. Some of the contributors were to become established writers, E.V. Timms, Jon Cleary, Ion Idriess, Tom Ronan, though perhaps the illustrators were better known, some as official war artists, and some were to become notable, Ivor Hele, William Dargie, Roy Hodgkinson, Frank Norton, Donald Friend, and Sali Herman. Hungerford contributed to the 1948 issue two stories, 'Splash of Scarlet', and 'The Best Boxer', and two short pieces, using his own name, and the pseudonym 'T.A. Guy'. The stories were of incidents of war in the islands, like those earlier in the *Bulletin*.

In 1949 he became responsible for the literary editorship of that year's issue, and contributed another story of the war, 'The Letter'. The following year Hungerford left the War Memorial and literary editorship reverted to Raymond O'Malley, responsible for the earlier numbers. Hungerford contributed two stories, 'To The Beach At Dawn', and 'Last Entry In Red'.

These stories tend to form two patterns, one in which the idea is discussed and explained, rounded off by explanation, very much in the tradition of the narrative story, or yarn, the other in which the story is shaped to its own conclusion, making its own point.

Of the first kind, the writer expressed some of the problems of this type of narrative in concluding his story 'The Nuns' Patrol', in *Coast To Coast* 1961-62, when his narrator remarks 'It doesn't seem much of a story, told baldly like that'. Hence the telling may be helped out by considerable description, or explanation. But the style is straightforward, laconic, factual, with an edge of humour that restrains sentimentality or forcing the point of the narrative. That this succeeds better in some instances than others shows in a comparison of 'To The Beach At Dawn', with its control and restraint, and 'The Nuns' Patrol'. Both could be seen with examples of the second type in 'The Letter' or 'Last Entry In Red'.

It seems that in these stories Hungerford was working with the material he was to use, and was probably already using, in his novels *The Ridge And The River* and *Sowers Of The Wind*. The stories do not shirk the harshness of war, the fighting is brutal, factual, non-human, but never used gratuitously, or for sensationalism. In some of the stories the enemy is seen as a fellow human being, caught in the same circumstances, in others as no more than a cypher, to be destroyed. But there is also the kind of compassion, the clear sightedness, an ability to see situations as they were, that made the novels notable. 'The Letter', and perhaps more particularly 'Last Entry In Red', similar in theme, give another dimension, an awareness of the point of view of an 'enemy'. 'Last Entry In Red' is an admission that in some things there is no difference between sides, nations, individuals. And ironic, with a note never far from the earlier *Bulletin* stories, that there may be no real winners to this kind of conflict. In 'Last Entry In Red' the last survivors are the green ants.

Turning to the novel at this time was for Hungerford something his stories had always suggested. It was true that publishers were not enthusiastic about the publication of short stories in book form, and few magazines devoted to short stories survived, but in Hungerford's case his interest in the novel was a natural development from his stories, offering the greater space and freedom his style and themes demanded.

The work that followed was a clear demonstration of this. In 1949 *Sowers Of The Wind*, the novel he had been working on, won the *Sydney Morning Herald* Literary Competition. It was a powerful and realistic account of the occupation forces in Japan. But the book did not find a publisher until 1954. Given the repressive climate of the fifties in Australia it was not surprising the publishers asked for something 'less objectionable'. The *Angry Penguins* trial of the mid-forties, and that of Robert Close later, on charges of 'indecent' publication, were warnings publishers were willing to heed. The trial of Frank Hardy for libel in the publication of *Power Without Glory* in 1951 added to the warnings and difficulties for writers and publishers. Almost any contemporary writing seemed threatened. *Sowers Of The Wind* might have appeared to contain material much franker than anything in Close's *Love Me Sailor*, but it was possible Hungerford's clear view in his depiction of the occupation forces, his outspokenness, were seen by publishers as, if not counter to general opinion of the time, at least likely to be viewed with little favour. They would hardly have been seen as desirable by officialdom. Nor, apparently, were they much appreciated by the newspaper sponsoring the competition. Rather ironically, the 1948 issue of *As You Were* published an article on the occupation which contained the statement: 'Following the charges of immorality and black-marketing made against the troops in Japan an investigation was made by an impartial body which found no evidence to support the allegations'. It may be significant that while Hungerford's later novel of the war in the islands has gone into many reprints, *Sowers Of The Wind*, at least as good a novel, has not.

In 1950 Hungerford, with his novel dealing with a different aspect of the war, *The Ridge And The River*, again won the *Sydney Morning Herald* prize, and this time found a book acceptable to publishers. It appeared in 1952.

In the previous year, January 1951, the *Bulletin* published the long story 'The National Game', an account of migrants and the migrant camp that was to feature in *Riverslake*, his novel published in 1953. Like *Sowers Of The Wind*, *Riverslake* was honest in its depiction, indeed a revelation of conditions in a migrant camp which at that time most Australians hardly knew existed. Perhaps the success of *The Ridge And The River* had softened the publishers' fears, or perhaps the topic was not one officialdom wanted dragged too plainly into public view through a publishing controversy. 'The National Game' has some variations from the same incident that appears in *Riverslake*. Hungerford may have modified it from the already written novel, or incorporated it into the novel.

A number of extracts from *The Ridge And The River* were to appear as short stories in different publications, and the novel's more episodic structure enabled this to be done successfully. *Sowers Of The Wind* did not lend itself to the same use. Certainly it is more difficult to extract, and some of the most effective portions are perhaps too long for separate publication. Chapter Four is an illustration of the style and tone of the novel, which might be felt to be Hungerford's best novel, though an extract does not give the compassion, the growing sense of understanding and despair of the central character, who finally must leave a country and people that are to remain strange to him.

Ironically, Seaforth Mackenzie's novel of the war was centred on the then unknown prisoner-of-war camp at Cowra. The novel was published in England in 1951 by the publisher of his earlier novels without objection. But the book was banned from publication or distribution in Australia. Mackenzie's *Dead Men Rising* may not have been as 'objectionable' to public opinion in Australia as *Sowers Of The Wind*, but it was more objectionable to official pride, and the restriction appeared to be mainly because of supposed identification of the principal figures. Oddly enough, the same might surely have been said of Hungerford's book, and might have weighed with the publishers. And there was considerable irony in the fact that *As You Were* had published in 1946 an account of the breakout at Cowra notable for its vindictiveness and lack of understanding, something neither Hungerford nor Mackenzie had displayed. The article concluded with the comment of the Minister of the Army: 'It appears to me that a difficult and delicate situation has been very well handled by the Military Authorities, and I desire to record my appreciation'. To which the writer, E.V. Timms, added: 'A tribute that all ranks of the 22nd Australian Garrison Battalion well deserved'. It was not strange that so much effort was made to keep *Dead Men Rising* out of Australia, or that there were doubts about the publication of *Sowers Of The Wind*.

Hungerford had written three important novels in a relatively short time. But writing novels in that period was unlikely to provide Australian authors with a living, and the work Hungerford took up in public relations and journalism, and with the Australian News And Information Bureau, while it gave him opportunities to travel and meet a variety of people, left him little time or energy for further work in the novel until the nineteen sixties, when in 1963 he published *Shake The Golden Bough*, based on experience in New York.

But he continued to write stories, as well as articles, and some excellent literary criticism. Some of these stories continued his themes of childhood and remembrance of that time, used in different ways, directly as in 'The Black Mountain', in 1956, or 'The Only One Who Forgot', from *Southerly* and in *Coast to Coast* 1951-2, or as in 'The Magnolia Tree', 1956, reminiscence of an earlier time shared by two men in the army, the present framing the past, a story foreshadowing very clearly in setting and time some of his later writing. Other stories of this period reflected topics from suburban living to imaginative, science fiction-like themes, though time has lessened the impact of the latter.

T.A.G. Hungerford has said his writing is concerned with Australian character. Australian character may be less easy to define than it once seemed. But his writing, particularly in the earlier stories, captured vividly through idiom, speech, humour, aspects of that character and of a time when it appeared to have a clear identity. The travelling he undertook both officially and privately after the war produced a different kind of writing of places he had seen and at times come to know. His close and sensitive observation and descriptive power found a focus on some of these places, perhaps nowhere more vividly than from the time he spent as a freelance journalist in Macau. These descriptive pieces stand clearly in their own right, but when they could be combined with remembrance of childhood, as in a story such as 'Green Grow The Rushes', gave some of the most successful stories of this period.

It may have been his well-known story 'Wong Chu And The Queen's Letterbox' which indicated the way to the group of stories centred on a past place and a past time, the suburban Perth of his boyhood. In *Stories From Suburban Road*, 1983, Hungerford discarded the device of narrator and the frame of another period, and returned to the vision of a past that had been behind so many of the earlier stories. He became his own narrator, and allowed what was for him the freedom of an admitted autobiographical view. The resulting stories, widely acclaimed, were clearly observed, the incidents closely described, sensitive, avoiding sentimentality, they reproduced the time so much a part of his awareness.

Now living at Canning Vale in Western Australia T.A.G. Hungerford gives all his time to work as a freelance writer. After *Stories From Suburban Road* he completed two further autobiographical books, *A Knockabout With A Slouch Hat* and *Red Rover All Over*, and has returned to work again at the form it seemed he might have abandoned, the novel. He has said of his stories, they were the result of a lifelong, fascinated observation of people, places, things and circumstances. That has been clear in all his work, and has given it a singular richness and vitality. It is something likely to remain as clear in what he is still to do.

Peter Cowan

VISIT TO THE LUTTS

Things was different in those days; wasn't no moving pictures and motor-bikes then; we had to make our own fun. The Lutts owned a farm about three miles from our place, and we used to go over to play with the Lutt kids. They was twenty in family, not countin' Mr and Mrs Lutt, none of your ones and twos and squawkin' about too many mouths to feed; they used to bake a whole sheep Sundays, and not a bone left to tell the tale. Them Lutt girls used to plough an' harrow with the men from daylight till dark, and would make two of you. Great hobnail boots they had and skirts above their ankles ... not proper it wasn't, then, but they had to work.

I remember they had a big red bull called Strawbry, what had grew up with them Lutt kids crawlin' all over it, slidin' down its back an' off its rump, and it used to lie in the yard near the house. He was the biggest bull I ever see; a neck like this ... an' horns like this ... an' eyes as big as y'r fist, blacklike, with red in them. Well, we was frightened of Strawbry, and used to stop at the fence, a post an' rail fence it was, and look at Strawbry, an' he'd look at us quietlike, an' we'd holler and squeal 'Are you there, Mrs Lutt?' till the Lutt kids came runnin' out an' all squealed back 'C'mon in, Strawb won't hurt you,' an' they'd run to the bull and crawl all over him, pull his ears an' twist his tail, but he'd never take any notice. We'd climb up the fence and drop over the other side and make a bolt for the kitchen door. Mrs Lutt always seemed to be bakin', an' we'd have hot scones and cream and home-made jam. They had about fifty cows, and an old mare an' a couple of dogs used to go to the river paddock and round them up night after night, and never leave one behind. The mare used to bring old Lutt home market days as drunk as a fiddler, an' no one ever interfered with her.

When we'd had our scones and cream, we used to go out with the Lutt kids to see what we could do. When Dad an' Mum came with us, like on Sundays, Dad and Mr Lutt would walk out in the crops an' talk about farming and pigs, and Mum and Mrs Lutt used to sit under an apple-tree in the yard an' talk about the marryin's an' funerals in the district, and every now an' then would lower their voices and laugh out loud like something funny had happened; Mrs Lutt was a laughing woman, with little brown eyes, and jolly for all she'd had all the little Lutts, an' was never happy unless she had kids all round her, an' all eatin' their heads off. We used to say 'No thanks, Mrs Lutt,' like we'd been told, but she'd say, 'Go on, there's plenty more where that came from. I never yet knew a kid that had enough!' an' she'd laugh and hold her stomach and wink at Mum, an' we didn't need much pressing to have more.

I remember they had a bull-calf down the paddock. We'd wait till he had his head down feeding, an' a couple of us'd creep up behind him and grab his tail, an' squeal blue murder. Off he'd go, like a shot, kicking and bucking, with us runnin' behind hangin' on like grim death till he spilled us off. Then his mother would come bellerin' up, and we would have to make a dive for the fence. Lookin' back, it don't seem so excitin', but it did then — we didn't have no picture books and clockwork trains; we had to make our own fun.

That's why we used to spend so much time at the swamp. There was birds galore and stretches of bulrushes where the reed-warblers used to hang their nests, an' in matin' season you never heard such warblin'. But, best of all, the wild ducks used to feed in the shallow lagoons, an' we used to trap them sometimes. You had to squirm pretty close on your belly, and you'd hear them quackin' and gobblin' quietly amongst themselves just like they was talkin' about how much food they was getting, or something.

This day I never did forget. We already had two ducks in a bag, an' Eugenia Lutt was carrying them. There was her and Alec Lutt and me. We come to a likely stretch of water, one we didn't remember goin' in before, and from a clump of reeds about the middle we heard some ducks quackin'. Alec, he was the oldest, said 'Ssh!' and stepped into the lagoon. I followed, an' 'Genie came after me. We was pretty intent on not scaring the ducks, an' everything was quiet as a hot Sunday afternoon, when we heard a squeal from behind us, and when we turned to bawl out ' 'Genie' all we could see was her hand clutching the bag with the ducks in it. I guess she had side-stepped a bit after a blue water-hyacinth that was growing near, an' gone into a deep hole. The ducks went up with a great splash and a squawk over our heads, but we never looked at them even. Alec made a dive into the pool, where 'Genie had disappeared altogether, and I splashed to the bank an' went screeching through the swamp at the top of my voice. I never knew mud to cling so, and bushes to be so thick. They caught my face an' hair, and although I didn't know it I was a pretty sight when I met Mr Lutt racing over the paddock on our old Smoky, who pulled the cart over from our place. He had heard me screaming, and dashed out and kicked old Smoky in the ribs and headed for the swamp. He yanked me up behind him, and I led him to the lagoon. When we got there Alec had pulled 'Genie out, and she was lyin' on the bank, still and white with her eyes closed, an' Alec was holding her hand an' crying. Old Lutt gave him a knock backwards, tipped the ducks outa the bag, pulled a feather out of one's wing and stuck it down 'Genie's throat. She choked, and brought up about a gallon of brown swamp water, an' after a while she was sittin' up taking notice. We stuck her on the horse and walked back to Lutt's, where Mum and Mrs Lutt were in a great stew. Mrs Lutt grabbed

'Genie, an' hugged her close, laughin' and cryin', and 'Genie said 'Anyway, I didn't let go the ducks!' and old Lutt said 'Just as well you didn't — if I catch you kids down the swamp again I'll knock your dam' heads together, ducks or no ducks, so don't forget!' and Mrs Lutt said 'Now, Henry, don't scold the children. They've had a big enough fright already. All's well that ends well, so let's go and have a cup of tea,' and she walked into the house and busied herself in the kitchen as though nothing had happened.

That night we was comin' home just after sundown. It had turned cold, and us kids was cuddled up under some clean chaffbags in the back of the cart, playing 'My Uncle Sam Kept a Grocery'; I couldn't spell very well, so I was lying there just listening to the jingle of the harness on old Smoky, and smelling the bags and the horse-sweat, and the sway of the cart was sending me to sleep, so that I just heard Mum, like she was a long way away, threatenin' '...and if ever I bring you visitin' the Lutts again it'll do you good!'

But I didn't worry ... she always forgot before next time, and as I went to sleep the evenin' star was shining still as you like above the trees, an' I could hear frogs croaking in a swamp just off the road.

THE WEDDING

There was eight of us in the family, and Mart was the only girl, so I guess when she married Herbie Lutt we was bound to make it something that the district would remember for a while.

Mart was the eldest, except for my brother Jim, who was drowned in the creek. I was only little then, but I remember it like it was only yesterday. Jim was out in the long paddock fixing the fence where the bull knocked it down trying to get at some stray cows in the road, and it started to rain. The rain- birds had been around for days, and they knew what they was whistling about. It poured from two o'clock in the afternoon, with great flashes of lightning that seemed to stand up quivering in the ground, and thunder like rolling an empty tank down an ironstone ridge, and the rain getting heavier every flash. The creek came up like one thing, and before long you could see drowned sheep bobbing along, and Dad was swearing out on the verandah, but Mum just stood at the window watching the creek and saying, like she was talking to herself, 'I do hope he don't try to swim Gipsy over the creek; I do hope!' Dad kept saying 'He'll be all right, Mattie; don't worry, he'll be all right'; but you could see he was worried too, and us kids didn't like to play our game of asking him if the lightning was really the angels lighting their pipes, and the thunder was them stamping on the matches.

Anyway, Jim never came in, and we just went to sleep on the floor in front of the fireplace, and I remember waking up some time and seeing Dad come in with the hurricane lamp, sopping wet, and putting his arm around Mum, and her crying. They buried him down the creek a couple of days later, and I nearly hollered out 'No!' when the parson says 'He's happier now where he is,' because I know Jim was happiest with us and Gipsy and having his egg collection and everything than he could be just standing around singing like in the holy pictures.

Anyway, when Martie was getting married to Herbie Lutt, for weeks beforehand, every night after tea, they'd spread clean paper on the kitchen floor and Mum'd be kneeling there with her mouth full of pins, gathering and tucking, and Martie suggesting this and that, and even then she looked lovely. Herbie used to ride over often, but he never saw her once in that dress because they said it was unlucky.

As the day come nearer us kids couldn't be held; you'd have thought we was getting married! Mrs Lutt came over two days before the wedding and lived at our place, and her and Mum cooked solid for hours, because even if it was only the Lutts coming over for dinner you'd need plenty, but there was the Williamses and the Tuohys from Balcabbin way, and the parson and his family, and a few others who, Mum said, would never have forgive us if they hadn't been invited. We killed a pig, and the Williamses reckoned you could hear him squealing over at their place when Dad cut his throat.

The morning of the wedding us kids went out in the bush and gathered armfuls of Christmas bush and gumleaves and decorated the dining-room until it was real pretty. Only the Lutts was comin' to midday dinner, but that made twenty-nine of us, leaving out Herbie, who, they said, musn't see Mart until he came over to marry her, on account of it was unlucky. It seems they had more ways of whipping up bad luck than there are days in a week. Anyway, Herbie missed a good time. They don't do things that way now — it's a bit of ham and a bit of chicken, with a bit of jelly and trifle to follow, and some little sausages on toothpicks, but nothing cooked at home. Lord, if you could have seen that table! Dad at one end of it carving a turkey and Mr Lutt at the other with a great leg of pork and in between them almost everything. Mum and Mrs Lutt and two of the girls was around the table all the time until everybody was ready to settle down, and you never heard so much laughing and going on. We was real happy, and I guess proud of ourselves and the food we could set there for the Lutts, and knowing that, if needs be, we could do the same tomorrow and the next day, and all grown and taken off our own place.

Herbie rode over late in the afternoon after everything had been cleared away, and the parson had arrived with his pale wife, who came from England and never really settled down. Old Charlie the goose was there. He got invited to all the weddings because he could play the accordeen.

Mum came bustling out of her bedroom after a while and whispered something to the parson, and he whispered to old Charlie and Mick Williams, who had his fiddle, and poor Herbie sort of half-grinned at the best man, who was his shearing mate, and he took a ring out of his waistcoat pocket. Then Charlie and Mick started playing and Martie came in, looking so lovely that I'd never have known her. She was all in white, with a bunch of the honeysuckle that grows all over our back verandah and some pink and white everlastings. She walked past Herbie, who took her arm, and when they were standing in front of the parson Charlie and Mick stopped playing. It was so quiet you could hear a blowfly buzzing and batting his head against the window, and right down the paddock a cow mooing softly, and a few birds calling, sleepy-like, in the hot afternoon.

I felt a tingle run down my spine, and when the parson started talking I snuck a look at Mum. She was crying quietly, and I straight away thought of the black, wet night when Jim died, but this was a different kind of crying somehow, just so happy. It wasn't long before Mrs Lutt had her hankie out too. And then it seemed that the parson had said all he wanted to, and Herbie kissed Mart and everyone rushed up to them, the ladies kissing Herbie and the men kissing Mart, and I thought if ever I did marry Lily Tuohy this is what will happen; and would I be glad, and would it make any difference if I wanted to run down the paddock or out to the swamp on hot afternoons like this.

Then there was the wedding breakfast, though why they called it the breakfast when it was nearly seven in the evening I don't know, and neither did Mum when I asked her. We all sat down, and soon they was making speeches. Dad made one and Mr Lutt too, and old Charlie, who had played at Mum and Dad's wedding, got up and said he'd never played for such a handsome couple as today, and Dad said 'That's what you said at my wedding,' and Charlie said 'Yes, Jim, but that was a long time ago.' Mum said 'Get along with you, Charlie; you make me out an old woman,' and everyone laughed.

Herbie got up and thanked everybody for everything several times, and told Mum not to worry — she was not losing a daughter, but gaining a son; and old Lutt sings out 'Well, where do we come in?' Then they started singing 'For He's a Jolly Good Fellow.'

Lord! if I close my eyes I can see every smallest detail of it. Mum and Mrs Lutt in their home-made dresses and their faces brown and sort of tired-looking, but just shining with happiness. Dad, a small, quick man, with a drooping moustache and going a bit bald, and old Lutt towering over him with one great hand on his shoulder and the other holdin' a glass of red wine. Old Charlie talking and laughing and never once stopping his playing, and Mick sawing away at his fiddle. I can even smell the drooping Christmas bush and honeysuckle coming through the windows.

No one stayed very late. They all had to be up early and working hard, and everyone was tired enough to want to be home in bed by midnight. There was none of your hanging around just to be polite and yawning over your shoulder when no one was looking. Everyone had had a good time, and we needed no telling, and soon hurricanes were bobbing around in the yard, and you could hear the jingle of harness and the men saying 'Whoa back, old girl!' as they backed the horses between the shafts. In no time the last light bobbed down the road and disappeared amongst the trees, and, my, the house was quiet! Mum said to Mrs Lutt 'We'll clean all this up in the morning'; and to me 'Come on now, Will, you've had a long day,' and she held me a bit tighter than usual, and came and tucked me in, which she hadn't done for a while. I remember thanking God for her and everything, and just as I went to sleep a dog howled on a farm miles away.

It was a warm moonlight night, and the sound just seemed to drift across the empty paddocks and fade away in the dark shadows, a sad sort of sound that made it good to be in bed and only nine, with years to go before you had to grow up and get married and leave home.

AND GERTIE DANCES IN THE MOONLIGHT

Leave ... it's all they talk about. Curley says 'I'd rather be down there with ten flamin' bob than stuck up here with a roll a Mosstrooper couldn't jump over!'

Down there. So long since you saw it that it is blurred and you can't remember which building stands next to which along the Terrace Hill. It would be cold down there, too; biting cold, with a keen wind off the water and fires indoors.

Someone says 'Anyway, Curl, you'd be apples; you c'd bite that old crow of yours in the city.'

A general laugh greets this one — Curley's old crow is a favorite joke.

'Yair,' he says, looking at the sky and acting coy. 'I'm sittin' in a plonk shop talkin' to a Yank. I'm tellin' him about the time Lofty bit the tail off the Persian cat in that milk bar, and he's buyin' the grog, see, when I looks up and cops this old sheilah winkin' at me, like this.'

He picks his teeth with a stem of dried grass. We are squatting by a track waiting for a move; all about us are the bare patches in the scrub where our humpies have stood. Funny how you get used to a place — you find out where the latrines have been dug, where you can get water, where the cookhouse will be, and the place takes on an air of permanency. You feel as though you have been there all your life, and never look like moving.

'But what was she like, Curl?' Someone always asks it.

'Beggars can't be choosers!' says Curley virtuously.

He flips two pennies and idly examines the fall. ''Struth, micked 'em again! She was a pensioner, too,' he adds. 'What!' yells Paddles. 'Old enough for the pension?'

Everyone laughs and we smack each other and say ''Struth, he's a riot!' but Curley looks offended.

'She was only about 35 or 40. The pension was for her hand; she couldn't use it much. She got about thirteen bob a week.'

'Couldn't expect a girl to live on that!'

'Well, she didn't exactly,' grins Curl.

And then along comes the transport and we clamber aboard. We are packed 22 to a truck, with all our gear. It's no picnic. Hot, too, and dry and dusty; and before long we're all caked with the fine red dust. It gets in your eyes — even under your plate, if you wear one — and the inside of your nose feels as if it is cracking.

Butch says 'I hope the creek isn't dried up'.

We think we know where we're going; there is a creek, but now the wet is over it might be dried up. 'Struth, the wet! A man was never dry. And the swamps! We all were rotten with tinea.

Now the days are all gold and blue with a few white clouds, and the nights all purple and silver, with stars near enough to touch, and cool moonlight that seems to drip off the trees.

Last camp, we had a goat named Gertie. Someone swiped her with an eye to milk, I suppose, although she didn't seem to have any udder. Maybe it was meat they had in mind, when the 'bully' got too much. Anyway, these moonlight nights you'd be awake looking at the sky and remembering other nights like these in other places with different company, and you'd hear a quick patter of little hooves and there Gertie'd be, dancing on her log.

She did it every night, her white coat glowing, tossing her head so that the pale light would twinkle on her horns and in her strange oblique eyes. Then she'd stop and listen to nothing, at least nothing you could hear, and you'd get the feeling that thin reed music was being made in the blue shadows of the pandanus. But all you could hear was the rustle of trees and the plop-plop of a grass-wallaby, and it gave you an eerie feeling about Gertie, as if she knew more than you did and was having you on.

But she was prosaic enough during the day — used to hang around the officers' tent for scraps, and when you came in there's be a neat pile of what we used to call 'currants' when we were kids, and bits of chewed letters and papers all over the joint.

Someone says 'Did anyone put Gertie on?'

Slats says '— Gertie! We don't want any damn' goats. We're going on leave, anyway.'

That starts it again. There's always some lame-brain with a rumor.

But before we get really stuck into this one the truck is stopped by a flaming provost because a few of the chaps have stood up to stretch their legs.

He compliments the lieutenant sitting in front, and says would he make the men sit down. As the truck moves on someone yells out 'Why don't you join up? Your cobbers need you!'

This is a favorite formula, and will usually start something. But the provost just scowls at us till our dust hides him. The chaps stand up again, and the discussion on leave resumes. We've hammered it all before, but there might be a new angle.

Mile after mile after mile of low red hills and burnt-out scrub. What a place! If it hadn't been for the war it would still have been lost in a quiet that stretches back to before history. When Alexander cried for new worlds these hills were sprawling here, red and dry, with kitehawks sailing above them in wide circles; but the billabong we passed along the road would have had a couple of fires or a wurlie on its banks.

That's about the only difference; the blacks have gone. Maybe in a few thousand years we'll be gone, too, and it makes you wonder why things assume such an importance when, after all, our whole lives are just a moment in time.

And that's a silly thing to say, because a two-hour guard between two and four in the morning is no moment whichever way you look at it.

Wally is on his favorite theme. 'Steak and eggs,' he says, with his eyes glistening. 'I'd sit down and have a double order, and then go for a walk and come back and have another.'

Our throats are cracking and caked with dust. Curley interrupts him. 'How'd you go a nice cool bar with a blonde slappin' the pots on the counter an'' — but he is shut up by a torrent of hoarse blasphemy from all quarters. Some things are too much to be borne.

Tempers are fraying a bit. We are all too dry and hot, and are tired of eating dust. There is nearly a blue when Harry has a drink out of Mort's water-bottle by mistake. Someone tries to open a tin of goldfish with a bayonet while the truck is going over corrugations inches deep, and a few of the boys get sprayed. When things are quiet again the discussion reverts to the eternal themes. The shadows are long by the time we reach our stop. It is where we thought we were going, for a change. It's a long, deep gully winding amongst the red hills, and is already filling with blue shadows.

It doesn't take long to chuck the gear off the trucks, and we don't bother to put up the tents, it's such a lovely, fine night. Mechanically, we look around until we see a fatigue busy with picks and shovels — the latrines. We passed the cookhouse further down the gully; the greasies came along earlier in the day, and the 'M. and V.' pick is well on the way. After that trip we'd eat horse, let alone 'M. and V.' pie.

There are a few bushfires around, and a thin veil of smoke is drifting amongst the trees, which are glowing pink in the last light. It's like being in the heart of a milky opal, all green and red, gold and blue.

After tea we just roll out our groundsheets and settle in.

Tich says 'Just like when I was a wrestler,' and Curley says 'You a wrestler! All you ever wrestled with was an old cow and a bottle of plonk on a park seat.'

But it passes; we are too tired to start anything. It is cool, and the stars are gaining in strength. On the hillsides around little red fires gleam, and the noises of the camp are subdued and sound far away — someone singing, someone cursing the mosquitoes and the rattle of loose stones as someone goes down the hillside.

A group of chaps a few yards away are discussing leave. '... and that's the good guts. Robbie's batman just told me.' The batmen are mines of information, usually fictitious, but we are suckers for it and always come in. Curley's voice can be heard. 'Yair, and this sheilah says she's got a cobber, so we pick up Tich and go out to their place and get stung; and some Yank that lives there dots me an' I wake up on the back lawn next morning with a beaut shiner, an' I get back to camp late, and they sting me ten bob and a day's pay; and you wonder why a bloke's crooked!' Which sets the ball rolling again — leave and sheilahs.

We forget so easily. Last night we lay down amongst the trees in our old camp as we had done for months and felt permanent. Now that place is forgotten and deserted; and this place, where last night it was quiet and only a few lizards rustled amongst the rocks and maybe a sly old dingo shadowed along, is noisy with our talk and laughter. Already we've forgotten what we did yesterday.

Perhaps we're not such big potatoes; all we left behind us was some bare patches in the scrub and Gertie dancing on her log in the moonlight.

LESSON BY FIRELIGHT

It is deepening twilight when we come down from the range, and cool and quiet under the trees.

A clump of pandanus where we intended to look for water is slowly merging into the blue haze that settles over the bush, and the quiet is so immense that you'd stop to listen. It is made up of all sorts of sounds that ordinarily you never hear ... the plop of a wallaroo in the grass, and the rattle of a disturbed stone on the slope; the tired hush-hush of the wind in the trees, and somewhere, sounding sad and miles away, a bird warbling.

You might call it desolation, but it's not that; it's just as it should be — we don't count. Standing there with the night coming on, and the old red hills brooding over the swamps and bush and open plains, it's hard to feel like 'lords of creation'.

I say to the Champ 'We'll leave the pandanus, I reckon,' and he says 'We'll go back to the waterhole. It's getting dark.'

The boss says 'Let's go!' and we get the big bluff squarely behind us, and set out for camp.

We've been going all day since before sun-up, through some hard country. When the platoon pulls up for the night alongside a little grey waterhole smelling of cattle, the three of us come on a few miles: the boss wants to know what's on the other side of these hills before we settle in. We find nothing except about thirty miles of blue and green bush between this and the next line of red hills, but at least we know.

It's exhilarating, hurrying back through the dim bush. The breast-high grass is cool and heavy with dew, which makes the going hard, so when we come in sight of the fire they've lit by the billagong we sit down for a breather. The smell of the broken grass is refreshing after the dusty day.

We have three boongs with us. They travel light; only a few blankets, a spear or two and a little bag of tea and sugar, all of which they load on to Munumcumbubbie, the youngest of the three. Old Woollamon, the sort of patriarch — and, I reckon, a wily old rascal — tells us Munumcumbubbie means 'The Burnt Behind', and shows us a long scar where he says a buck hit the boy with a firestick. We call him Charlie, and, in spite of his stiff leg, he's a cheerful cuss.

When we reach camp there's a couple of billies of tea waiting for us, and some bully and vegemite stew with an onion chopped up in it. We finish off the tucker, and I go to the fire, where Greg is poring over some letters. I haven't had a letter for donkey's years, and I say sarcastically 'Private courier, huh?'

Greg just says 'Pull y'r head in, mug; it's old mail,' and goes on reading.

The mossies are bad, and some of the boys are drifting over to where Woollamon, Charlie and Tommie are lying around their smoky little fire, heavy with food. During the day they bowled a big goanna and three shags on a creek we passed, and we shot them some flying-foxes; a pile of green fruits from a vine, some bully and biscuits — and they scoffed the lot!

They smile to each other as we come up and exchange a few words that sound like water running over mossy stones, so softly and easily do they speak. They only whisper, too; sometimes it seems they're merely thinking aloud; but the others understand easily enough.

'Hello, Woollamon!' says Curly, squatting down. 'Mosquito no good!'

Woollamon just waves his black paw toward the waterhole.

No words are needed — he couldn't have said more plainly 'What in hell do you expect, camping right on top of water?' He adds a few rippling sentences to Tommie, just sighs them out, but Charlie, who is gathering long stems of grass yards away, hears them and laughs silently. It is not hard to make them laugh, particularly Charlie.

Cisco comes up and squats opposite Tommie and rolls a smoke, looking all around him meanwhile. 'What name?' he says, and his eyes stop at the waterhole. 'What name that fella?' He points at it.

Tommie looks at Woollamon and grins slowly, then back to Cisco. 'Bacca?' he inquires softly, and Charlie chuckles.

Cisco hands Tommie the smoke he's made, and Curl gives Woollamon a tailormade; and, as Charlie sidles up and grins at me, I have to hand him one, too.

Tommie inhales luxuriantly and says, so quietly that I have to listen hard; 'Quordarrie!'

'Quordarrie?' says Cisco, and I see the boss take out his pencil and notebook. 'Well, what name this fella?' and he holds out his hand.

Charlie, wide-eyed and motionless, watches, ready to laugh. Woollamon is scratching his leg — he has had a couple of draws and parked his smoke behind his ear.

Tommie spreads his dusky paw and examines it minutely, as though he's just seen it for the first time. You could hear a pin drop. 'Daman,' he says.

Charlie laughs and repeats it softly. 'Daman.' He stands up, dark and skinny, and selecting one of his stems of grass, launches it straight into the heart of a water-lily at the edge of the pool — a distance of about thirty feet. It's his contribution to our entertainment, and, judging by the way he laughs, he reckons it's pretty good. They're so willing to teach us what little we're capable of taking in that I can't help thinking of another teacher I used to have — she taught me another language years ago.

Mam'selle D'Erot, she was; a little dried-up woman with a pinched nose and tired brown eyes; not much hair to talk of; and she'd carry her head on one side like a bird watching a beetle. In the three years she had us I recall her in but three dresses, a new one at the beginning of each year, and always the same dusty black stuff, made high at the neck, where she used to pin a great big cameo brooch and what looked like a white lace hanky.

'*Attendez!*' she'd say, and rap her ruler on the board, trying to act fierce, and one of the sheilahs up the back would say '*La mauvaise fille* — it means the wicked girl, doesn't it, Mam'selle?' and all the other girls would begin to chant '*La mauvaise fille*, the wicked girl! *La mauvaise fille*, the wicked girl!'

She'd jump up and down like a toy monkey on a stick and beat the desk, poor old sort; if only we'd stopped to think ... she wasn't any chicken, and hadn't any bloke or kids of her own. I suppose things were a bit too much for her at times. She'd say '*C'est incroyable!*' and smooth back her hair nervously. 'Tomorrow I tell the head!' But she never did. '*Maintenant!* We count! *Un, deux, trois, quatre*' —

'Ookamar, waharrie, warrak, mayeninka; one, two, t'ree, four,' says Tommie, counting off on his black fingers, and old Woollamon nods in agreement. 'T'ree,' repeats Tommie, holding up his third finger. 'Woollamon ... t'ree gin!' and Woollamon smirks at us — a bit of a doer in his own quiet way, I bet.

Tommie is warmed up. 'Charlie,' he says; 'Charlie, no gin! Byembye, Woollamon givem!' Charlie is wriggling and giggling like a sheilah; he reckons this is all right.

Creek, hill, friend, track — the lesson goes on, and the light from the little fire dances on their black faces, and on Cisco and Curl, and on the boss, copying it all down, and on the white trunks of the paper bark.

Just outside the circle of light are the bush and the old hills, and the ghosts of a million quiet years straining over our shoulders; and I think: all those years these words have been whispered around here, unchanging, like the hills; they will disappear, words and misty folklore, simply because they would not shout out and be heard, preferring to whisper and laugh.

Cisco says: 'What name "yesterday"?'

Woollamon looks puzzled, and Charlie wrinkles his forehead.

Tommie murmurs something anxiously and shakes his head. They don't know yesterday — all life is just today for them, today and tucker and sleep.

It's late, and we've had a hard day. The boss says good night, and one by one the chaps drift off. The fire has died down and Tommie heaps green leaves on it, and the three of them lie almost on top of it.

Cisco laughs. 'They'd better be careful,' he says, 'or they'll 'munnum' their 'cumbubbies'!'

'Pull y'r head in,' mutters someone sleepily, and Cisco says 'Okay, darlin'; meet you at the G.P.O.'

The G.P.O., I think, as I gather grass for my bed. Sydney! Light and music, noise and a girl to dance with ... wind and darkness, trees and the glittering stars!

HAPPY SUMMER DAYS

It was close to the wet; the jumpy wind that swirled down the gully carried dead leaves and fine grey dust with it, and as Brock walked over to the Rec. tent he thought 'It must rain soon, it must.'

The oppressive heat of midday and the cloying warmth of the nights were too much altogether, although it would be no better when the wet did come; but anything to break the monotony of blazing days that sucked out your energy and left you limp.

He entered the big tent, where Bluey was fiddling with the wireless. 'Hello, Brock,' Bluey said. 'Stinker, isn't it?' He couldn't get anything decent on the air, either; it wasn't much of a set.

Brock walked over to the bookshelf. The two inadequate kerosene lamps were smothered by clouds of insects dancing, whirling, frizzling, and the smell of them was nauseating. He looked over the titles.

'This all you've got, Stan?' he said to the lance-jack in charge. Stan kicked the box at his feet. 'Some new ones in there, Brock,' he said; 'haven't had time to look 'em over yet; only come up yesterday.' Brock lifted the lid and took out the first book he came to and opened it.

'Don't tell me,' he said aloud to no one in particular, and no one listened to him. They were playing draughts and chess and Chinese checkers, and talking about what they did on leave, and what they would do on their next leave ... 'What in hell do they think we are? Listen to this, "Awarded to Effie Lucas for the most consistent attendance, Christian Endeavor, St Mark's, third of May, 1913" '...

Dim ghosts of a long-gone Sunday,
and the warmth of a faded summer.
Listen...

Effie cuddled down in bed, knowing it was Sunday morning. She sniffed the starchy smell of the sheets, and wriggled her toes in the warm nest she had scuffled for them; it was quite early yet, not long after sun-up, and the whole house was quiet.

She could hear the ticking of the kitchen clock and the rustle of the blinds and all the secret sounds that go on in a house not fully awakened. Somewhere a rooster crowed, a long way away, and Effie snuggled closer; it was such a lonely sound, and sad.

She didn't mind their own rooster; she knew what he looked like, and, although he chased her, she could laugh at him, because Ella said begod what a fine tail he had, and it would look a sight better on a good woman's bonnet than dragging around in the muck; but those roosters that crowded in the half-light, miles away, sounded lost and somehow frightening, and you couldn't be sure they *were* roosters.

Effie looked over to Meg's bed and saw the fair pigtail draped over the pillow.

'Margaret!' she whispered hoarsely, 'come over and play, Meg.'

Margaret stirred, and her brown eyes fixed on her sister. 'Play what?' she said. 'I been awake hours!'

Effie ignored this evident exaggeration. 'Oh, anything,' she said. 'Come over to my bed and you can nurse Emmaline Constance.'

'There, there,' she soothed the doll as she passed it to Meg; 'it's the wind, poor lamb!' She didn't know exactly what this meant, but Mrs Potter said it about her baby, and it sounded very good.

They could hear Ella in the kitchen now, pattering around noisily, and the flip-flap of her slippers as she waddled between the pantry and the stove.

'Meg,' said Effie, 'd'you remember what today is?' Meg, without taking her eyes off Emmaline, said 'Yes, of course — Sund'y!'

Effie wriggled excitedly. 'Yes, of course; but what else? You know — Prize Day.'

'So it is, too! D'you think you'll get a prize?' Margaret was out of the running herself, since she had missed a number of Sundays on account of small illnesses.

Effie wriggled again. 'I think I will,' she whispered. 'I've only missed one Sunday, and Mamie Stone has gone away...'

'What's this, what's this?' Ella said as she bustled in. 'Playing again? Now up you get, and Effie, you tidy up your bureau before you come to breakfast. Now come on, show a leg or your Mama'll be having my hide!'

She whisked back the curtains at the window and bustled out. Effie pictured her genteel Mama 'having Ella's hide' — Ella spread out like the bearskin in the drawing-room, only not so hairy.

Sunday had spread its quiet charm over the breakfast-room — on no other morning did the curtains flutter so softly nor the sun shine so warmly on the linoleum beneath the window.

Papa was seated at the table with his glasses on reading the paper, and Mama was pouring the tea. As Effie walked in she was saying '...and of course it's been apparent for a long while; I don't know what Mary's mother can have been about not to have noticed it. She must be blind. And as for Arthur' —

Papa coughed and rattled his paper, and Mama, raising her eyes, continued, 'And don't drag your chair, Effie; lift it. Where is Margaret? She is always last.'

'Mama,' said Effie. 'Mama, may I wear my pink ribbon today, please? It's Prize Day.'

'We'll see,' replied her mother; 'but remember, you don't go to church to show of your hair ribbon. And stop picking all the strawberries out of the jam.'

'Yes, my lady,' Papa rumbled as he put down his paper and stirred his tea, 'but I think we might manage the pink ribbon today, eh, Mother? Are you going to get a prize?'

Effie put down her glass of milk. 'Yes, papa; I mean, I hope so,' she murmured shyly. Papa always seemed to be making fun of her. 'You see, Mamie Stone has gone away.'

'Oh,' said Papa, 'I see. That makes it quite clear!'

Effie smiled gratefully at him and having finished her milk, put down her glass and said 'Please may I leave the table?' and in a few minutes was busily braiding her hair.

'Meg,' she said when she was joined by her sister, 'what happened to Mary? I heard Mama say her mother must be blind, and as for Arthur' — Arthur Andrews played the organ at the church, and was secretly very much admired by Margaret and Effie.

'Oh, I don't know,' said Meg. 'It's just the way they talk. Where's your ribbon?' 'No, wait a minute!' cried Effie. 'Not that one — it's the pink one today!' And she lifted it reverently from the drawer and gave it to Meg to tie on.

When Effie passed demurely through the front gate on her way to Endeavour she was very conscious of her shiny Sunday shoes and spotless white Sunday dress, but, above all, of the pink ribbon. If she swung her head she could see it over her shoulder, dancing at the end of her plait, and she wanted to skip; the sunshine and the Sunday calm, the green gardens and somewhere the homely sound of a lawn-mower filled her with a happiness that she felt must bubble over somehow, but young Miss Lucas did not skip in the street, so she sang happily under her breath.

Down the street Charlie Graves was sitting at the front gate sucking a lolly-ball, which, as she passed, he took from his mouth, reverently noting the change of colour.

The Graves family added a piquant touch of evil to an otherwise blameless street, since Mr Graves, who worked at a bank, was addicted to drink, and the Graves children never came to Christian Endeavor or Sunday-school except on wet days in winter when, as Effie had heard her mother say, Mrs Graves could not stand them in her own house, so packed them off to make a nuisance of themselves in God's.

Charlie popped the lolly-ball back in his cheek and gave it a few vigorous sucks.

'Where you goin'?' he inquired of Effie, and she stopped, for, although she was years his senior, Effie was always thrown into near panic by Charlie. Of every other house in the street, she knew the secrets of the back garden; who had fish pools, rose gardens, grapevines; but, because she was not allowed to play with the Graves's, the area behind the trellis at the side was a mystery, and the Graves children, whose dolls she had never nursed, and whose tricycles she had never ridden; were almost as creatures of another world, and, be it admitted, a very alluring world at that.

Effie could not even guess at what lay behind the trellis, but it was something monstrous, she felt sure.

Charlie's unwinking gaze had not shifted from her face. 'You c'n come in, if you like,' he volunteered, 'we got kittens' and he indicated a deal box on the verandah. Effie glanced up and down the Sunday-stricken street. Kittens! She crossed the forbidden threshold, Charlie treading on her heels in his eagerness to show off his treasures. They nestled, five of them, on an old knitted blue skirt in the box, and in no time Effie had a warm little kitten snuggled under her chin.

'Oh, you lovey!' she crooned, and wondered why there were never any kittens at home, nor pups; all they ever had was chickens, and then they mustn't touch them ...

A door opened behind her, and turning around she saw a lady walking slowly along the verandah towards her, a pretty lady with red lips and cheeks, and black hair, and a fine white dress with lace at the throat like the ladies on the chocolate boxes and — Effie felt her hypnotised gaze drawn to the cigarette that dangled between the lady's long fingers.

A cigarette! Effie felt horror trickle down her back like cold water.

Charlie was grappling with the lady's hand, not even noticing the cigarette. 'She's come to see the kittens, Mum,' he babbled. 'She's Effie, from up the road. Perhaps she can stay and play?'

'Yes, dear,' said his mother, and to Effie's ecstatic surprise, inhaled deeply from her cigarette and let the creamy smoke trickle from her nostrils, lazily inspecting the visitor through the haze. 'Does your mother know you are here, Effie?'

Effie started. She had been peering down the hall, which was disappointingly like theirs at home. At least there might have been something. 'No,' she replied, feeling herself blush. 'I was on my way to Endeavor when Charlie' —

'No,' murmured the lady, half to herself, 'I didn't think she would.'

Her tone was bitter. She walked to the edge of the verandah and plucked two blood-red geraniums and pinned them to her bosom, and she said again 'I didn't think she would!' She stood still, looking out over the geraniums into the sunny street, and Effie thought she had forgotten her, but presently she gave a little laugh and turning to Effie, smiled and said 'Look, Effie, would you like to see me make smoke come out of my eyes?'

Effie nodded, not trusting herself to speak.

'Well, put your hand here, on my chest, and look right into my eyes,' said Mrs Graves. Effie complied, and when the lady drew deep on the cigarette waited breathless for the miracle.

Charlie suddenly started to jump up and down. 'Look out!' he cried, 'or Mum'll burn your hand! It's a game!'

Effie snatched her hand away and fled up the path to the gate, the pink ribbon dancing over her shoulder as she ran. Behind her the pretty lady stood on the steps and laughed till suddenly she stopped and, putting her hand to her cheek, turned swiftly and disappeared through the door.

Only when she was two houses away did Effie realise that she still held the kitten against her heaving chest. She could not take it back; not for worlds would she again set foot in the Graves place, so she hurried on, and reached the church just as the minister was shepherding in the last of the late-comers.

'Why, Effie, you are late,' he said smiling. 'What's this ... a kitten?'

'Yes, Mr Douglas, I found it,' murmured Effie; after all, she had found it in the box. 'And Mama says Margaret can't come today on account of her cold.'

'Well, well, I'm sorry to hear that. Tell your Mama, will you? Now, we'll put your kitten in a box until afterwards and go in, eh?' And together they walked into the cool church.

Effie noticed, as she tiptoed down the aisle, that Mary was not in her place; Mary's mother stood by herself, and now and then jerked her head upwards as if throwing something off, and looked defiantly around the church. Arthur sat at the organ with his shoulders hunched, and his fingers straying idly over the keyboard, instead of grinning and winking over his shoulder as he usually did.

But soon the music of the first hymn banished all thought of Mary and Arthur from Effie's mind, and she sang lustily, opening her mouth very wide, and closing her eyes to get a better effect in the parts she particularly liked; although during the address that followed, she found it increasingly hard to keep her mind off the fact that it was Prize Day, and conjecture as to whether Mama would let her keep the kitten. The minister droned on about the stark necessity of succoring the heathen, and noises from outside drifted in, the barking of a dog, pigeons in the roof and the hollow clippity-clop of a horse passing the church.

Another hymn, and at last Mr Douglas's voice announcing the prizes.

'Effie Lucas, for best attendance!' and somehow she was out in front of a haze of faces, curtseying, and back in her place, but in her lap now lay a dull crimson book; on its cover, in ornate gold lettering with a fairy swinging from the middle of the capital 'H,' the title *Happy Summer Days*. The organ chanted, and Effie felt her heart lift and soar as reverently she opened the cover. There, in the spidery cript of the minister's wife, was her own name. 'Effie Lucas ... St Mark's ... Third of

May, 1913' ...

Brock closed the cover of the book quietly and looked about him. Blue was still fiddling with the wireless, and the swirl of frenzied insects around the lamps was still unabated.

Stan said 'Found something you like, Brock? What Name?'

Brock shook his head. How long had he been standing there? He seemed to have been listening to a story, or something; it seemed somehow as if the simple things of his childhood had come flooding over him, calm and serene; and now, of all things, tears burned in his eyes. 'Yes, Stan,' he said, holding up the back of the book, 'think I'll take this one. Seems okay ... a bit old-fashioned maybe' ...

Outside in the darkness a rising wind eddied around the crooked knees of the ghost-gums, and a few big drops of rain fell into the deep grey dust. The wet would soon come.

'GOING BACK,' SAY THE WHEELS

'Good-bye, darlin'; good-bye, love!' she whispered, the plump lady who stood on the platform waving to the train as it moved out. She held one hand at her breast, and fluttered the other, and as Jack settled back in his seat and writhed out of his shirt, he wished vehemently she had had the sense not to come to the station.

He never grew used to them, the mothers and sweethearts of these men who, when the station faded into the noise and steam behind them, shed their home-life like a garment and donned the khaki that in most cases was all they knew or remembered... Most cases; a few sat like stunned magpies and stared at their gear and shuffled their feet, and remembered, like young Stedley in the corner, who carefully packed some cakes and oranges on the luggage rack without actually knowing what he was doing... perhaps he was the plump lady's son.

Jack didn't know who she was, he had just happened to hear her whispered words as he slid past her, for she was talking almost to herself, but he felt that a thousand grieving women could be no more tragic than that one, with her small homely words of endearment being spoken to a retreating train, and lost in the noise of wheels, the wheels that chanted 'Going away, going away, going away,' faster and faster as the train moved further from the station.

That was two days ago; since then they had covered a lot of the continent, and felt as though they had lived all their lives cooped up in this rocketing little box, six of them, with nothing else to do but look out of the windows at the eroded farmlands and desert, with now and then a small town squatting in the emptiness.

The last day's travel had been pleasanter; torrential rains had made miles and miles of desert into soft green pasture, wide and cool, and the sky had a pale washed look about it. Jack loved to lean back in the corner and watch it flash by, green and red and blue, with scuttling rabbits in the grass and hawks circling above them.

Yesterday evening they had pulled in at a little siding that crouched beside the line like a group of huge boulders in the red and purple dusk; a couple of trees, no roads, and underfoot the hard weathered stones of the desert. All about it the frightening immensity of the night welled up from the plains, grey and brown and velvety black.

The stop was a fairly long one, so Jack took his towel and walked to a bore about 50 yards up the track for a shower. The water was warm and had a strong taste, but a light wind off the desert cooled it on his body as he stood naked in the darkness. He was reluctant to dress and lose this moment in time when it seemed he stood alone with the awful forces that had fashioned the stark dead hills and winds that swept over them, and by the time he was ready to return to the train, lights were gleaming dully in a few shack windows, and music from a wireless floated on the warm air.

There was a big peppercorn-tree standing in front of one of the houses, and as he passed it Jack was aware of a girl standing in its deep shadow. A shaft of light fell for a moment across her face, and he saw that she was gazing, lips parted, at the long line of lighted carriages, and he wondered was it his fancy that made her expression seem wistful.

He had passed in a moment, saying softly, 'Good evening,' but she didn't answer.

'Thinks I'm on the make,' he mused, as he sought his carriage;

but as he lay on the floor later on, while the train rocked through the night and the wheels and the iron rails sang their unchanging duet, he could not drive her face from his thoughts, wondering what she did, what was her life, that she stood in the shadows and watched while a trainload of troops cut a swathe of light and noise through her life.

Over breakfast next morning he had mentioned this, and the talk turned to the track and the people you meet on it.

'Remember that screw up Cairns way?' said Fisher, taking a fork-full of bully out of a tin on the floor; and so many laughed that Jack thought, 'Hell, most of my section are bagmen!' 'Remember him?' one said, 'I'll say! Useter walk alongside the train swingin' a billy an' sayin' softlike "Who'd like a mug o' chi, boys?" and if any poor cow pipes up, he'd pull back the tarp an' say, "Right-ho, you bastards! Out you get!" Well, I seen him crowned a beaut once. We was pulled up by a station, and he comes his old trick, an' a mug up an' says "Yes, mate," before we can stop him. Well, when he sees he's in he crawls over to the side of the truck, and when the screw pulls back the tarp he crowns him with his nose-bag. Gawd knows what he had in it, because it dropped that screw like a maggot; an' serves the lousy cow right!'

'All screws ain't bad,' said Fisher, but at that moment the train began to slow up, and the men turned to the windows. It stopped with a jerk, and Jack walked out to the platform. Before long, there was a game going beside the rails; they'll lose their pennies in that red dust if they don't look out, he thought as he stepped down.

The train had stopped in a grassy valley between two long low slopes; it was cool and green, and as the men scattered from the train rabbits leapt from the grass and bolted in all directions.

They got away easily, but the game was on. Some Yanks who were travelling with the convoy joined in, and the blue and khaki figures streamed up the slope. Jack watched them till they disappeared over the crest, and then sauntered down the length of the train.

It seemed inconceivable that only 50 years ago men had staggered over these wastes, and died and gone mad in the solitudes where now he stopped and started, and travelled so unconcernedly between water and water, feeling, sometimes vaguely, the hot threat of the desert's breath, but only guessing at the parched lips and swollen tongue and black despair of a dried waterhole. Such agony happened to other people a long time ago, and was not so much as a cut finger, or the tea-coppers not being lit, or any of the trivial things that could make him forget that pain and death never gave up the chase, that always, just outside the circle of security, they waited hungrily for the stragglers...

A rabbit came bobbing over the brow of the hill, a palpitating dark speck among the red stones, and was followed, lumberingly, by half a dozen soldiers. A wild view-halloo rose from the men in the train, who had a grandstand seat, and amidst loud ribaldry the little cotton-tail disappeared into a hollow log, thinking in its naive way that it had found a safe harborage.

But it didn't count of the blood lust that had been aroused in the breasts of the hunters, the slumbering lust that had slept so long while meat could be passed over a counter instead of being won by skill and stealth and savagery. So while the light wind from the desert turned the tossing new grass into green flame that ran up the hillside to be quenched among the red rocks, and the restless shadows of the amber-eyed hawks flickered again and again across the slope, the soldiers busily stopped all but one entrance of the log with sticks and stones, and proceeded to smoke out their quarry that lay, wide-eyed and with twitching whiskers, in the cool mould at its heart, sharing his refuge with three pale lizards who listened to the noise fearfully, little pulses thumping in their smooth throats.

Practically everyone around the train was now interested in the progress of the chase, except the two-up players, whose monotonous chant of 'Dollar the mick' or 'Bringin' him in, gents,' sung in a high voice, supplied a sporadic Greek chorus to the little tragedy that was being acted out on the slope.

The group was far enough off as to appear like puppets to Jack, blue and khaki figures slightly obscured by the mounting ripples of heat that arose between him and them. Suddenly a cord was pulled, and all stood stock-still except one, who held a brown wisp above his head, and for a moment the group was as if painted against the green and red backdrop of the hill, with the creamy smoke writhing amongst them.

Then the spell was broken, and Jack saw a stick raised, and could picture a keen knife making the first slit in the soft white belly, and the sleazy pelt slowly leaving the little carcass.

Interest had left the hunt now. Faces left the windows and turned inwards; the train was due to start again any time.

The chap who had been in wheat said, 'I knew a cruel cow once; useter tie a stick of jelly each side of a rabbit and let it go down a burrow. Useter blow th' warren sky high...cruel cow!'

'I dunno,' said Jack. 'You got t' do something about the little bastards, and, when it's a case of them or the crops, cruel or not don't enter into it; Gawd knows there's enough of them that a few warrens don't make any difference.'

The train had started while he was speaking, and he glanced back at the hillside, but all he saw now was the restless shadows of the hawks flickering across his face.

Stedley touched him on the knee, offering a box of home-made biscuits. 'They're not much good now,' he said, 'but they're still not bad.' Jack took one and put it in his mouth, and as he said 'Thanks, Sted,' he blew out a cloud of fine crumbs.

'That's orright,' Stedley replied. He placed the box between them, lid off, and motioned Jack to help himself. 'Mum makes beaut cakes. That was her at the station the day we left. I saw you looking at her.'

'Yes,' Jack lied unconvincingly. 'I thought she looked like you.'

'D'you think so? I got a bonzer photo of her while I was home on leave. Gosh, it was good home, wasn't it? How did it go with you?'

'Fast!' said Jack. 'Too ruddy fast! And now we're away again.'

He turned to the window while they were speaking, and noticed that they had drawn away from the grassy plain; now the whole landscape lay in three broad bands of colour, red desert, purple hills and blue sky, joined by whirling pillars of dust that faded and shimmered and merged in the late afternoon heat.

Out of the corner of his eye he looked at Stedley, who sat with one hand in his lap, the fingers extended; with the other hand he pulled the little finger away, and then let it snap back into place, and his eyes were blank. Remembering again, mused Jack, and aloud he said, 'Penny for 'em, Sted!'

Stedley started, and said shyly, 'I was just thinking. You know how you get feeling lousy, and never knowing where you're going or anything, especially like now when we're going away from home...in...well, I got an antidote, sort of. I just think that, whatever happens, some time we must be heading home again, and if...if we don't make it, then I guess we don't know much about it, do we? Even going away like this really brings us nearer home, because, anyway, that's what's at the end of this bloody business — home; for most jokers, anyway.'

His voice trailed away, and, strangely, the carriage was silent except for Fisher, who was telling a yarn about Tich trying to sell his pig-sticker.

All up and down the long train they would be 'bashing' each other's ears like that. What they did on leave.

Jack turned and looked out of the window again into the deepening twilight; he didn't want any tea, and sat there until the last light went out in the carriages and the last song dwindled away, and the vast cool night enfolded the train and bore it on swiftly to the unmarked spot in the desert where it would meet the morning. He lay back and the song of the wheels came to him, clear and insistent, 'Going...Going away'...

He thought of his talk with Stedley, of the calm surety with which Sted had reckoned 'One day we will go back,' and suddenly — so suddenly that he wanted to sit up in the dark and tell someone, anyone — he was burningly aware that, no matter what happened, time must pass; no matter what misery and dirt and tiredness, no matter what fear of death and fear of being afraid, seconds and minutes, added up to days and brought nearer the end of the war when, as Sted said, they would be going back...going back.

Why, even now the wheels seemed to have changed their song; and while they sang 'Tickety tack, going back, going back' the train sucked in the miles, and disgorged them, and in the calm of the sleeping desert Jack slept.

THE WOOMERA

About the middle of the morning the little dark Sister hustled into the tent where Rex was lying, and said 'Come on, Galahad, your good deed for the day. Take Rose her morning tea.'

Rex looked up from his paper, laughing, and said, 'Break it up, now, Sister; I did it yesterday. I think you're a bit of a matchmaker.'

The Sister, already half-way to the next tent, said over her shoulder, 'Look out I don't nab you for myself, Sergeant,' and as Rex picked up the bucket of lemon-juice he thought, 'you could, too.' Then he walked over to Rose's tent.

Rose was a half-caste lubra from one of the outlying stations. She had long, slanting eyes, and her black hair, instead of being a wild frizz, hung in long waves, which she plastered with brilliantine.

There was no civilian hospital within hundreds of miles, and so the abos were admitted to the A.G.H., where a line of tents was set aside for them. Rose's husband was camped by the creek behind the hospital, a grizzled old buck, who spent the entire day pottering around her tent.

As Rex walked in she looked up from the cards laid out on her blanket and said, 'Good morning, Sergeant Rex,' in a high lilting voice.

Rex smiled. 'Good morning, Rose. Like a drink?' He poured

it out, and as she leaned over to take it from him he was enveloped in a cloud of the cheap perfume she used.

'Phew,' he muttered as he walked away from the tent, 'what a crow!'

He noticed that the tent next to Rose's, empty last night, now had an occupant, and he caught sight of the newcomer as he walked by...a woman's enormous brown eyes staring from a pinched black face, and one ludicrously skinny leg hanging from under the heavy army blanket.

He picked up the hose and began to water the young pawpaws which the little Sister had bullied him into planting around his tent.

Someone said softly, 'Good morning, boss.'

He turned around and saw a black boy leaning against the tent-pole. He wore a faded pink shirt, tattered army trousers and high-heeled stockman's boots, and was smiling questioningly.

Rex said 'hullo,' and the boy's grin broadened. He pointed to the young pawpaws.

'Soon grow...nine mont's, year, maybe...fruit!'

'Well, I hope I'm not here to pick 'em,' said Rex. 'What you here for? You sick, too?'

The boy shook his head. 'Me not,' he said, 'T'resa, my wife. She too sick, longa that tent,' and he looked at the tent where Rex had seen the little gin.

'Oh,' said Rex, 'you married. How old you?'

'Dunno...twenty maybe; I got two piccannin', little boy, little girl.'

'Kicking on, aren't you?' said Rex, and when the black boy looked at him enquiringly said hurriedly, 'What your name?'

'Peter,' said the boy. 'I live longa Mission.'

Rex lit a cigarette, and gave the boy one, which he carefully placed behind his ear. 'My word, you have come a long way.'

'Yes, I come longa aeroplane,' Peter said proudly. 'T'resa, she very sick.'

'Oh, well,' said Rex, laying the hose at the roots of a big pawpaw-tree, 'I'm going to lie down. See you after lunch.'

'Yes,' Peter replied, walking away, 'I go see T'resa.' He walked over to the tent, and Rex heard a plaintive rippling voice, and, craning his neck, saw the black boy leaning over his wife fanning the flies away with an old newspaper.

After lunch Rex sat in the shade of a casuarina, and idly watched the black boy's deft fingers scraping patiently at a slender stick with a piece of a broken bottle.

It was still and hot, and the amiable conversation of the creek and the narcotic hum of thousands of insects in the grass made him sleepy. He sat up with a jerk and said, 'What you make, Peter?'

The boy looked at Rex quickly and held out the stick. 'Woomera,' he said, 'for t'row spear.'

Rex took the weapon, and ran his fingers up the smooth haft, marvelling at the patience that had fashioned it out of a knotted stick. He gave it back to Peter, who started to scrape a groove in the base.

'How's T'resa, Peter? What Doctor say?'

The black boy continued scraping for a while, measured the depth of the groove with a small stick, and said, 'Dunno... He don't tell me, ever. T'ink T'resa too sick, too much.'

He spoke quite without emotion. He fished in the pocket of his ragged trousers and found a small piece of quartz, which he placed in the groove, leaving a projection of about a quarter of an inch. Rex watched in silence, interested.

'Who show you how to make woomera, eh?' he said, and Peter replied without looking up, 'Old man live along Mission.'

He paused, and his black eyes swept over the plain and the hills behind the hospital, and Rex followed his gaze; red and green and blue, mile upon mile of it, the imperishable sheet upon which was written the only record of the black man's history, and now ... who could read it?

'I piccannin, then; little fella,' Peter said. He patted the air around knee high with his open palm and laughed, showing his pink tongue and even white teeth; then he took a lump of bitumen from his pocket and, kneading it soft in his palm, pressed it into the groove around the quartz, and proceeded to bind the whole with copper wire.

Rex watched him. A piccannin. He tried to picture the black boy as a child, but could not. Hell, they were much the same age — but Peter was married, had two kids and his wife was dying; not that he seemed to care much. Or did he? Rex could not fathom the boy's blank gaze when he spoke of T'resa.

'What your name, Peter?' he said suddenly.

Peter looked at him strangely. 'Peter,' he said.

'No, I mean your ... what your people call you?'

'That one? Weeharrie.'

'And T'resa?'

Peter looked at him again and said abruptly, 'Neeloona. Look, you see.' He rose, and, taking a long, light stick from the grass, fitted the end against the quartz and, raising the woomera, launched the stick straight at the dog that lay outside Rose's tent. The cur ran howling, and Rose's husband came out. Peter called to him gaily, and laughed, then said to Rex 'I go now. See T'resa.' Rex watched him as he wandered over to the tent lines, his bare feet splashing in the soft dust — he had not worn his stockman's boots again since he arrived.

Soon the heat and the drone of the insects sent Rex to sleep, and he lay in the shade, not even waking when a Sister tip-toed out and laid a rug over his legs.

Half a dozen of the patients started a game of pitch-and-toss outside Rex's tent after tea that night, and he stood watching them in the fading light. Mosquitos were abroad, and the little dark Sister was whisking from tent to tent, putting up nets, and spraying.

'Got your net up, Sergeant?' she said to Rex as she passed him. As always, the sweet, clean smell of her starched apron and the touch of powder made him feel giddy and he wanted to lay his lips against her hair.

'Come on, boys, nets up,' she called to the players, and ducked as one of them plucked a flower from a pawpaw tree, and tossed it at her.

'Cripes, Sister, what about putting our nets up for us? We're sick.'

She made a savage grimace at him and, crushing the bloom in her hand, held it to Rex's face. 'Sweet, isn't it? Like tuberoses.'

Rex looked at the fine blue veins in her wrist and mumbled, 'Yes, like tuberoses.'

He turned away and saw Peter standing at the side of the tent, watching intently. As he caught Rex's eye, he smiled and murmured, 'Goo' night, boss,' and, when Rex nodded, they sat down together on a log to watch the pennies.

'Must be my first toss,' said one of the players, spinning the six pennies high into the dusty air. 'Come up heads! You beauts ... four.'

'You're unnatural,' said another, bending to pick up the tails. He took a cigarette from his mouth, and flipped it away; it lobbed almost at Peter's feet. The black boy stooped, picked it up, and was putting it to his lips when Rex knocked it out of his hand.

'Don't do that,' he said, 'it's dirty. Here, have one of these.' He took a packet from his coat pocket and gave one to Peter, who tucked it behind his ear.

The pennies player walked over. 'What y' mean — dirty?' he said, standing over Rex. 'It's good enough for the bloody boong, anyway. They should be glad to get that much.'

Rex felt the black boy start, and the red rushed to his face.

'Ah, pull your head in,' he said savagely; and the other muttered 'All right, don't do your block.' As he walked back to the game, Rex stood up, and moved in the direction of the Red Cross tent. Peter overtook him.

'Boss,' he said, 'what that feller mean, 'boong'?'

Rex looked up at the first pale stars and said 'I dunno. Just a name.'

Peter said 'Teacher longa Mission tell me white man, black man same, all same God. Me Cat'olic, look.' He pulled an old boot-lace from his shirt. On it hung two tiny silver medals, and a little leaden saint. He displayed them anxiously on his dark palm. 'That feller say wrong. Me not bush blackfella!' His voice was troubled, seeking assurance. Hell, thought Rex, what am I supposed to say? 'P'raps that fella don't know, Peter. You all right, don't worry.' He walked away and said over his shoulder, 'I write letter. See you later.'

But he went to his tent and lay down on his bed. Poor cow ... didn't know whether he was coming or going ... why did they interfere? One tells him he's all right and another slaps him down. Well, he couldn't do anything about it.

He lit his lamp, and picked up an old magazine but couldn't read.

Beetles and mosquitos were hitting at the lamp and getting in his hair. The game had stopped and he threw his book on his bed and went to stand outside the tent in the cool dusk, and watch the darkness seep up from the hollows and blot out the warm glow that still lingered on the red, barren hills.

In the still gloom the strident racket of cicadas was harsher than ever and overhead the flying-foxes flapped in an unending stream out of the east, dragging after them on the shadowy night. They passed over quietly, like a flight of soundless black bombers; in the morning, the ground beneath the mango trees would be littered with half-eaten fruit, and the trees starred with splashes of bright yellow where the big bats had been feeding. Rex had shot them, often, in the colony out on the river, but they never fell out of the trees, just hung there screaming shrilly.

A slight noise behind him made him turn around, and he saw Peter's white teeth gleam. He said 'How's things?'

Peter came closer with his noiseless tread. 'Goodnight, boss,' he murmured, 'Me sad.'

'Why? T'resa not too good?'

The boy said nothing, but traced invisible lines in the dust, with his bare toes. Rex could hear, faintly, coming from the Red Cross tent, a gramophone playing 'Melancholy Baby,' and the half-heard refrain brought back things only half-remembered that filled the night with a sadness he could not define ... scattered memories of nights just like this, on a high sand-hill over-looking the sea, and his girl singing softly; carnival dances on New Year's Eve, the streamers and the lights, and the determined gaiety: booze and the fresh breeze early in the morning, and the Cross fading slowly into the sea.

He took out a smoke and lit it and in the flare of the match he saw Peter's black gaze was fixed on him in a meaningless stare.

'Poor cow,' he thought, 'what the hell can I say?' Aloud he said 'Doctor he come today ... what he say?'

'I dunno,' Peter muttered. 'T'ink T'resa she die tonight, tomorrow, maybe.'

He said it very quietly, without selfconsciousness. What *did* he know? thought Rex. How *much* did they know? What secrets did they hide beneath the eternal 'no savvy' and meaningless grin?

Perhaps death came to them as a buzzing in the ears and a warm silence, or a blinding flash and a black curtain or just sleep. They said it was like that with animals — they didn't think about it, or about what happened after, and so didn't fear it ... nice way to be! In the dark trees by the creek the fireflies were busy weaving their glittering decorations in the branches, each one Morse-coding his palpitating song of love into the shadows. Rex picked up a couple of letters and smiled.

He flipped his butt away, and watched it describe a hot arc in the gloom, and burst against a stone in a shower of tiny sparks.

'Goo' night, Peter,' he said. 'Think I'll hit the hay.'

The boy said nothing, and Rex walked into the tent. He could feel the black eyes upon him. As he turned Peter stooped and picked up the glowing butt and inhaled deeply from it, then walked aimlessly towards the creek.

Some time that night Rex was awakened by a soft moaning from T'resa's tent. Hurricane-lamps cast awkward shadows around the lines, and made the pawpaws dance drunkenly. He heard the swish of the Sister's skirts, and the subdued rattle of a basin or a bucket, and, all the while, the soft animal sounds of suffering.

He got up and peered down the lane between the tents. Peter stood in the disturbed darkness outside and, as the Sister or the Doctor brushed by him, he would make as if to speak — put out his hand and half-open his lips — but what he wanted to ask wouldn't come. Perhaps he didn't even know himself, and while Rex watched he turned away and faded noiselessly into the shadows.

In the morning T'resa's tent was empty. The hard iron bed was stripped down to the mattress, and the flaps were rolled back. Rex breakfasted and shaved, and was standing out in the warm early sunshine watering the young pawpaws when Peter came up from the creek.

He had his stockman's boots on, and walked awkwardly. In one hand he carried a bundle wrapped in a red-spotted neckerchief, and in the other the woomera. His face was blank, impassive, and Rex could not even guess what was going on behind the smoky eyes.

'T'resa die las' night,' he said, as he approached closer to Rex. No more — just that, and said it as if he were remarking on the weather. 'What *does* he feel?' thought Rex. 'Yes, Peter, I know. I'm very sorry.'

The boy said no more, but stood still and looked at the white man. The little dark Sister bustled by, raised her brows at Rex, and said to Peter 'Off now, Peter?'

He answered, without taking his eyes off Rex, 'Yes, missus,' and then they were enclosed in a little world of uncomfortable silence, around which the activity of the hospital flowed unnoticed. Rose's husband walked up from the creek with two of his mangy dogs, which scuffled a hole in the dust outside the lubra's tent and settled down to their scratching; an ambulance pulled up at the Administration block, and four or five new patients got out; a Sister called out clearly and gaily to one of the orderlies. It all passed over their heads.

'What you do now, Peter? Go home?'

'Yes, go along Mission, p'raps,' said Peter.

'How far — one day, two days?' Rex was glad to find something to talk about, something that would lead the conversation away from the empty tent down the line. He felt that the boy wanted to ask him something, and he wouldn't know what to say in answer. 'You walk, or you got horse?'

Peter stared up the road. 'I get ride longa truck,' he said, 'no go there' — waving to the shimmering eternity of bush and hills, behind the hospital — 'bad blackfella there, maybe kill this boy.' His black fingers wandered up and down the smooth haft of the woomera. 'T'resa dead. My wife.'

Rex said hurriedly 'Your piccaninnies — they live longa Mission?'

'Yes, longa Mission — learn sing, Bible, Peter n' Paul. Boss, you tell me somet'ing?'

'Here it is!' thought Rex. 'Yes Peter,' he said casually, 'I tell you if I know.'

Peter turned away and looked at the empty tent, and then at the ground, a furrow in his brow. 'Boss,' he said softly, 'they put T'resa, my wife, longa graveyard?'

'Yes,' said Rex, 'I suppose so.'

'They put her longa grave with soldier, boss; he no touch her?'

Rex stared at him astonished. A kookaburra was croaking hoarsely in a tree near by, and snatches of talk and laughter drifted from surrounding tents, and between them the white and the black, the dim past and the present, there could be only silence.

'Holy smoke!' he thought, 'so that's it! Poor cow' ...

As he looked into Peter's eyes he was touched by the plea he saw there, the struggling understanding that was caught between two worlds so totally different, and unable to believe either one; and his anger rose against the people who had stripped the boy of his code and given him in return something half understood and a troubled memory of something his people had believed in since time began.

He put his hand on the black shoulder and said softly 'No, Peter, no one touch T'resa ... you don't worry, she safe. She sleep all right, I tell Father Riley.'

'T'ank you,' said Peter simply. 'I go now,' He held out the woomera. 'For you,' he said. 'You good man.' He turned abruptly and shuffled out towards the road, and was soon lost to sight amongst the dusty trees.

Rex stood looking after him with the woomera in his hand. A good man ... first time anyone had called him that ... funny! The little dark Sister walked past him, stopped and came back.

'He gone?' she inquired, and looked in the direction of Peter's tent.

'Yes, he's gone,' said Rex, 'he gave me this.'

'What, his old bow and arrow? What a card!'

'Yes, his old bow and arrow,' said Rex, more to himself than to her, and she hurried away. 'His supple black fingers made it while his poor damned bewildered head tried to grapple with something he couldn't understand; and now he's given it to me for something I didn't do for him, and I'll just heave it away. As you say, Sister, what a card!'

'IT ALWAYS TAKES TWO'

As the darkness faded into pearl-grey, the dense green mangroves stood out more and more distinctly where they marched right out into the water on gnarled black legs. Soon the rising mist that curled above the trees showed plainly where a tidal creek wound back into the jungle, and, as the water beneath the boat became less opaque, Adam could see a fantastic world of coral and weed, colourful and serene beneath the surface.

Two lakatois sped out of the mouth of the creek and, dipping and bobbing through the light surf, glided at length under the bow of the corvette. The boys in them stood up and waved their paddles, and their voices rang out clear and happy in the cool morning.

Adam thought of Lae...no welcome committee there; and yet he seemed almost to have forgotten it already. It must be the mind, building up a defence against what it didn't want to know or remember; shying off the things that would make it throb with hate and misery, and make the heart race madly when you woke up in the night with the water up to your armpits, and the surf sucking you back, and stabs of flame like a bright amber necklace along the edge of the jungle...no; you had to forget or go batty. And so you forgot, just like that, and started the next phase with a clean slate — almost; you remembered the things that your body had learned to ensure its survival, every time something new, until it grew, like everything in the army, to be a drill: *On 'One!' leap clear of the ramp...*

'Nice an' quiet, ain't it?' said Bob at his elbow, and Adam replied 'Yair. Wonder when the Mayor an' brass band will show up?'

More lakatois were shooting towards them, and one of them carried a wiry, red-headed soldier in shorts and boots. His hair hung down the nape of his neck, and he was conversing fluently in pidgin with the natives who paddled his canoe.

'Hi!' he yelled. 'Nice work! Just in time for breakfast,' and he swarmed up the landing-net that hung over the side, trailing in the clear water.

He was one of a party which had been patrolling back of the beach for a couple of months. As he reached the deck the boys were crowding around him — how were the boongs? Were there any Japs close in? How close?

The stranger turned and pointed to the frowning mountains that poked their woolly crowns through the clouds a few miles back from the sea. 'Up there,' he said, 'any mount of 'em. In a bad way, though; poor skinny brutes'...

Adam looked at the hills again. Some of the upper slopes were flushed deep pink in the growing light, and harsh gashes of indigo showed where jungle-matted re-entrants cut far back into the ranges. Again he experienced the queer feeling that he was being irresistibly drawn toward them; that, no matter what he did, it was another link in the chain of events that would one day confront him with his destiny.

He had felt it first when he stepped on to the corvette that had brought them here, a sudden realisation that the step he took, severing from the land was the first move in a new round. Death or fate, whichever you preferred to call it, had chased him halfway round the world, from the Middle East to New Guinea; but now he knew that it was he who did all the chasing, and that fate just sat in its pre-destined place and waited for him to come, jerking him like a manikin on the end of a string that stretched through four years and thousands of miles; and something told him that the end of the string was somewhere in this island...up in those hills, maybe...

He had been in other, bigger shows. There it had been whole battalions that had fought out their destinies, which were inescapably the destinies of every soldier fighting; but here it was different, more personal, somehow, and Adam felt fatalistic about it. Whatever happened in the big war all over the world, for him things were going to come to a head. He had come halfway to his appointed climax — or almost.

Someone else had travelled the other half, someone whose slit eyes might even now be fastened on the corvette from the dark hills.

Wally had said the other night, 'I wish I was a pilot, up there in a world all your own.' But no man ever lived in a world of his own, and Adam had replied 'We're too much the creatures of circumstance, and, no matter how much we kick, it's what the other fellow does to us, as much as what we do to ourselves, that makes us either this or that. It takes two to make a cycle complete.' Someone kills you, whether he breathes a 'flu germ down your neck or drops a grenade behind you, whether he knows it or not; and through all the years and all the places he went, every move he made was designed to bring him to just that place at just that time when he would complete your run, and then move on till he found someone who would clinch the deal for himself; and so the game went on. No matter how you fancied yourself, you simply were not the master of your own destiny.

The hills held Adam's gaze, so lonely and withdrawn, and yet seeming so lovely and fragile where the white clouds clung to the rain forests on the upper slopes and the pink glow turned to gold.

He found himself thinking of his opposite number, up there, crouching in the dripping undergrowth. I suppose he'd be about the same age, he mused; but that's about as far as it would go.

What did a Japanese youth do — leave school, start smoking and take his first girls into the back seats of the pictures to play at love in the close darkness, and then proceed to dances, grog and maybe a car, and then marriage? Or did this black-eyed enemy dedicate himself to the spreading of the seed of Yamato, as Adam had read; work and study, and deny his body for the Emperor, and take his holidays in some national shrine in the quiet of the cedar woods, marvelling at the beauty of a spray of blossom etched against the grey sky? All that was most likely heifer-dust, anyway; and yet, they were a queer crew.

Adam had lived in Broome, on the north-west coast, when he was a youngster, and had known plenty of Japs, especially the quiet, grave, button-eyed kids, children of the divers who worked the beds for shell, and, as it turned out, systematically plotted every shoal and inlet, reef and tidal creek along that wild, lonely coast, right up around Arnhem Land, where they went after trochus and beche-de-mer, to the grey waters of the great Gulf. Plotted against the day, twenty years later, when they would walk in; only their plans had gone astray. Few had dreamed about that then; and if they had, had been howled down. One night every year the whole town had turned out to watch them parade in the feast of the lanterns.

In the velvety tropic dusk they gathered on the white shell road down to the beach, young and old, mostly dressed in vivid kimonos, and each carrying a coloured paper lamp on a pole — glowing flowers of light, red and green, yellow and gold, that swayed and bobbed in the soft dark as they walked in procession to the beach. They sang as they walked, plaintive songs in a minor key that mingled uncertainly with the dull throb of the sea and the sad cries of night birds, and the pale young moon that stood on tiptoe to peer over the feathery tops of the palms.

When they reached the beach, glowing palely in the gloom, they lit strings of fire-crackers, and then the wives and children of divers who had lost their lives during the season in the warm waters from shark or groper or the dread bends would stand at the water's edge, where the turning tide lapped quietly in the dark, and launch a tiny oil-paper ship that carried a light.

The tide carried the fairy fleet offshore, lonely points of golden flame that danced on the ripples like giant fireflies, and the people stood on the beach in perfect silence and watched them out of sight. Some sank, some just disappeared in the night; no word was spoken, and the only sound was the hushing of the tide and the sigh of the wind in the palms...

Funny coves, all right; loving beauty with one half of their souls and wallowing in beastliness with the other. The things he knew about them made Adam's blood run cold. No wonder the boongs said 'Japan — no good! Me kill!' and drew the back of a finger across their throats, grinning and rolling their eyes. A motor launch had been lowered and nosed along the side of the net where the boys were going over four at a time. It filled and moved off, and its place was taken by a big lakatoi, and another, and soon the whole company was formed up on the beach to march to the village.

It wasn't far — a smooth coral path that wound between the palms, under a couple of huge old lime-trees, and gave on to a clear space with a bit of a rise between it and the sea. The houses, the few that there were; were new, and a few were building; some distance off the blackened ruins of others showed where the Nips had passed.

Adam saw only a couple of Marys, the rest were most likely out in the taro-patch, but there seemed to be no piccaninnies at all except a few very young ones. As a rule, you'd see two or three outside every hut, rolling in the dust, annoying the scrounging pigs or just sitting in the warm sunshine, gravely regarding the phenomenon of their own distended little black bellies; but here there were none, and Adam found himself thinking again of the yellow men in the hills.

His section was assigned to an area on the far side of the village, and soon had things shipshape. Adam had dug a hole and stowed his gear handy, and was sitting in the shade of a palm studying a map of the island which had been given him on board, when the lieutenant walked over to him.

'Look, Adam,' he said, 'You'll take out the first patrol. The cutter's broken down, and number four section is out loading, otherwise they'd have gone. Now, here's the dope...'

Adam looked out to sea. 'I told you so,' he said to himself.

Number four couldn't go ... another link. Mechanically he listened to what the lieutenant was saying: '...An old Jap track; not shown on the map. Find out where it goes and map it ... be careful, still plenty of Nips around in the hills.'

Well, that's how it was. Four section couldn't go, and so you ... Adam sat for a while, looking at the map, although it didn't tell him much; spurs and contours were apt to be any old how, and creeks and rivers were very sketchy. He stood up, and went over to warn his section, thinking as he went 'This is it.'

Before the war, when crisis followed crisis, and every day started and ended with the threat of hostilities, the thought of dying had appalled him. What? Leave all this to lie cold and still and forgotten? And he'd plunge with greater abandon into the business of living, just as people fill tanks and tubs when there is a threat of the water being cut off. But now, if ever he did think of it, it was with nothing but curiosity — at all events, he would know what he didn't know now; only, his body would cool, ants and beetles would wander unmolested over his face, and his eyes would see nothing, and he'd be like ... well, anything left by the tide of war — an old boot, a busted gun; people would soon forget, and in the long run it wouldn't make much difference to the course of history.

The mind again ... telling itself since death appeared likely that after all it wasn't so bad. Don't worry; if you come through — all right; if you don't, then you don't know much about it, do you?

They left the village an hour or two before midday. In preparation, just another patrol — check the gear, ammo., tucker; tell each man where you're going, and show him the approximate route. 'You'll take over, Ted, if anything happens; and after you, Ernie. Okay; then let's go.' But all the time the feeling of unreality, as though this time, at least, it really didn't matter.

It was hot, hard going, and the afternoon was already well advanced when they struck what appeared to be the old Jap track and plunged into the foothills. Adam didn't like it much, slopes all around, and good ambush positions every few hundred yards.

When a single shot rang out, rattling the echoes of the hillside, and a slug spat viciously in the dust beside him, he wasn't greatly surprised. The section went to cover, and the echoes died away in the ravine, and a few moments later Ern rustled through the bushes and stopped a yard or so away from him.

'What's the set-up Ern?' Adam inquired. 'See anything?'

'Only the smoke,' Ern replied. 'About two hundred yards up the track, and just into the right ... better take a look-see.'

'Right.'

Adam glanced up the track. On the left a very steep slope, with little cover; couldn't go that way without being picked off. On the right an even rise with sufficient cover, boulders and some creepers — better go that way.

Ted had brought the rest up in cover behind him, and Adam said over his shoulder. 'Bring the Bren up and cover up along the track, Ted. Sandy and Art can take the left, and Wal keep a look out behind. Ern and I will go around the right and see what's there. If anything goes wrong scoot back down the track and try to by-pass this place. All right? See you later, then.' If anything happens ... another link. Must be just about the end of the chain.

Adam wormed cautiously forward, ears and eyes alert for what lay ahead. Ern was about five yards off to his right, body sloped forward, Owen at his hip. Almost two hundred yards, he'd said ... should be about on them now.

He looked over at Ern and raised his hand, making an O of his thumb and forefinger. Ted and Ern would take the section through. It was like reading a book of which he had been told the ending, so sure was he of it; and, try as he did, he could not keep his whole mind on the job. He edged round a boulder, and came face to face with a Jap.

Time stopped while they stared at each other, the blue eyes and the black.

Automatically, Adam's finger, ready curled around the trigger, contracted, and the bolt shot forward with a futile click. Stoppage. Faulty round or something. The last link ... if that round had been fed in one or two later, if he'd picked up the ammo. box on either side of the one he had taken, if ... but he hadn't; and as the Jap's weapon swung deliberately to cover him he thought — surely this slant-eyed bastard would have some mark of identification, a red carnation, or the other half of a cut coin, especially since they had both come so far? He found himself grinning; it was almost perfect.

There was a sudden ear-splitting burst of fire from his right, and the Jap's hands clutched at his belly. Adam watched in a curious daze; the yellow face puckered like a baby's, crying, and a strangled word or two tumbled from his lips just ahead of the blood. He lurched to his hands and knees, head down as though looking for something in the grass, and with a soft moan, rolled over, one hand twitching grotesquely, trying desperately to grasp the thread that was slipping so quickly between the fingers.

No more shooting; must have been a lone wolf. Adam stood and stared at the body, trying to focus his thoughts. What had happened? He had come halfway; so had the Jap, but destiny had slipped him up. It was the Jap who had completed the journey, and he, Adam, who would go on. His premonition had been all screwy, must have been nerves.

A sharp stone struck him on the shoulder, and Ern rasped from behind a rock, 'Adam! What the hell you doin'? For God's sake, get into cover!'

Skinny little runt, the Jap was; covered with sores, too. Well, thought Adam, he's out of it, and I go on. He turned and looked at Ern, who stared back, lips parted, eyes questioning. 'Adam!' he whispered again, 'what's the matter? You crook?'

'No, Ern, I'm apples,' Adam replied. 'Looks like that's that, eh?' He looked up the ravine where the shadows were thickening. 'Better get out of here before it's any darker. Think we'll go back to the entrance.'

They started to pick their way back, and Ern said 'What's was wrong with you then? You were like a stunned gosling.'

'Was I? I had a funny feeling about that Jap. I dunno' —

'What d'you mean, you dunno? Dunno what?'

Ern's words trickled into the cool silence that had settled on the ravine with the dusk, and it was some moments before Adam answered. From where they were he could just see Ted crouched by the track; the others were there, but hidden in the shadow. 'It's hard to explain,' he muttered, more to himself than to Ern, 'but somehow it seemed like the wrong ending to a story' ...

They merged into the gloom, and the Jap was left wrapped in stillness on the hillside. The fingers of his outflung hand clenched, and a green lizard wriggled over them, paused on the skinny wrist to listen to the watch that still ticked there, and then ran up the arm inside the sleeve looking for the warmth that was not there. This was where the story really ended.

THE LETTER

Mort squatted on his heels in the flickering gloom and listened to the guttural drone of the kanaka's voice, roughened and slurred by betel and tumbling across his thick lips in shuddering jerks and starts that made it almost impossible to understand him. Outside, the night was wild; a high wind lashed at the trees, swinging the trailing vines like pennons before it and covering the muddy track a foot deep in great glistening leaves. Rain fell intermittently, in driven gusts that snarled on the tattered sac-sac thatch just above his head, dripping through the rotted patches and snaking in an inquisitive finger through the hole in the wall that served as a door. It was a bush kanaka's hut, low to the ground, stinking with smoke and stale tobacco and the acrid kanaka smell, unfloored, unlined, with just a row of bare poles on the ground for beds. They'd been living there for the past night and day, waiting for this bloke to come. Silver had been interrogating him for the best part of half an hour, since just after sundown when he had loped into the hut, streaming water from every pore, to tell his story. Mort listened in, although Silver would have told him anything of interest later on.

''Long morning time, masta,' the man muttered, and spat a stream of red betel juice on to the floor. He looked at it for a moment, wrinkling his brow, and then rubbed it into the closely packed earth with a splayed, calloused foot, and continued with his story — how, in the morning, twenty Japanese left a village called Kikimogo and walked along the Government road to another kanaka place called Ramaka, reaching it at about sundown. Some of them were armed, and the rest carried packs; in some of the packs there were papers — he had seen them some time before.

'Orright, Rukwa. Talk-talk 'e finish!' Silver waved the kanaka to the far end of the hut, where their stores were stacked high to keep them out of the water, and raised his voice. 'Give the coon a tin of bully and some biscuits, Bert, will you?' He turned then to Mort, who looked up at him with a questioning smile.

'Well, what you think of it, Silver?'

The long man squatted down beside him, his skinny legs hunched almost to his shoulders, like the back legs of a grasshopper, and tugged at the lobe of his ear, a habit he had when he was weighing something up. The off-again-on-again flicker of the little slush-lamp splashed deep shadows around his eyes and over his gaunt promontory of a nose, and rioted in the long ash-blond hair that gave him his name. The boongs called him Masta White-grass — like the Greeks they had a word for everything.

'I dunno, Mort,' he answered, drawing his brows down into a perplexed expression. 'Could be Okay, could be phoney. Long way into Jap country here, you know — coon might be working for 'em. Still, Luluai down Samanai reckons he knows him. Could be.' Could be what, he didn't say, but left it to the other's imagination. Where one word would suffice, Silver considered it a crime to use two. Mort smiled to himself. The old clam!

'Sounds interesting, china. He reckons he saw the papers go into the packs — they might be anything, order of battle, strength returns, instructions for attack or movement — *anything!* He says there's twenty in a patrol; well, say half of 'em are armed, one weapon to one carrier, well, we got six ... should be able to do 'em over!'

'Yeah.' Silver blinked at him in the dull light. 'Not just shoot and scatter, Mort. Got t' bowl 'em over, finish, otherwise they'll just go to ground other side of the track an' we'll never get near the packs, see? Hard to arrange!'

Mort picked up a stick and scratched on the hard floor between his knees. Silver watched him. A capital 'D' first, with a wealth of curls and flourishes, then a tentative 'a' and then a 'y'. Next another 'd', followed quickly by 'awn'. Daydawn. Daydawn Station in the Murchison, Western Australia. Home. Red soil, not black, and the stark whiteness of the river gums, not the lush unhealthy green of the jungle. Purple hills, with columns of ochrous dust holding the red plain and the pale blue sky apart. Home.

'We could get over it, Silver, easy,' he said, dropping the stick and looking up. 'Let them get right in amongst us, and after we open up and what's left of the pongos hit the scrub, we hurl a few grenades after them to keep their scones down and then four, say Bert, Arch, Wacka and you, keep firing, but back into the jungle. That way there won't be any danger of hitting whoever's out on the track, and it'll make the Nips keep down. Then me and Mike hotfoot it out on to the track and hurl in the packs. Then we gather as many as we can hump and leg it. Might even be able to send the coons back later for the others. The chinese soldiers won't wake up you're firing the wrong way for a while. It's a chance.'

He stopped talking; the only sound was the soft murmur of the others in the far end of the hut and the thud of rain and jungle berries on the roof. Silver sucked in his breath in a sharp, deep sigh.

'Risky, Mort. Long way from home for casualties!'

'Course it's risky — what the hell isn't? But it's not as risky as it might be, nor as other jobs we've done!'

'Wonder what the road's like there — need a fair bit of cover close in to the track!' No question or argument as to who should do the more dangerous job out on the track — if Mort did it one day he would do it the next. It evened out in the long run.

'Soon find out,' Mort looked up and called to the kanaka, beckoning him. 'Quick-time!'

Rukwa put down the bully beef tin he had been eating out of, wiped his greasy hands on the dry lap-lap one of their coons had lent him, and walked over to the white men. He stood respectfully until they spoke.

'Rukwa,' said Mort, taking his weed-tin and his cigarette lighter out of his pocket. One he placed on the floor and, pointing to it, said 'Kikimogo!' The other he placed a couple of feet away, rested his finger on it and, looking at the kanaka, said 'Ramaka!' Then he picked up a stick and joined the two with a plain furrow in the dirt saying, as he did so, 'Guv'man road ... you got savvy?'

The big coon wriggled and grinned delightedly — they loved this sort of thing. 'Yes, masta,' he burbled. 'Me got savvy, true!'

'Orright now. This-fella Guv'man road,' Mort ran his finger along the length of the furrow, and looked questioningly at the big native. Was there plenty of timber close to the track?

'Yes, masta, 'e stap!' Rukwa nodded his head vigorously. 'Japan, 'im 'e no got akis, no can rous'im dewai!'

'Go on!' Silver muttered. 'So they don't keep the timber cleared away from the track, eh? I wonder why — that's asking for trouble! Orright, Rukwa, finish!'

'Perhaps because like the boong says, they got no axes!' Mort grinned. 'Although I can't see that. Anyway, it's the green light, eh?'

'Start early, first light, be best?' the other decided. He wouldn't waste words, by saying yes or not to the suggestion. The mere fact that he went on with the plan signified that he would be in it. 'Give us time to get a good possy. Plan when we get there.'

'Yeah ... Okay. Tell the others, will you, mate?'

'What you goin' t' do?'

'Oh, finish off a letter ...'

Silver grinned. 'Flamin' letters!' and Mort grinned back at him. As Silver, bent almost double, went to let the other men in on the plan, he took an oil-silk roll from a long pocket he had sewn on the inside of his shirt and extracted some sheets of paper and a stub of pencil. He licked the pencil and studied what he had written the night before. He did a bit every night, when he got the chance, and sometimes even during the day. He'd even written close on three pages of a letter once while squatting beside a track waiting for some Nips to walk into an ambush. It passed the time and steadied his nerves.

'*I'm glad about the new tank,*' he'd written. '*I was worried about it for a while. Thank Mr McKenzie for doing it for you, will you? He's a good old stick. You say you're going to try some wheat? Don't overdo it, dearest — we'll scratch along somehow. Just be there when I get back, and never mind about the bank balance. The last photos of Graham and Merle were beauts — I've got them in front of me as I write ...*' he looked hungrily at the snapshot on his knee; a leggy little girl of about eleven and a fair-haired bruiser of five; behind them, grinning, obese, vigilant, Veronica, the old station gin who had looked after him when he was a kid. '*...glad the weather's been so good, it'll mean plenty of good feed. I'm toying with the idea of sinking my deferred into a good young Hereford bull after the war — polled of course. What do you think, dearest? Should go well on our kind of country ...*'

The wind scratched in the thatch and worried the tree-tops, and the slush-lamp jumped and quivered, sending grotesque shadows cavorting over the roof as moths and beetles in suicidal hordes battled its struggling flame. Acrid smoke drifted up to his nostrils from the tiny fire the kanakas had built in the far, dark end of the hut, voices murmured, a ration tin clanked, and the snaking rope of water gathered in a pool about his feet as he licked the stump of his pencil and began to write. '*Hello, darling, it's another night, now, pretty squally outside, but we're snug as cats in a crib. I wish you could see us ...*'

They moved off in the first pale light, when the pigeons were still drumming eerily in the deep jungle — 'balus 'e crai', the boongs called it — when the pigeons cry. A long indistinct snake of men moving jerkily along the overgrown kanaka pad, silent, still numb with sleep, miserable from cold and damp. Rukwa in front to guide them, then Silver, Bert, Arch and Wacka, then three coons laden with their stores, and then Mort and Mike, who, since they were going to do the job on the track together, brought up the rear.

They wanted to hit the patrol about midway between the two villages, Kikimogo and Ramaka, to ensure the minimum chance of interference from either end, consequently they did not have very far to go from where they had been bivouacking. They found a spot, a nice, level stretch of the road that might almost have been made for their purpose, with the spoil from a shallow drainage ditch that flanked the track making a low earthwork in front of where they would lie. Silver concertinaed his long frame behind a small tree only a few feet from the edge of the track, and just in advance of the rest of them who were strung along fifteen or so yards, lying flat, partly concealed by the low embankment and partly by the leaves and ferns they had jammed down the sides of their gaiters, into their belts and under their hatbands. The boongs were a couple of hundred yards into the jungle, out of the way of stray slugs.

'Silver!' Mort whispered harshly. There was actually no call to whisper as they could see a fair bit of the track in both directions, but it was a habit, and a wise one, to do so. 'You're too close, if they're on their toes!'

Silver shook his head and grinned.

'Shrink when they come along — that wide!' He held up his little finger. 'From funk. Won't see me!'

Mort grinned back at him, and dropped his head on to his arm. He still wasn't satisfied about Silver's spot, but, apart from dragging the old goat back by the heels, there was little he could do about it. The sun was up well and truly now, and hot. It broke through the leaves above and warmed him, then made him hot, drawing the stink out of the shirt that he hadn't had off his back for four days and nights. Yet funnily, when you took it off, the skin wasn't dirty, but clean, smooth as satin; all the dirt went into the rag, and cripes, it smelled like it! But *his* smell, *his* body — thank God he could still raise a sweat. He breathed deeply of it, acutely conscious of being alive. One day, perhaps years ahead, he would take life for granted, like he used to before the war, but not now. Now it was something that they renewed every day, not a matter of a ninety-nine year lease, and the rank smell of sweat in his nostrils was his assurance that his body was still his own, and a going concern.

Birds and insects were abroad now; the birds, flapping and squawking in the high trees, dropped half-eaten nuts and berries to the ground about the prone figures, and the insects, invisible on bark and twig all around, solemnly rubbed leg and wing together and produced a rising din of clicks and rattles that acted like a lullaby. Warm and still, lulled by the insects, he lay with the sun on his back, and presently picked up half of a red berry that had just plopped beside him and lobbed it gently against the cheek of the man next to him, Wacka.

'Keep nit!' he whispered. 'Having a snooze!'

'Okay!' Wacka made a circle of his thumb and first finger, grinning. 'C'n sleep your ruddy head off!'

He didn't know how long he slept — it might have been an hour, it might have been a few seconds. Something touched his cheek and he was awake, like a wild thing, instantly in possession of all his senses, knowing where he was and what he was there for. Men got that way. Wacka nodded briefly along the track, and Mort heard the clatter and rattle that almost invariably preceded the Japs in the jungle. That they should move on the Government road in broad daylight was bad enough, he mused, but why make a noise like a flaming Labour Day procession? Well, it was their funeral. Yeah, their funeral, all right!

He craned his neck a little, cautiously, but could not see them yet. His eyes dropped to the ground beneath his nose, and he saw an earwig scurry out of a matted jungle of twigs and rotting leaves, its tail over its back and its pincers gaping wide. A couple of ants were conducting a struggle over a piece of seemingly valueless dry bark until, dropping it suddenly and simultaneously, they raced off busily in opposite directions. His eyes rose from the teeming mould and up his Owen to the foresight. Good old 37842, the paint long blistered off her tacky barrel, the jerry-built wooden butt worn and hacked about.

Where the heck were the ruddy Japs — they should have

been in the ambush by now... He peered cautiously again down the track but still could not see anything, although the noise was, if anything, even greater. He looked sideways at Wacka and saw him snake out an arm to pick up a pellet of paper that had just been flipped to him by the man one beyond him. He watched Wacka's face as he read what was written on the paper, saw the grim smile wreathe his eyes and saw his lips form a familiar oath. Then he rolled the pellet again and flipped it to Mort.

'The bastards are having a brew,' he read off the grubby slip of paper. 'Wouldn't it?' Wouldn't it, all right! Mort rolled the paper and carefully flipped it to Mike, the only other man on the far side of him. A cold sensation sat in his belly and loins, and his breath came a little quicker. Twenty or more Nips having a cup of tea a few yards away from the end of the ambush was not the kind of thing calculated to calm anyone's nerves. One of them was certain to wander off into the scrub a bit for something or other — Mort grinned bleakly as he imagined the reactions of the Jap who first discovered an Australian soldier stretched out beneath a bush overlooking their tea-party. Well, there was nothing to do but to sit still and weather the storm; strung out as they were, like Farmer Brown's ruddy cows, they were in a bad spot if anything started — masked each other's fire and hadn't anything like a decent getaway. His eyes narrowed as he heard a burst of shrill laughter from along the track, followed by a string of guttural Japanese. 'Having the time of their ruddy lives!' he thought malevolently. 'Hope the ruddy tea chokes them!'

What seemed like hours passed; the sun shone hotly on his back, the birds flapped and squawked and the noise of the insects was intensified by the mounting heat. The strain was becoming almost unbearable when Wacka, without turning his head, whispered out of the corner of his mouth, 'They're coming!'

Mort's eyes, strained on the track, saw a single Jap first of all, walking easily but cautiously towards the ambush, trailing his rifle and peering from side to side. Presently behind him, the rest came into view; as the boong had said, about half were armed and about half were cargo-men carrying great bulging packs that looked as if they might contain all the secrets of the Japanese Sixth Division. Mort started to feel an interest in the business again.

Suddenly, something happened. Usually their forward scouts loped along, rifle over the shoulder and quite often with a dixie of food swaying from the barrel, head down and mind somewhere in the sacred Thousand Islands. Not so this one — he walked a little way, then stopped and almost sniffed the air. He couldn't have seen anything, or he wouldn't have stopped in the middle of the track. It was some sixth sense — perhaps the very air was so charged with anxiety at that particular spot that he'd run into it like he'd run into a brick wall. Whatever the cause, he motioned backwards with the flat of his palm without turning around, and the noisy cavalcade behind him stopped too, bunched up into a Bren gunner's dream. Mort could imagine Arch fondling the trigger of his Bren, his black and hairy cheek nestled snugly against the butt and his pale blue, murderous eye glaring through sights chock-a-block with yellow-bellies.

The forward guard was moving again now, steadily, stealthily, as though drawn by a rope around his neck to the very tree where Silver was hidden. It was uncanny. Mort could see the long man's face in profile — it was as if carved out of stone. The Nip drew nearer, and Mort could feel the intensity of the six pairs of eyes watching the scout's every move, the cold menace of the ugly muzzles training on his chest and belly. He reached the edge of the track, peered about and took a step towards Silver's tree. Silver raised himself on one knee, gently, said softly, 'Howdy, stranger!' and, almost knocking the Jap's popping eyes off with the barrel of his Owen, blew his head off with a good burst.

A split second after Silver pressed his trigger Arch was ladling it into the group down the track, supported by every weapon in the ambush. There were a couple of hoarse shouts and an animal scream of agony that crinkled the skin on Mort's spine, then an infinitesimal lull in the firing. Changing mags, his mind said, while his hands automatically unhooked a grenade from his belt. No movement from the track, as far as he could see through the swirling cordite fumes — good. A quiver in the grass on the other side — bad.

'Grenades!' he yelled, slipping the pin out of his and holding it for a couple of seconds before lobbing it gently across the cleared space. A line of savage bursts growled and rumbled on the other side of the track, and another scream of agony split the shuddering air.

'Come on, Mike!' he shouted, and bounded out of cover, his words almost drowned as the others started to fire back into the jungle, their muzzles pointed at the tree-tops.

The cordite stung his eyes and nostrils, and he almost tripped over a ghastly sprawling body, the one that Silver got with his first burst; then another, and then a pack, lying abandoned on the ground. 'Here, Mike!' he rasped, and together they heaved it into the bushes. It weighed a ton. His eyes darted ahead; the fumes were clearing and his mind counted thirteen bodies while he thought, 'Thirteen dead; that leaves seven in the grass if there were twenty', and his hands groped and swung at the packs. They wouldn't be able to get them all — best make sure of what they had. 'I'll get a couple more!' he gasped as they swung one in, 'you drag the others farther in and tell Silver to get the coons up to take 'em back! Go on!' as Mike lingered a moment, and, turning his back on the other, he started to race up the track, but stopped dead.

Right in front of him there was a tree across the way, about belly high. As he crouched, staring at it for a split second that seemed like a year, he saw the crown of a khaki cap rise above the top edge of the wood until a small blood-coloured circle was disclosed and began to move stealthily, stopping and starting, along the log to the Japs' side of the track. Below the log, he could see two black canvas, two-toed shoes moving in company with the cap.

He crept swiftly to the log, raised his head and shoulders over it and poked the muzzle of his Owen into a startled, round yellow face. With his teeth drawn back unconsciously in a terrible grin, he pressed the trigger and the bolt shot forward with a futile click. *Jesus! He'd forgotten to reload!* Quicker than thought he swung the butt around and crashed it into the Jap's bewildered face. The yellow man slumped behind the log, groaning and whimpering, and Mort stood over him flailing at his round black skull with the butt of the weapon.

Suddenly he realized that he was in a cone of terrible silence; no birds, no insects. Only an occasional bubbling groan from the other side of the track.

'Mort, for Chris' sakes, come in out of that!' It was Wacka, his face peering urgently, uglily, from the bushes. 'Come in, damn you!'

Mort stood with his Owen poised for a moment, and the Jap behind the log lurched drunkenly to his feet, blood streaming through his hands where he held them against his battered head. There was a roar at his side and a belching cloud of cordite enveloped him as he felt the slugs from Wacka's gun go past him, heard them thud into the screaming Jap, who toppled at his feet, threshed and lay still. Almost without thinking he leaned down, grasped the man's collar, and, yanking savagely, dragged him into the cover at the edge of the track.

'Oh, Jesus! you fool, you fool!' Silver was saying, but Mort hardly heard him.

'You got the packs?' he demanded, and Silver said, 'Yes — yes, the coons got 'em! Come on, there's a team of 'em, must be twenty or more we didn't get. They'll wake up in a minute!'

'Frisk 'im!' Mort gritted, pointing to the dead Jap who lay hideously at their feet. 'Bert, Mike, you others! Keep a lookout while we go through this bastard!' They dragged the body farther off the track into the shelter of some rank grass; he lay on his belly, one arm outstretched, the other cradling his battered head. His helmet, which must have fallen off in the terror and excitement of the first volley, lay near him.

Wacka stood in the ditch, with one foot on the low parapet, and leaned on his knee, his drawn face turned to the track, his restless eyes flickering up it and down it, in and out of the cover crowding close on the far side; Mike was at the Jap's feet and Bert and Silver were on the other side of him. Mort, and Arch who had dropped his beloved Bren on the grass, crouched over the body. It was a tense, tearful job; blood still oozed spasmodically from the Jap's mouth and perforated back, saturating the belt of a thousand stitches that was wound around and around his waist. They were beginning to feel the reaction from the strain of the last couple of hours, and hands were inclined to fumble a bit. Arch kept muttering through closed teeth, while his hands ratted the corpse: 'C'mon, get out'a here! Nothin' here ... c'mon!' and when one hand became smeared with glutinous red, he wiped it convulsively on the grass, and then on the seat of his reeking pants.

Mort's hands ran expertly over the dead man's pockets — trousers, jacket, inside and out. From an inner pocket of the coat he withdrew a roll of oiled silk; it fluttered open, and a piece of white paper fell out. As he stared at the closely packed Japanese characters which covered it, he heard Arch gasp, 'Grenade, *duck!*' and flattened on the ground as the grenade burst in the mud a few yards away. He felt the hot blast, nothing more. They weren't much worse than fire-crackers.

'You dirty yellow bastard!' Bert shouted, his voice shrill with indignation, and Mort grinned as a hail of what must have been vitriolic abuse hurtled from the other side of the track. Once, the Japs had seemed dangerously near in Malaya, then Singapore, then New Guinea. Now, across the narrow strip cleared through the jungle, they were as remote as the South Pole — but it didn't do to take chances. 'Come on,' he said, rolling the paper in his own oil-silk pouch and stowing it hastily in his inside pocket, 'let's get going — they're waking up!'

One by one they faded silently into the jungle behind them, treading softly, there one moment, gone the next. Wacka was the last to leave; he crouched, tense, peering up and down the track, searching the cover on the far side of the track, a green wraith hardly visible against the green behind him. Then, suddenly, he too was gone, and the dead Japanese sprawled on the trampled, reddened slush, a slight wind rustling the square of oiled silk that lay beside him.

'Well, this is it,' Mort said, holding up an envelope and examining the writing.

'This is what?' Silver inquired lazily from his stretcher. 'What you expectin', your commission?'

They had been back in camp for four days, with only a short job two days ago to a garden a few miles away — out and back in the same day. They were beginning to feel that the war had passed them by. It was the short twilight hour before the swift tropical dark fell to hide the jungly hills and the deep ravines, the pale green sky and the wavering strings of black flying foxes that beat steadily across it. The camp was quiet, with pearly smoke from the cookhouse hanging palely amongst the towering trees. Mort slit the envelope.

'That paper we got off the Jap,' he said. 'When we sent the others in, I put in a note to Bracken at Int. and asked him to send me a copy of the translation if he could get hold of one and if it wasn't too top secret.' He turned the page to the light. 'See what he's got to say.'

He read through the first page rapidly, chasing the fading afterglow, and then came to what he was looking for.

'That Jap document you marked,' he read. *'It won't start or stop any ruddy wars. It was just a letter he'd written to his missus — routine stuff you married codgers give out with — how's the kids, how's the crops, how's the weather? Look after the old man and all that guff. The funny part of it is that he wrote it over a year ago, and must have been carting it around waiting for a chance to post ever since — what a hope! It was in good condition, though — did he have it rolled up in oiled silk or something ...'*

Mort stopped, and looked up. Silver raised his head and sucked deeply on his cigarette, expelling the blue smoke in a luxurious cloud.

'Well,' he inquired, 'what's Brack got to say about it? Hot stuff?'

Mort said nothing. Since they had come in from that patrol, no boong-line had left the camp, so that no letters had gone to the coast. His eyes were fixed on a pale oblong of white on the box alongside his stretcher. He could see the address, even in the dark. Daydawn Station, Murchison, W.A. *How's the kids, how's the weather, how's the crops?*

'Nothing, china,' he said flatly, as he folded the pages of Brack's letter and stowed them in his pocket. 'Just an old letter.'

LAST ENTRY IN RED

Before the Third Division took over from the Americans in Bougainville the whole of the island was the stamping ground of the Japanese forces under the command of the astute General Kanda who, realizing the impracticability of keeping such large forces in concentrated strength, divided them into innumerable small groups that took over the best of the villages and gardens from the kanakas and lived as self-sufficient units. This worked out well while the Allied forces were content to remain inside the Torokina perimeter but, when the drive towards the south began and Australian patrols started to finger out into territory that had been so long sacrosanct to the Japs, it proved something of a boomerang, for as soon as the kanakas learned that the Australians were there for no other reason than to liquidate the 'puk-puk' men they were only too pleased to lead offensive patrols by hidden ways to the gardens and villages occupied by the Japs, and the 'dawn attack' was developed into a fine art.

The following story was woven around extracts taken from a diary captured on one such raid. The Japs were by this time obviously feeling the strain of the long inactivity. Their lines of communication and supply from Japan and Rabaul were breached in a dozen places; they were literally prisoners on the island they had captured and were reduced to living off the land. Entry by entry the story was unfolded in translation ... until the last entry, which was written in red ... but not in ink; which had no words, but was most easily translated of all ...

In the long run we didn't learn much from the diary, except that the writer's name was Ayashi, and that he was about twenty-nine when his life came to a sudden end in the coarse grass outside a sac-sac hut in Monokoro; that he was a tiny cog in the glorious Army of Imperial Japan that rolled invincibly over its enemies until it bogged down inextricably in the last island that was to have become the spring-board for the assault on the great land of the south. Not much, really, but it also unfolded a tale of cunning and desperation, hunger and homesickness, that was tragically enacted in the jungles, where the ceaseless drip of water on to the ageless mould might slowly send a man mad, and in the eerie, lifeless green twilight of the great swamps where the night watched his every move with a million unwinking phosphorus eyes.

We know this because one night, perhaps when the swift tropical dusk welled out of the eastern sky and the smell of wet grass from the river reminded him of home, of a white temple on a knoll amongst the paddies, hot *sake* and the tang of frosty persimmons, of women, smiling and scented, the clatter of *geta* on the roadway and bowls of steaming, snowy rice, he wrote ...

I dream constantly of home. It seems impossible that men of the Japanese Army could be reduced to such straits. I remember Nanking, and the glories they heaped on us ... now I dream always of the women at home, and bowls of white rice, heaped, steaming ... food is becoming increasingly scarce; we should not have destroyed the gardens when first we came, but who was to know ...?

Lieutenant Ayashi stalked out of the jungle with a party of stumpy soldiers at his heels and stood surveying the clearing.

The few sac-sac huts were mouldy and falling apart, and an old lapun sat in the shade of a wilted papaw-tree and stared vacantly at the Japanese; a tiny pot-bellied piccaninny with pipe-stem arms and legs sat in the dust, petrified with fear, its great eyes fixed unwinkingly on the ground, and a few marys who had been working the kau-kau and straggly corn stopped their labours fearfully to watch the intruders. Ayashi stared angrily at the huts. No young men! Gone to the hills, the black swine, with their long bows and spears. He swaggered over to the lapun and shouted:

'All-a boy b'long this-pella place ... w'ere 'e stop?'

The old man shook his head and muttered, 'No got!'

Ayashi spat at him, walked to the kau-kau patch and stopped by a young mary, full-breasted and far gone in pregnancy and his eyes flaming over her body, repeated his question. She looked fearfully along the worn path leading out of the clearing into the jungle, and cowered behind the handle of the hoe she had been using.

'No got savvy!' she muttered. 'Boy 'e go walk-about ...'

The Japanese shouted savagely and punched her in the breast. She fell with a low moan and the piccaninny ran and crouched wimpering where her brown body lay half-covered by the green froth of the kau-kau leaves.

Ayashi pointed to a cluster of coconut palms.

'Cut those down!'

As the keen machetes of his men bit into the tough trunks he kicked over a cooking-pot and stood with folded arms while greedy tongues of fire licked the sides of the sac-sac huts. The kanakas looked on expressionlessly ... the rains were due and a score of moons would pass before new palms bore fruit ... aie-e-e-e!

The soldiers, laden with the great golden nuts, filed past Ayashi as he stood in the first line of trees and looked back at the clearing. It lay perfectly still in the hot hush; the lapun still sat in the dust, the marys stood motionless around the garden and the piccaninny whimpered softly by a still brown splotch on the green of the kau-kau. With a harsh oath he turned and disappeared into the jungle.

... and we have no contact except with small parties in conditions as bad as our own. There is something afoot amongst the men, some plot; they are sullen and hostile, and betray themselves in a thousand ways. It most likely concerns food ... it is all we think about, these days ... food ...

Dull brown trees pressed in around the clearing and a few pale stars gleamed in the green evening sky. Deep in the jungle night insects spasmodically tuned their instruments, and streams of black foxes strung across the heavens on their way to the soft ripe papaws of some deserted garden.

Private Tanaka sat up suddenly in the hot gloom of his hut and peered fearfully through the uncurtained doorway.

'Stop!' he whispered harshly. 'Who is that?'

'Be quiet!'

A slow and stealthy footstep sounded by the doorway, and the pale afterglow was shut out by the head and shoulders of someone entering the hut.

'Quiet! It is me ... Corporal Okura.'

'Ah!'

Tanaka lay back heavily on the filthy pile of ginger leaves that served as a bed, and fireflies stitched the silence with a pattern of palely glowing green. The visitor sat on the bed and laughed bitterly.

'It was good for supper tonight,' he muttered, bitterly, his voice sarcastic, 'the chicken and *sukiyaki*! They feed us too well ...'

Tanaka said nothing and the corporal continued.

'How long do they think that we can keep going like this, our guts chewing on grass and kau-kau leaves? This morning I passed blood, and Nigato did, too, and Wanatabe. There is plenty of fish in the store, and rice too, barrels of it. I have seen it; enough for all of us, but that swine Ayashi keeps it for himself and his lick-spittles ...'

The hot silence of the hut was unbroken except for Tanaka's

quick breathing and the nervous shrilling of a tree-frog on a bough outside the window. Okura coughed softly and laid his hand intimately on the private's shin.

'Sergeant Higashi sleeps in the ration hut,' he murmured. 'If he were not there ... if something happened to him ... I should be in charge of rations, and my friend should not want for rice and fish ...'

Tanaka shifted fearfully in the darkness.

'If something ... what do you mean, Okura?' he muttered. 'What can I do?'

The corporal laughed softly.

'I have a grenade ... you will know where to find it, in my hut. Late tonight, when the moon is down ...' his words trailed away, and he rose softly and left the hut, pausing in the doorway to whisper, 'Remember, there are barrels of fish, and rice; Ayashi should not get it all ...'

Only the highest of the trees were splashed with silver when the moon sank into the pools of darkness, and the clearing lay deep in gloom when the savage roar and hungry red flash of a grenade burst the silence into a thousand shivering fragments and strewed them amongst the trees. The echoes died away and no one stirred; they lay in the dark and listened and sweated and trembled, waited for the evil red flower of another grenade, and another, and the cold flame of steel clawing at the heart, but never moved or groaned or whimpered. They lay in the dark, and listened ...

With the first light Lieutenant Ayashi walked abruptly into the ration store. The sergeant was sitting on a keg of fish with his round cropped head in his hands. One of the kegs of fish was split, and the bags of mouldy rice were pitted with small holes.

'Sergeant! What happened here last night?'

Higashi raised his head and stared owlishly at his officer.

'I .. don't know.' He waved his hand toward the kegs and the bags of rice. 'Someone threw in a grenade last night;

fortunately I sleep between the two stacks, otherwise ...'

The officer shook his head impatiently.

'Have you checked the stores? No? Well, I shall do so!' He moved over to the stacks and counted swiftly. 'As I thought ... a bag of rice and a keg of fish are gone. Whoever threw the grenade took them, do you suppose?'

'Yes, yes!' cried the sergeant, eagerly, passing his hand before his eyes and staring out at the door. 'That is it ... I was dazed, I didn't know. Corporal Okura ...'

Ayashi looked at him intently for a moment and said, 'Corporal Okura? You think that he might be mixed up in it?' He walked to the door.

'See if you can devise a bar for the door ... on the inside. Immediately!'

Higashi bowed and sucked his teeth, tiptoed silently to the door and watched the officer as he strode away across the clearing.

... what day is it? I have almost lost count of them. Each one is just like the others, sickness and hunger and quarrelling amongst the men. I don't know how I hold them, in fact I don't; their condition does that for me. As I thought, there was a plot to seize the rations ... I have disposed of Sergeant Higashi ...

Lieutenant Ayashi sat at the soiled table in his hut. It was hot and close, and hundreds of flying insects whirled around his head and sweat trickled down the stubble of beard on his sallow face; a dull haze lay over the clearing, and thunder growled in the bruised purple hills in the south. He looked up impatiently as a footstep fell across the entrance.

'Come in,' he grunted, 'what do you want?'

Private Tanaka shuffled toward the table on his dirty bare feet. His sunken eyes were red-rimmed, and he wiped his hands ceaselessly down his greasy jacket.

'Well?' barked the officer, and Tanaka passed his tongue over his lips.

'I know things ...' he said, glancing nervously over his shoulder at the doorway.

Ayashi slid his stool back and moved swiftly and silently across the opening, but by the time he looked out Corporal Okura was leaning against a dying papaw-tree yards away. He returned to the table, sat down, and asked wearily, 'What things?'

Tanaka sucked in his breath.

'Corporal Okura gave me a grenade to kill Higashi. He said he would give me fish and rice. Then, that night, Higashi stole a keg of fish and a bag of rice and hid them by the river. I have watched him. I never got any ...'

Silence settled on the room and a great scorpion fell from the thatch with a fat plop. The officer leaned over and crushed it beneath his boot and his eyes remained glued to the disgusting mess on the earthen floor. Men ... lying, cheating, thieving reptiles. They did not deserve to live — if only he could crush them all, like that, under his boot. He raised his head and stared at Tanaka.

'Why do you tell me this?' he asked softly, brushing the crawling beetles from the table with a trembling hand. 'What do you expect to get out of it?'

The private walked backwards towards the door, frightened by the expression on Ayashi's face.

'Nothing,' he stammered, 'nothing. I just thought ... I ...'

'Then get out!'

Lieutenant Ayashi sat at the table and watched Tanaka shamble across the clearing to the men's huts, where he was joined by Okura. The first heavy drops of rain were falling on the sac-sac when he took up a brush and wrote on a piece of dirty paper, 'This man is a thief, a cheat and a liar. Shoot him immediately. Ayashi.' He dropped a blob of hot wax on the folded paper, pressed it with a seal delicately carved from amber and called through the door to Higashi.

'Sergeant,' he said, when the man stood before him, 'take this despatch to Lieutenant Nakama, at Mevai. Waste no time, it is most important!'

The sergeant glanced through the door.

'It is getting late, lieutenant,' he said. 'Shall I stay overnight at Mevai?'

Ayashi looked at him and laughed suddenly, uncontrollably.

'Yes, sergeant, you will stay overnight at Mevai ...'

... and yesterday Corporal Okura shot Private Tanaka — he blamed the kanakas who are daily becoming bolder. The day before yesterday, two of them appeared at the edge of the clearing and shot Private Wanatabe who was digging for kau-kau. They were using captured Japanese rifles. Our position is hopeless; patrols of the Australians are seeking us out, and nearly every dawn we are awakened by gun-fire as they attack one of the gardens. Only last week it was Mevai ... soon it will be our turn. I do not mind, but it will be hard to die without once more tasting the hot sake and eating clean white rice. It is all I dream about or care for ...

Creeping softly through the dripping undergrowth in the darkness of just before dawn, a kanaka stopped suddenly and raised his hand; the file of dim figures behind paused in the shadows. From deep in the jungle came a full, throaty throbbing — pigeons stirring in the first light. The kanaka leaned close to the Australian patrol officer and whispered, 'You hear 'im, masta? Balus 'e cry! Be'ind, sun 'e come!'

The officer grunted and turned to the sergeant just behind him.

'Almost first light, Nig. Better get into position right away!'

'Okay, boss!'

Before long the party of ten had melted into the shadows, moving silently to positions planned for them in close reconnaissance during the past few days. Directly in front of them was a clearing with a few tattered huts just becoming visible, and so close that the deep breathing of the occupants was plainly heard.

'Never wake up, do they?' whispered Number-two on the Bren to his mate Number-one. 'You'd think that they'd be on us by now, wouldn't you?'

Number-one was about to reply when a single shot rang out, and a split second after it a torrent of lead poured into the huts from every weapon in the party. It stopped jerkily, fading from a solid blast into spasmodic shots; the sergeant shouted, 'Okay! Grenades!' and a moment after scarlet flowers of flame blossomed in and around the smoking buildings.

A figure dashed from a little hut, isolated from the rest, and had almost reached the shelter of the jungle when an Owen stammered in the thick silence and he lurched to the ground, heaved desperately once or twice, and then lay twitching in the long grass.

'In we go!' cried the officer. 'Be careful, make it snappy, and pull out on the whistle. You know what to look for!'

'I'll say!' muttered Number-one to Number-two. 'Me for a ruddy sword ... I ain't got nothing yet!'

As they poked their way into the indescribable shambles inside the hut, someone shouted from outside, 'Hey, boss! Look at this ... this chap's an officer, or something! Got what looks like a diary ...'

'Give it to me,' replied the officer. 'Intelligence might be interested in that!'

Two of the Australians had found the ration store and the grim thing guarding it. One of them kicked a keg, and they watched the dried fish run out on to the floor.

'What flamin' tucker!' one of them muttered, almost in pity. 'No wonder the little runts are so skinny ...'

What tucker ... men had coveted it, and schemed for it, cheated and lied and murdered to get it, and had lost it; now they lay in the burning hut beyond all hunger and hate and longing.

A shrill whistle rang out, and the green-clad figures faded into the jungle as silently as they had come. Lieutenant Ayashi sprawled on the coarse grass with his head on a crimson cushion and already the jungle had started to claim him; a green beetle walked over his lips and disappeared into his nostril, and a waving tendril of kau-kau, blown in the cool morning wind, swayed over him and fell across his chest. In the store-room hordes of green ants struggled to and fro, busily removing a pile of dried fish that had escaped from a shattered keg.

THE WILLOW OF BREAM CREEK

It was cool and overcast, the afternoon we mashed Bream Creek, just ideal for the job, but ideal, too, for a game of football. There was a scratch game on over the oval at the dog-park, but my uncle didn't believe in Sunday sport, and we never even suggested it to him. He'd stretch his conscience, though, to do a bit of fishing on the Sabbath after he'd come home from church in the morning and lowered the big feed that my Aunt Foebe stayed home to rustle; he reckoned that if we got a few boxes of bream to send away on the night train to Sydney we'd done a good job — for him, not the Lord or us, because we didn't get any extra for working Sunday. After tea, if the mashing had been good, he'd praise the Name in between hawking into the bunch of gumtips in the dining-room fireplace until I could have cut his damned unctuous gullet.

You'll gather that there wasn't much love lost between him and me, or him and anyone. He was a big black hypocrite who drove us like mules, and used anything from quotations out of the Bible to a clip under the lug that would have floored a bullock to get the work out of us. He had hot black eyes, and what with his ragged black eyebrows and the full moustache and beard that he wore, he looked like a rogue bull glaring out of a bush when he was angry, which was most times. Aunt Foebe was the only person I ever knew had a kind word for him, even to his own two sons, Aleck and Willie, who hated him nearly as much as I did.

I owed him for nothing except that he'd raised me from when my own mother had died and my old man lit out into the backblocks and never came back, or wrote. I might have owed him for the gesture, but, holy smoke, he'd made on the deal, what with me milking and carting wood and working around the place until I was big enough to haul a net without rupturing myself and involving him in unnecessary expense with doctor's bills; since I was fifteen, I was out on the Lake nights and days with the men, storm or fine, and made the trips down the coast in salmon-time, and worked round the clock in prawning-time catching and packing. Odd times I fixed the meshes where the sharks and big rays snarled and tore them, pulled mangrove bark to tan the nets, and belted old lead sewer-piping flat and thin for sinkers until my arms damn' near dropped off.

I was eighteen when I began to spark Maid Warburton. She lived a few blocks along the side of the hill, and her old man's land ran down, like ours did, to a muddy bit of a creek where most of the fishermen kellicked their boats. Years ago, long before I was even born, I suppose, there'd been a big argument and talk of a law-suit between Uncle Seth and Maid's old man and the bad blood never worked out — not out of Uncle, any rate, although Jeff Warburton must have swilled his out with grog in the years since. My uncle still hated Jeff's guts as hard as ever, and never lost a chance to run him down and rub the dirt in, especially as the old bloke was such a tiger for the liquor. Uncle hated the sight and smell of it and made certain that we never got within coo-ee of it, even on the dark sleety nights on the Lake when your hands got stuck to the bloody oars with cold, and all the other boats carried bottles of rum in their lockers.

But there was something else to it besides the lawsuit, and I only found it out after I started tracking with Maid. She told me that her mother had told her that my uncle used to spark her until Jeff Warburton came along with his laughing, easy ways and song-singing and won her away; that was the real beginning of the bad blood, and Maid said that before the wedding my uncle had tried to kill Jeff by running him down in a buggy. It was a long time ago, and most people who knew about it had died or forgotten it.

When Uncle Seth knew that I was sparking Maid he acted-on as if I was setting up to live in sin with some fancy woman or other instead of just wanting a girl and maybe later on a wife, like any normal young feller; he roared and raved until he had all of us nearly tripping over our bottom lips, except Aunt Foebe, who just looked at him fond and placid whatever he said or did. To shut him up I stopped seeing Maid open in the day-time, but it didn't stop us nights after he'd gone to bed, walking around the grassy shores of the Lake, her hand in mine, wondering at the stars and the fresh wind from the paddocks sweet with the soft noise of cowbells and sometimes the sleepy baa-ing of sheep; many a night I crept into the house in my sock feet, still seeing the moon through the willows down by Bream Creek and feeling her kisses on my mouth. But it seemed pretty hopeless. He'd never pay me enough to get married on, and I knew nothing but fishing. This afternoon I spoke of, when we mashed Bream Creek, we were all sitting in the dining-room after midday dinner, overfull and hot, waiting for Uncle Seth to tell us if we could go off somewhere or hoe into some work on the nets, when there was a knock on the back door. Aunt Foebe, who was darning socks, didn't get up but just sang out, 'Come in!' and Mrs Warburton walked as far as the door and stopped.

She was a poor thing of a woman, browbeaten and timid to the point where she was afraid of her own voice half the time, and she twisted her aprons into ram's horns until, watching her, I could have shaken her until her teeth fell out of her poor silly head. We didn't hear her walk up the passage — she must have tiptoed like a mouse, because a moment after Aunt Foebe called out she just appeared in the doorway, wringing nothing out of her apron as if her life depended on it, and looking nervously around the room with a smile that could have been brushed off her face with a moth's wing.

'Sit down, Grace,' said Aunt Foebe, 'What's the matter?'

It was automatic to ask Mrs Warburton what was the matter because nothing other than trouble ever dragged her out of her house, particularly to our place; and whenever local people saw her around and about they began to speculate on what trouble she was in. It was usually her old man, drunk in town and kicking the inside out of the Greek's.

'No, I won't stop, thanks, Miz Franklin,' she said, and her voice was just like the rest of her, small and trembling like the last drop of water that hangs on the lip of a tap not knowing whether to drop off or not — and about as colourless. She shuffled her bare feet, and looked at my uncle like I've seen a calf look at me many a time just before I pole-axed it.

'I jus' come across to see if any of you'd seen my ... seen Jeff; if you been in town Friday or las' night you might've? He went down Bream Creek after lunch Friday an' we never seen him since. I thought you ... Capt'n, or maybe the boys, perhaps ...'

The local people called my uncle Capt'n, I suppose because his grandfather was a sea-captain. He wrecked on the sand-bar at the Lake's entrance and set up fishing in one of the ship's boats, my uncle reckoned, and his son, and now his grandson, Uncle Seth, was in it after him. When Mrs Warburton stopped speaking, or rather when her soft, frightened voice just got so low that we couldn't hear it although we could see her lips working, Uncle Seth hawked and spat in the fireplace.

'No, we haven't seen your husband, Missus,' he said abruptly, and his hot eyes burned practically through her. 'If we went into town, which we ain't, having a living to make, we wouldn't go to the same places as he'd be in, not being in the habit of drinking ourselves and our family into the poorhouse.'

The woman's lips dropped apart and her worn, skinny hand picked aimlessly at the bosom of her dress. Aleck and Will watched her with interest, but I had my eyes on the old man, wondering how it was someone hadn't knocked his skull in before this.

'You hitch up an' drive in an' ask the police sergeant,' he went on, and his full lips curled back from his teeth, pulling his moustache aside like the curtains of a stage, 'an' he'll most likely be able to put you on to your husband's tracks!'

He belched and settled into his chair, and just looked at the poor woman until I thought she'd collapse on the mat, there and then, but Aunt Foebe put down her darning and walked over to her.

'You just go home and stop worrying,' she said crisply. 'He'll mos' likely be waiting for you in the house.' As she spoke she edged Mrs Warburton down the passage and I found myself wondering who was the worst, her or my uncle, for all her soft ways. She never even offered the poor woman a cup of tea.

'We'll mash Bream Creek this afternoon,' my uncle said as Aunt Foebe walked back into the room, and I saw Aleck's face fall and Will stuck out his bottom lip. The old man pulled out a big old gun-metal watch and looked at it. 'Close on two. That damned silly woman and her drunken sot of a husband.'

'It must be a worry,' my aunt said, biting through a thread of wool on her short white teeth. 'Always wondering when he's likely to be home, and if. Well — well.'

'She knew what she was getting when they married,' my uncle said harshly. 'Once a drunkard, always a drunkard. It's in the meat and bred in the bone, and that lily-lipped brat of theirs won't be no exception. If it don't come out in the drink, then it will someways!'

He looked full at me when he said that, and, God help me, I never batted an eyelid.

'You boys go and get your things on an' be down the creek in ten minutes.'

'Dad, I wanted to go' — Aleck began in his high, complaining voice, but the old man cut him off with a roar.

'I know where you was wanting to go, but you'll go mashing first!' A secret sort of smile flickered around the ends of my aunt's eyes, and I knew then what she looked like — a well-served old cow when the bull puts on a show of stamping and roaring. 'What d'you think damn' well keeps the roof over your head and your backs warm an' your bellies full? Bagh!' He stood up with his head thrown back and ran his big fingers through his beard. 'Now go get into your things — no son of mine'll go titty-rattin' around the dog-park on the Sabbath!'

As the boys trudged out of the room looking just as black as they dared and not a shade blacker, Aunt Foebe looked up placidly.

'Seth — you leave me that coat of yours if you're going mashing. You notice you lost a button off the bottom? After all these years!'

My uncle looked down quickly, and felt the ragged edge of the hole where the button had been pulled, and his heavy eyebrows came together in anger and concern. For a moment he looked at it absently. It was a heavy black jacket I never remember seeing him without, with big horn buttons he said had come off the coat his grandfather was wearing the night of the wreck.

'Damn!' he said softly. 'Now, where the name of Judas d' I lose that button?' He looked up and saw me watching him. 'Go on, you, Mark! Get out and get your things on! Unless' — his lips curled away from his teeth again — 'you want to go lolly-lobbing around the dog-park, too?'

I got up and walked out without a word. Two o'clock. We'd be four hours mashing Bream Creek; it'd be nearly dark by the time we come in, and then whatever we got had to be boxed and sent away, and, even if we finished by eight, I'd be too tired to — under my breath, I cursed my uncle and bitterness crept up in my throat like gall.

Bream Creek was a wandering deep-water creek that ran back from the lake between the flats into the hills. Up as far as the bridge it was deep with cloudy brown water and steep red banks that had been gouged out like bloody wounds by the winter floods. The bream loved it, and you could always get a few boxes mashing. Every hundred yards or so, sometimes closer, there'd be a big old gum toppled into the water where the bank had been washed out from under it, and they got in amongst the branches underwater for protection, and to feed on the weed that grew there.

Mashing, you'd row quietly up the centre of the creek, and then glide in alongside one of these fallen trees and lay a weighted net around it from bank to bank, then stand off and mash the top of the water with long poles and poke them in amongst the submerged branches, rattling and twisting them to make the fish dart out bang into the net. You'd never miss getting half a dozen or so from a tree.

It being Sunday there was a lot of people with rods fishing the creek after bream, and you could understand they didn't take too kindly to us disturbing the fish — rod-fishermen are funny that way; they reckoned that mashing for fish was as bad as dynamiting them. But it was our living and only their sport, and any day but Sunday I'd agree with Uncle Seth as he stood in the bow of the rowing-boat and sneered at them on the bank. Some of them shouted abuse at us and shook their fists, but they were the strangers, people out of the town for a day's fresh air and sunshine, and a bit of fishing; any of the locals shut up, whatever they thought, because my uncle was a bad man in a quarrel and never forgot an injury.

About half-past three we had better than two boxes flapping in the bottom of the boat, I reckon, and we were well up the creek about a quarter of a mile higher than where old Jeff Warburton's land ran down to it. Young Aleck leaned out over the bow, looking ahead.

'This is it!' he whispered softly, pointing to where a big old willow trailed its long whips of leaves across the top of the water. The bank around it was a twisted mess of curling black roots so that even the fiercest winter floods couldn't get at the soil to topple it, and you could imagine the nooks and crannies among them going right down into the brown water for the bream to feed in, and hide in — dozens of them blinking and wagging their fins in the darkness. Besides, the tangle of roots caught and held all sorts of things to attract them — banks of drifting weed, grass, and sometimes dead sheep from up the creek.

'This oughter fill a box for us!' Aleck said.

His eyes were shining, and I suppose mine were, too — it's a funny thing, no matter how much you hated being there, you couldn't shake off the little excitement of a good cast or a likely spot, and I guess when I'm ninety I'll still hold my breath as the net snakes out of the water, wet and brown and heavy, empty for a while and then spangled all over with fish, hanging and flapping by their gills, silvered like jewels by lamplight and sunlight and moonlight. It gets into your blood, I suppose, like drink or collecting pictures.

My uncle just stood staring straight ahead and said, 'No, we won't cast there.'

None of us understood him. We were listening but it was just words, and we didn't understand. Will was rowing, and he feathered the boat in towards the willow so gently as you'd never see a ripple or hear a sound, and Aleck, who was in the bow, guided him by hand signals over his shoulder. I was in the waist with the net coiled loosely at my feet, waiting to slip it silently over into the brown water. None of us was making a sound, holding our breath almost, and all you could hear was the sound of sheep across the flats and, far off, a woman laughing — one of the fishers from the town.

'I said we won't cast here!'

My uncle roared the words, and we all jumped as if we'd been shot. Will caught a crab and almost flopped backwards into the silver pool of fish in the bottom of the boat, and I just looked at the old man with my mouth open, the net dangling from my hands.

'Pull away, Will!' he ordered, his lips folding back from his teeth, but not in a smile.

'But, Dad!' Aleck was peering over the prow into the brown depths. 'They're *thick!* There must be a sheep caught, or something. Crikey, they're *everywhere!* Hold on, Will, hold. We'll get a box here!'

He turned around, his face flushed and lively with excitement, and looked at his father. Uncle Seth reached across me and hit him hard with the flat of his great hand across the cheek, and he reeled against the gunnel, his hat slipping off into the water and drifting away towards the bank. A little fleck of blood showed on the corner of his pale lips, and he let out a whimpering noise.

'Learn to do as you're told, you bloody galoot!' Uncle Seth said coldly. 'Now pull those poles in or I'll take the hide off your useless back come we get home!'

The mashing-poles, long, slender gum-saplings trimmed of their leaves, had got all awry in the boat during the scuffle. 'Will, pull out into the creek and make for the blackberry bushes down by Harvey's!'

As the wake bubbled under our stern and we drew away from the big willow, he looked back and Aleck's gaze and mine followed his.

'That spot's alive with wire,' he said. 'Old Warburton's been tipping it in there because he knows we mash it. I don't want my nets torn to threads.'

When the war was on they'd dug ditches all across the flats and spread barbed-wire in case the Japs landed there with tanks, and when it was all over some of the farmers just rolled it up and dumped it in the creeks. The fishermen who fished the creeks and the Lake were mad about it, but they couldn't do much, and we were always getting our nets snagged and ripped on it. But not at that spot. It was thirty feet if it was an inch, and we'd never snagged a net there yet, so I couldn't think why Uncle Seth got so cagey about it. I had my mouth half-opened to say something about that when he looked at me coldly.

'When you're paying out your own money for nets you can do what you damn' well like with them,' he said. 'But while you're using mine you'll do what I say.' He looked at Aleck and then at Will, and none of us said a word.

The next day we spent down at the creek caulking one of the boats and mending nets. Uncle was in a good mood for him because he got four boxes and then some on Sunday, although it was half-past eight when I got back from the station after sending them to Sydney. About four o'clock, while there was still plenty of light for working and it was still hot and sunny, he put away the ball of twine he was mending with and stood up.

'Knock off,' he said. 'Clear this net into the shed and we'll call it a day. You, Will, lay a fire under the copper and we'll tan the new net tomorrow.'

It seemed almost too good to be true. My mind began automatically to juggle with time, and I was thinking if I got a shave and a sluice in before tea and got in plenty of morning's wood after we milked the three cows, I could say that I was going line-fishing with Steve Attwater and spend hours and hours with Maid down by Bream Creek. Usually by the time I'd finished my chores and had tea and everything it was dark and it didn't give much time for getting out.

We hurried through the work and jog-trotted up the gentle grassy slope from the creek to the house. Uncle had left just before us, and as I crossed the back verandah I heard my aunt say, 'They found Jeff Warburton all right. In Bream Creek, with the side of his head hit in.'

'In the creek?' my uncle replied, and there was a harsh timbre to his voice, but no regret. You'd have thought that death would have softened him a bit. 'Just where did they find him? Did they say?'

I tried to stop, but they'd seen me through the doorway, and I had to walk on into the kitchen, so I did my best to pretend I'd heard nothing of what they were saying. Aunt Foebe just closed her soft mouth and turned to the stove, where tea was cooking.

'You're off early this afternoon, Mark,' she said evenly. 'It'll give you time to get in a good stack of wood for my washing tomorrow, instead of me having to cut it myself, as usual. Don't dawdle, boy.'

That was a lie about her having to cut the wood, and she usually brought it out in front of visitors to make us boys look silly, but I'd heard it that often that it slid off my back.

'I'm going line-fishing with Steve tonight,' I lied, to get my spoke in early. 'But I'll have time before that, I guess.'

'You'll make time,' my uncle said sourly. 'And be sure you strip the cows properly, too; any damned thing's good enough for you boys lately.'

I walked over to the dresser and took a fig off the platter there, and as I did so my aunt turned around and picked up my uncle's coat from the settee under the window where she'd been doing the mending.

'Here, Seth,' she said, holding it out. 'Put this in the room — I couldn't find a button for it; you'll have to see if you can match it next time you're in town.'

The coat hung almost in front of my face for a moment, and the jagged hole where the button had been torn out just jumped out and hit me like a fist between the eyes. I felt Uncle's hot gaze on me, and something tore my eyes away from the coat a split-second after I'd seen the whole world laid out flat under a blinding light, and our place and Jeff Warburton's and Bream Creek standing out black and large above everything else.

Uncle Seth took his coat and clumped off into their bedroom, and I stood still in the hot silent kitchen with the smell of stewed rabbit in my nostrils and looked down at the blood-red, mashed heart of the fig in my hand. The side of his head hit in. I knew then where they'd found Maid's old man, and what had happened to him. 'Don't stand there mooning, Mark, if you want to go lining,' my aunt said gently, and I never hated the softness of her voice more. 'Get out and get the morning's wood!'

'Yes, Aunt,' I said cheerfully, but once outside and down behind the sheds I made a bee-line for the paddocks to Bream Creek and then followed the yellow clay path until I came to the big willow.

That night after tea, when the table had been cleared and Aleck and Will were in the kitchen doing the dishes, I sat in the dining-room listening to the wireless. Uncle Seth sat under the standard-lamp looking at a paper and Aunt Foebe had her mending-basket in her lap as usual. It was almost breathlessly hot, and the thin music of the radio didn't drown out the clatter the boys made with the dishes. My Aunt looked up.

'You'd better hurry if you're going lining, Mark,' She said. 'It's almost dark now. Where you meeting Steve?'

'I've changed my mind,' I said. 'I'm not going fishing.'

'I thought you'd give it away,' my uncle grunted, without looking up from his paper. 'Rather lie on your back and read some damned useless trash.'

'No,' I said, and stood up. I spoke calmly, somehow, but my hands in my pocket were wet in the palms. 'I'm going over to see Maid Warburton. She'll be upset about her old man.'

For a moment neither of them cottoned on to what I'd said, and I stood just outside the circle of light and watched them. My aunt stopped darning, the needle poised over a half-mended hole in one of my socks; she didn't look up, but after a moment Uncle Seth's great shaggy head jerked away from his paper like something on a spring.

'You what?' he said, with a curious soft harshness. 'You're going *where?*'

I was glad the light didn't come up as far as my face. 'Over to see Maid!' I repeated, holding my voice steady, God only knows why.

My uncle's eyes glowed almost red.

'Have you gone mad, you galoot? Haven't I told you time and time again you're not to have anything to do with that namby-pamby, white-skinned drunkard's brat?'

Cold water trickled down my spine and I pulled my hand out of my pocket and opened it in front of them, against my thigh. In the palm the horn button nestled, the one from Uncle's coat, smooth and glossy in the yellow light. My breath seemed too big for my chest for a moment, but when I spoke, I spoke evenly, somehow.

'I found it down by the willow where you wouldn't let us mash yesterday afternoon, Uncle. I got there just before you did, I reckon.' I pointed to the rim of yellow clay that just touched the uppers of his black rubber boots. 'The willow where they found Jeff Warburton.'

You could have heard a cat walk on feathers in that room; the rattle of dishes from the kitchen and the thin whine of the radio just made no impression on the silence. It was a solid thing that seemed to encase the three of us like glue, and for one awful moment I thought I was going to burst out crying and give them the button. Aunt Foebe stopped me.

'That's good!' she said, and her voice was thin and dry, like puddle-ice on the roads, cold mornings. 'Give me the button, Mark, and I'll put it straight back on your uncle's coat.' She held out her yellow hand, palm up, for me to drop the button into.

'Just as well you mentioned about the button being off Uncle's coat,' I said and ignored her hand; it returned softly to her lap, although now the fingers were tightly curled. 'I mightn't have recognised it, and I might've took it to the sergeant in town. I was going to.' I walked over to the door and stood with my hand on the knob. 'It all right for me to go over and see Maid?'

I'll bet my uncle's face under his whiskers was as white as frost, and his eyes were like coals.

'If you want to,' he said, and it was like every word was dragged out of a sixty-foot well with an iron kellick tied to it. 'Don't be too late home, though. We got a lot of work to do tomorrow.'

I slipped through the door and closed it behind me, with my skin crinkling on my back, and leaned against it for a moment breathing hard and listening for anything they might have to say inside the room. It was still as the grave.

I could see now that I'd have to watch my uncle like a hawk or I'd finish up in the Lake one dark night among the sharks when we was pulling in the nets, or among the roots of the willow on Bream Creek with my head stove in, feeding bream like Jeff Warburton. But I knew, too, that I wouldn't be working for him much longer; there wasn't a man over at Maid's place now, and her mother wouldn't mind me moving in. They had two old boats that I'd be able to patch up, and Uncle had all the money I needed for new equipment.

I ran lightly across the verandah, through the garden and vaulted over the fence into the paddock. It was heavy dusk now, and the air was full of flitter-mice chasing the gnats. The Lake was calm, the colour of a mullet's belly, touched with crimson, and the willows were a brown smudge along the banks of Bream Creek. Underfoot the grass was long and warm and damp; I was barefooted, and as I ploughed through it dandelion-heads clung between my toes. I fingered the worn, smooth edge of the horn button in my pocket and laughed, a funny hot feeling flowing from my feet up through my thighs and belly into my chest in jumping waves that would have burst me like a ripe squash if I hadn't shouted aloud to the darkness and the new stars.

Paddocks away, I could see the light shining out of Maid's window.

THE NATIONAL GAME

Eastside Camp squats on the top of a red gravel hill and droops in untidy folds of unpainted wooden buildings down the slope to where a road skirts the willow-lined river, its ugliness masked partly, in the summer, at least, by the heavy foliage of half-grown oaks and soaring poplars, some elms and pines and pin-oaks and a stand of ragged gums that drip their tatters of grey bark on to the gravelly paths between the huts.

Behind it is the sky, and in front of it the road and the river, and the lush greenness of the lucerne flats. Dotted with red and white cows, they stretch almost unbroken to Duntroon and the aerodrome. A lovely, gentle prospect, but hardly ever seen by Eastside's inhabitants, the laborers and clerks and tradesmen and timekeepers whose monstrous task it is to change the wide and smiling valley into a city. They have other things on their minds.

In the late afternoon of a summer day one of them, Mick Ransome, walked down the slope from the mess-hut and stood for a while to look out over the paddocks, golden with the last light; it was something he loved, in a curious way. He was a curious fellow. The pale grey eyes that now wrinkled against the hot glow on the hills could take as much pleasure from the contemplation of a row of bottles on a wine-shop shelf, and the stringy frame that was never more at home than when it was draped comfortably against a sopping bar had many a time lain lonely on a dark hillside while his eyes sought the stars and the wells of black desolation between them and beyond, and his head and his heart wondered about them and many other things that his wanderings and unlettered life had never fitted him to understand. The marvel of it was that he even knew they were there to be sought after and wondered about, and that he could stand, as he did now, with the raucous noises of the camp crowding the air of the hillside, and lose them and the day and himself in the softly-coloured stretch of silence below him.

Paul Kernow sat on the steps of a wooden hut a little further down the slope and watched him. Not with much interest, nor much understanding, but with idle curiosity about what he was looking at. Without getting up and walking out on to the path he could not have seen it, so he sat and waited, for, although he was only young, his experience of life had taught that it was more often than not the safest thing to do — to sit and wait.

He had been a farmer's son in Poland until he became a refugee in the chaos of Central Europe, and then a member of a Resistance Movement and then a laborer in Germany, and then, after the peace, driver to an American colonel and a blackmarket operator. That was all in the first twenty years of his life; in the next two he was a D.P., a New Australian, a Newcomer and a Balt. Drifting on currents over which he had no control, and recognising this fact, he lodged in Eastside, and lived out his two-year contract clipping hedges along with two Lithuanians, a Latvian, a Hungarian and another Pole, who were all lumped by the Boss under the name of Balts.

They tolerated the Boss, a conscienceless middle-aged soak, because he did not worry them. They were in the main fastidious, and were offended by his bulbous red nose and loose mouth, the pathetic eyes that swam like two uncooked eggs in the whiskery ruin of his face, the ever-present stench of stale beer and stale sweat and slops of all kinds; they edged away from his greasy flannel and the greasy trousers that hung like a dishcloth beneath the awning of his pot-belly, miraculously supported by a greasy leather belt. He could not understand them, nor make himself understood by them, so after first making vague clipping motions over the hedges and shrubs, jerking out inarticulate words in English, and waving a stubby hand in the general direction to which they were to proceed, he left them to their own devices and settled into a hotel — even if he had to catch a bus to reach one. No one ever bothered.

On his return he was inclined to be maudlin, and, dropping a hairy black arm across the shoulders of the one nearest him on arrival amongst them, was given to commiserating with them over the 'crook deal they got', and promising them the world, rolling his tragic eyes and running his blue tongue clumsily over and over his spittle-whitened lips. This, too, they tolerated, relieving their feelings by abusing him in Polish or Lithuanian or any one of half a dozen tongues which were common to them all, smiling broadly the while, for in his absence they sat amongst the shrubs, smoking and talking, one or two working occasionally to give the impression that something was being done. Paul Kernow found the life easy enough. More than once he had planned and had his plans smashed. Now he was content to wait.

Ransome, turning away from the view of the valley, saw him and waved. Circumstance had made them friends, a curious compassion on the part of the Australian and loneliness on the part of the Pole, and nothing had happened to part them. A couple of months had cemented their relationship and each got something out of it — amusement, company, instruction — so they knocked around together. Pictures, dances and beery parties made up the social round at Eastside.

'Hi'ya, Paul,' he said as he approached the hut. 'Why'n ya go inside?'

Kernow shrugged. He knew that any other, any Australian, would have gone into Ransome's room, hunted up a smoke, stretched out on his bed and even read any letters that might have been lying around; but even now he could not take the liberties that seemed so commonplace to the Old Australians. He always thought of them as that, sometimes with secret amusement — *if we are New then they are Old. Garay!*

'Come in,' Ransome said, and Kernow followed him through the door, along the narrow passage that divided the hut lengthways into two and into the tiny cubicle that was his home. It was almost filled by a bed and a chair and a tiny table and a wardrobe; two dusty ports teetered on the top of the cupboard, a plane and a wooden mallet crowded the chair and two towels hung with the curtains across the small window. Boarders at Eastside did their own cleaning-up — or didn't. The room had a musty odor, and dusty working-boots and unwashed, undarned socks littered the bare floor. Kernow stood with one hand on the doorknob.

'Sit down, for heck's sake,' Ransome said, 'You make the joint untidy!'

'Untidy?'

'Oh, forget it.' Ransome still found it hard to remember at times that the other couldn't follow his slangy talk. He hooked the toe of his boot under a rung of the chair and pushed it along the floor. 'Shift them and sit down. What's new — what you want?'

'Nothing I want,' Kernow said, raising his fair eyebrows. 'Just, what you do tonight — you pictures, or somet'ing?'

'Somet'ing,' Ransome mocked him with a grin. 'I'm going up the game — up to Ainslie.'

'Game?'

'Yeah, the game. Swy — two-up, you know, with the pennies? At Limestone Hostel. They run a big one there in the scrub, behind. You want to come?'

Kernow shrugged, and Ransome felt like saying, well, don't put yourself out! 'No, I don' know this game, this two-up. I hear sometimes men speak about it, only you win money at it, no?'

'Yeah, or vici voce,' Ransome said, and grinned again. It was like tagging around with a school-kid, with Paul, and he was slowly getting into the habit of explaining things that others took for granted, and of searching his meagre vocabulary forwords that would take the place of the ones that the Pole didn't understand. 'You bet — gamble. You know?'

Kernow nodded, so he went on. 'Well, you want to give it a burl — you want to come? You'll have to learn some flaming time if you're ever going to be an Old Australian.'

It was an old joke between them, and Kernow laughed. Privately, he divided everything into New Australian and Old Australian, and laboriously sorted it all out, only half-knowing what things and words meant, but carefully watching what he did and said, and stacking it all away for future use. Sometimes he would bring out something he had heard weeks before, sometimes he would be right on the beam, and sometimes so comically wrong that Ransome would laugh. When that happened, he was never sure if the Pole resented it or not.

'Then I come,' Kernow said, 'and maybe I show you Old Australians how to play this — swy.' Ransome could see that another word had been ticketed and filed away under the fair hair, bleached almost white by the sun. 'Maybe I win enough for buy' —

He stopped, and Ransome said: 'Not for buy, Paul. To buy — that's the shot. Buy what, anyway?'

'To buy something I think about,' Kernow said, standing up. 'Someday, I tell you.'

'A motor-bike, I bet!' Ransome said with a swift grin. That was what most of them bought, after they had got a good suit and shoes and gloves and a heavy-belted overcoat. The Australians did it in reverse order — went into hock for a flash bike, sometimes a car, and drove it around with the seat out of their trousers, some of them, while they saved up for clothes that wouldn't laugh at their vehicle. 'You'll finish up breaking your flaming neck, that's what!'

Kernow shrugged, flushing slightly with half a smile, but said nothing. It was something else he found strange, still, this frank discussion of each other's means and hopes and plans. While he would have liked to discuss it with the Australian, he found himself unable, so Ransome watched him for a moment, speculatively, and then turned away with a shrug. He was not overinterested in what the other was saving for — his question had been routine. Most of them were saving for something — some for clothes, some for marrying, some to send things to their people, those of them who lived in the parts of Europe not yet swallowed up by Russia. It was their own business.

'You be down here by ha'-past seven,' he said, 'and we'll get away.'

'Okay,' Kernow said, and walked out of the room. As he went, he said aloud, as though he had forgotten Ransome's presence, 'Swy — two-up.' He said it a number of times, trying it out on his tongue and his ears, finding a spot for it in his head, and Ransome, listening, grinned at his back.

Limestone Hostel backed on to the low scrub and deep gullies on the side of the mountain, a good spot for the game. Not only the men from the hostel played there; often Ransome, who was a regular visitor, recognised men he had seen in offices in the departments sitting behind big tables with girls to take their notes. They were easily distinguished by their general cleanliness, but they didn't earn much more than the men who crowded around them in shirts and singlets and ragged shorts and possibly worked a lot harder.

The game usually started just after tea, with a couple of petrol pressure-lamps on boxes on each side of the ring. It was in full swing when they arrived. Half a dozen men lounged at intervals along the path from the huts, and if Ransome had not been recognised as a regular they wouldn't have got near the ring, which was a narrow gully hung over with gum-trees a couple of hundred yards beyond the farthest hut. It was hard to find, for the lamps didn't show through the mat of leaves around them, and only close in did the hum of betters, and now and then the voice of the ringkeeper, seep out.

Ransome took five notes out of his pocket, and didn't ask Kernow how much he had brought with him. It couldn't have been much, in any case, for he didn't get much, and although he was not mean, he was cagey about money — on Eastside standards, where it was made to be got rid of in the most flamboyant manner possible. They stopped at the outer edge of the crowd for a while, Ransome having a look at how the pennies were falling and searching for the tail-betters and faces he knew. Some of the players drifted away, and before long they had edged right on to the side of the ring.

Ransome had stood on the edge of a ring like that more times than he could remember, and in some funny spots, especially while he was in the Army, but the curious drama of a two-up ring at night was never lost to him. Perhaps it was just the light that palely gilded the two circles of disembodied faces, of the men kneeling at the ringside and of those standing behind. Perhaps it was the faces themselves, all naked expression without a visible body to water it down — he found himself thinking, as he had done a thousand times before, *if I make a killing tonight, I'll be damn careful getting away from the ring and back to camp!*

Kernow stood staring around the ring, listening to the babble of talk and betting, half-understanding it. On the way across from Eastside, walking along the dark road between the warm fragrance of the lucerne-paddocks, Ransome had patiently explained as much of the game as he was able, and now a quiet smile wreathed the Pole's lips as he remembered the earnestness Ransome had put into it, the pauses while he searched for words to make it clear. The only friend I have made in a year and a half among the Australians, he mused, the smile on his lips deepening into mild bitterness. And him one who can talk only about women and drink and gambling. God, I am still a stranger!

Staring straight ahead of him he became aware of a small, skinny man in a grimy singlet who squatted on the opposite side of the ring, his hands red with the red dust of the hillside, his eyes black and button-bright with inquiry in the light of the lamp. A wet, foul butt drooped from one end of this thin mouth and he spoke around it, looking straight at Kernow.

'Ten-bob he tails 'em!' he said, the butt wagging raffishly as he spoke. 'I got ten-bob to say he tails 'em — ten-bob the micks!' He raised his brow and shook the notes in his hand.

Kernow, as though he had been doing it for years, slowly peeled a note off the roll he had in his hand and tossed it across to the other side of the ring.

'Set,' he said, as he had heard the others say, and Ransome, standing alongside him, grinned. The pennies flickered in the air, the ringkeeper's mate stooped over them where they lay on the ground and sang out, 'Heads — heads 're right!' The thin man smoothed out the two notes on the ground in front of him and looked up at Kernow.

'Double up?'

'Sure, double up,' the Pole said.

He won that bet, too, and a few more. When the spin worked around to him he turned to Ransome with the lift of his shoulders that said all he wanted to without his opening his mouth. Ransome took a quick look at the roll of notes in his hand, and his eyes popped — he could see at least three five-pound notes without searching for them.

'Yeah,' he said. 'You get in and spin, for Chris' sakes, you got plenty.'

'How much I spin for?' Kernow demanded. By now most of the side-betters had got set and there wasn't much noise around the ring. Everyone was looking at them, waiting for the new spinner to come in. 'Ten-bob, is enough?'

The ringkeeper looked them over impersonally. 'Come on, gents,' he said, but softly. He was a big hulk of a man, built like a church, and dressed in a clean white singlet to advertise the fact. He could afford to talk soft and call the animals around the ring gents, but in that company he'd need to be able to back it up. 'Come on,' he said again. 'Make up your mind, Digger — a fast game's a good game. Spin if you're going to.'

Ransome whipped one of the blueboys out of Kernow's hand and tossed it across to the ringkeeper. 'Five,' he said, and grinned. 'He don't know!'

The ringkeeper looked at the five-pound note in his hand and grinned back. 'He'll soon learn!' he said.

Kernow stood in the middle of the bare patch of red dirt, still as a rock while the ringkeeper's mate put the pennies on the kip. A couple of late betters called their bets, and were set; silence settled over the ring except for the hissing of the lamps. He looked at the two tiers of palely luminous faces that surrounded him and remembered without volition the tale his father used to tell him, as a child, of two hunters in the back wood of Poland standing back to back in a circle of grinning wolves.

'This's where you begin your flamin' education, Swede!' one of the onlookers called out, and he grinned.

'Sometime, must begin — maybe, pay for learn!'

'You ain't kiddin'!' the ringkeeper's mate muttered, and stepped back from him. 'You right, mate? All set on the side, gents? All right, come in, spinner!'

The two rows of faces around the ring, Ransome's among them, lifted and dropped again. Kernow headed them, and no mistake; two lovely pictures of Victoria looking up at them from the red dust.

'Heads're right!' the ringkeeper's mate called out, and the player next to Ransome laid two pound-notes on the ground in front of him, took two more from his pocket and raised his eyebrows.

'Yeah, sure,' Ransome said. 'Double up, and more if you want it.'

The man shrugged a refusal, and Ransome set a tail-better on the far side of the ring. He had that queer, untraceable feeling that seemed to start somewhere in his belly, that Kernow was set for a trot of heads. The middle was set in no time, and they were away again. Heads. And then again. The tail-betters began to fold up.

'You want to drag, Digger?' the ringkeeper asked Kernow. 'You got thirty-five now.' He had run rings in a hundred different camps and knew that the only man who ever won was the ringkeeper, but wasn't afraid that they'd ever wake up to it. He had seen men mad with excitement and hiding it with a soft smile and a lifted eyebrow; he had seen men bitter over losses and letting everyone know it, men avaricious, men spiteful, men desperate, but he had never spoken to them in anything but a soft, slow voice, nor looked at them in any way but with a mild, amused disinterest — as he looked at this one, now and said, 'It's your dough, Digger.' Take your dough, pass the kip, go home and never come near another ring. But of course you won't. No, I thought not.

Kernow shook his head and the ringkeeper looked away from his serious face to the mob around the ring.

'We want thirty-five, gents. Get the guts set, before you bet on the side — he's a good spinner. I'll take any part of thirty-five.'

There was still a fair bit of money around the ring, although it was not pay-day, and he got it in three tens and a five. A sour-looking big animal at the edge of the ring just behind him rolled the three tens into a ball and flung them at his feet.

'I'll take thirty of it,' he said sneeringly and looked at Kernow as though he was butterflying the pennies. 'He can't keep going for ever. It's a bad show when it's left to a bloody Balt to skin the ring.'

A few of the players laughed, and Kernow went red as a beetroot, standing there in the centre of the cleared space. The ringkeeper just looked at the better, and, extending his foot, pushed the notes back through the red dust.

'Beat it,' he said softly. 'You've had your time here.'

'And you can — !'

The ringkeeper's hand moved so fast that it almost crammed the foul words back between the lips that had spoken it. 'Watch the box, Jerry,' he said quietly to his mate, and stood over the other while he scrambled to his feet, blood pouring over the front of his shirt. 'The Balt's dough's as good as yours, Mace, and if you can't do yours without screaming, then best you leave it at home. Now beat it, and don't come back.'

The man addressed as Mace beat it, and Ransome, watching him go, didn't blame him. The hand at the end of the ringkeeper's iron arm was big as a small pumpkin and shaped much the same.

The middle was set, and Kernow now spun again. Heads. And again. Again heads. The tail-betters folded up and the ringkeeper was having difficulty covering the stake. 'All right, gents,' he sang out, 'there's one hundred and forty quid in the guts — get it set before you bet on the side. Any part of one-forty quid — I'll take it in singles.' He grinned, knowing that the market had closed up. 'I'll take it in deeners!'

There was no response, so he turned to Kernow. 'You'd better drag, Digger. We're wasting time.' Kernow nodded and the other counted the money into his hand. He stood there, looking at it, not sure what to do, not even knowing that his spin was finished.

'Snatch it, Paul,' Ransome said from the side. 'Come on out — your spin's finished. Hand 'em the kip.'

Kernow shrugged and walked out of the ring.

'Sling, Paul,' Ransome said, and when the other looked at him, shoulders and eyebrows raised, he whipped a ten-pound note out of the bundle the Pole held and handed it to the ringkeeper. 'He don't know,' he explained. 'It's the first time he's played.'

'Then for Gaw'sake make it his last!' the little man in the singlet, who had taken Kernow's first bet, said ruefully, but without spite. 'What he's done to me's nobody's business!'

Those within hearing laughed, and the ringkeeper tossed the ten-pound note into the box negligently. 'Thanks, Digger,' he said.

Kernow's trot had broken a lot, and figures started to drift away from the game. The track was dark and swallowed in shadow for most of its length, so those leaving the ring occasionally flashed the thin beam of a torch in front of them as they went; Ransome, his attention attracted from the game for a moment, followed a stabbing flash and saw a dark clot of figures crouched in the black shadow of a drooping gum — among the three, one which he would have sworn was that of the big yob the ringkeeper had called Mace. They could only be waiting there for one thing, and that was for the biggest winners to leave the ring. Ransome shrugged; it was something that they would have to take care of when the necessity came up.

Kernow started to back the tails, on his own initiative, and it was a good hunch. After a few losing bets the tails rained down and it looked as if the pennies had been made without heads; so much so that the head-betters who had survived his run of heads now tumbled for the run of tails, and before long the game began to peak. Ransome, who was holding Kernow's money for him, threw the ringkeeper another five-pound note and nodded to the Pole.

'Come on, Paul,' he said, 'We'll slope — we'll go home.'

'Not much use you stopping,' the ringkeeper said, but without any scarcasm. It just wasn't any use their stopping — they had collared most of the money around the ring and had waited a fair while to give the losers a chance to get it back. 'You got just about all the mazuma here. You be Okay, you think?' His eyes flickered out from the lighted ring and along the shadowy track; he too, apparently, was thinking of the man called Mace.

'Yeah, she's apples,' Ransome said casually, although he was not feeling too easy and nodded to Kernow. 'Come on, Paul.'

They left the glow of the ring behind them, and the subdued murmur of the few betters left there melted into darkness and silence. Passing the three where for a brief moment he had seen three figures illuminated in the swift beam of a torch, Ransome glanced sideways but could see nothing; however, they had not gone more than a few yards, stumbling on the uneven surface of the track, when a stone, dislodged in the darkness, clattered a few feet down the slope and came to rest.

'Come on,' he rasped, grabbing Kernow's arm. 'Run! Run like hell!' As they began to pound along the gully the clatter of footsteps behind them joined in the noise of their own flight.

They reached the first of the darkened huts, dodged down between it and the one next to it; reaching the other end, Ransome stopped sharply, and followed by Kernow, tiptoed up the steps, along the central passage and through the far door.

There they stopped, listened for a moment above the rasping of their chests and the thunderous thump, thump of their hearts, and then darted across to the hut opposite, through it and out the other end into the low gumtrees that crept up to the edge of the camp.

'Wait a mo,' Ransome panted, and again they stopped together and listened. All the noises of the camp around them drifted out to them — drunken singing, the hum of talk and laughter and the rattle of table-tennis from the rec.-hut, the purr of a car leaving on the rough track down to the road. But of sounds of pursuit there was none. They had shaken off whoever it was that left the game just behind them.

'What is this, then?' Paul whispered, the first words he had spoken since they left the ring. 'This running?' He could only vaguely make out his companion's outline, and the doubling, twisting chase had puzzled him and lost him completely. 'It is like the days of the resistance, now! I remember' —

'Come on,' Ransome interrupted him shortly. 'We'll talk about that back at Eastside — if we get there in one piece. Some of those animals thought they'd pick us off, I reckon, that big ape that had a shot at you, Paul. They mightn't have, but then it's just as well to be on the safe side.'

'Pick us off?' Kernow repeated the unfamiliar phrase. 'What is this pick us off?' But the other was already edging through the low scrub away from the camp. Kernow looked behind him at the darkened buildings, listened and felt the cool wind that rustled in the leaves around him and tickled the long fair hair across his forehead. This dark, warm Australian night sent a shiver down his spine; the stars, so near and clear and bright, were strange stars, and the lights of the city, scattered in festoons beneath the looming shadow of Black Mountain, were only the pale reflection of those stars in the black heart of a sea of tremendous distances and inconceivable isolation.

It was so big, with a bigness that frightened him and made him long suddenly for the tight neighborliness of the Polish countryside, the small fields and the stone's throw between houses, the hour's walk between villages. And for people he could understand and who would understand him; not the Old Australians, hard and big and incomprehensible like their country; who could begrudge him the money he had won at a game where they might all have won as much if it had been their luck to do so. He shivered again, sensing the affinity of bigness and hardness between this country and its people, an affinity so close that he felt he would blunt his years trying to force his way into it. He shrugged and plunged in among the trees in pursuit of Ransome, whose passage was marked for him by the swaying of branches and the clatter of stones in the darkness.

In the safe closeness of Ransome's room they counted the pile of crumpled notes that Kernow tumbled from his pockets and the front of his shirt where he had stuffed them in the excitement of the game; a tattered, dog-eared collection smeared and gritty with the red dust of the hillside. They had walked home, down the hill and across the bridge at Scott's Crossing, up the rise and in amongst the scattered and darkened huts of Eastside camp. They had not spoken much, their few words chased quickly into the silence by the metallic clatter of their iron-shod working-boots on the hard road surface. Ransome, glancing sideways at his companion, grinned occasionally; Paul walked with his hands behind his back, high up, and his head sunken on his chest. Thinking, the Australian mused. What's he cooking up now?

In the pale golden light Kernow stood staring down at the scattered notes that covered the counterpane, shrugged and looked sharply into Ransome's questioning eyes.

'Mick,' he said, 'this man call me bloody Balt. Why? Always Australians say bloody Balts. Why? Are they opposite us?'

'Against us,' Ransome said automatically.

'Against us. I am sorry. Because I win so much money?' He waved his hand above the bed and shrugged again, disdainfully. 'This only money. If Australian win money in Poland we do not say bloody Australian. We are proud, we show our country, we are not crook for other country. But all Australian say bloody

Balt — here, in camp, at job, in picture t'eatre, playing this swy. Bloody Balt. If I win tonight, bloody Balt. If I lose, silly bloody Balt. Why?'

'Why? I don't know!' Ransome shifted uncomfortably under the other's sharp, questioning gaze.

'I dunno, Paul,' he said half irritably. 'You're strangers, I suppose. In a while it'll be apples — it'll be all right. Then you'll be Old Australians.'

But Kernow didn't rise to the old joke. 'In a while,' he said with a bitter grin. 'I am already here one year and a half. How much longer? My friend, who I know in Germany, is here nearly t'ree years. Is finish his contract. Still people say to him bloody Balt. Why?'

'Australians don't trust foreigners,' Ransome said deliberately. 'Australian workmen think you'll hook all the jobs. That's why.'

'Jez' Chris'!' Kernow exploded. 'That's silly! Every day papers say, 'Canberra Times,' many men for work wanted, build dams, build roads, build railways. Still many newcomers arrive and still more jobs. One Australian in one job only — he cannot have more.'

'Count the dough,' Ransome said, sitting on the side of the bed and beginning to pick out the red ten-pound notes from the mass before him. He could find no answer to Kernow's question and so ducked for cover. 'You've got a pile here.'

'Enough for go back to Germany,' Paul said softly and bitterly. 'To Germany, I go, Mick. This, what they say, this great experiment what the papers call is finish for me. I finish my contract, kaput.'

'Don't talk bull,' Ransome said impatiently. 'You were never better off in your life.'

'Talk bull?' Kernow echoed him with bitter scarcasm. It was a term he had heard often enough to know what it meant. 'I don't talk bull, Mick. If I have nothing to eat, if I have nothing to live for, still I am man, I am not bloody Balt in Germany. You ask other newcomers to see if I talk bull. I tell you, Mick, ninety-five precent.' —

'Per cent,' Ransome said.

'Per cent, Okay. Ninety-five per cent of New Australians not happy. Finish contract, go to U.S.A., Sout' America, back to Germany. There, maybe not so much food, not so much work, but I say we are not bloody Balts.'

Ransome shrugged. There was nothing to say. 'Count the dough,' he repeated, and Kernow knelt on the floor beside the bed to sort out the notes. Ransome watched his hands, big, capable hands, strong to work. Hands to work with, and suddenly between his eyes and the hands hovering over the notes there was superimposed the wide view of the lucerne paddocks below the camp, the fields of deep-brown soil that reached forty feet down to the water and produced five crops a year, rich soil that was always there, come rain, hail or snow, depression or bloody Balts. He knew what he must say to this man who had known the goodness of the soil and forgotten it — he, who had never known to this moment what the soil meant.

'Paul,' he said suddenly, knowing that if he didn't say it now he would never say it. 'This's different here, to anywhere else. Canberra's a tough place for an Australian, even, when he's new to it — everybody's here for what he can get out of it, they don't put nothing back, and everybody's scared some other —'s going to jump him for his job, or his sheila, or something. You understand?'

Kernow shrugged, and Ransome looked down at the wad of notes in his hand. The bed was cleared of money, and Kernow held a similar wad.

'I got one-eighty-five quid here,' he said. 'How much you got?'

'One-twenty-five, I think.'

'Over three hundred quid.' Ransome took the Pole's empty hand, pressed the money he had counted against the palm and closed the unresisting fingers on it. 'You saved a bit in the last eighteen months, haven't you?' he demanded. 'A couple of hundred?'

Kernow nodded silently.

'Well, five hundred'll buy you a bit of land somewhere away from this flaming dump — Australia's a big place, Paul, and the people are kind, most of them. That's the shot — buy some land and grow things. It's good people who do that. Only the drips settle in dumps like this, and Sydney, and Melbourne — they don't know any better, God help them.'

'Drips?' Kernow queried.

'Drongos — oh, hell, forget it!' Ransome sat on the bed and kicked off his boots. 'Don't forget what I tell you — buy a bit of land and you'll never look back.'

Kernow held out his two hands. 'Half of this is yours, Mick.'

Ransome looked at him obliquely, about to say, oh, don't be so damn silly. But the man looked pathetic, slightly ridiculous. He's offering me a couple of acres of land, Ransome thought, and the idea softened him. 'No Paul,' he said gently, 'we don't do things like that here — you won it and it's yours. Thanks just the same. Whack it in the kick and don't forget to hide it well until you can whack it into the tin tank.'

'Tin tank?' Kernow began, but the Australian stopped him with a laugh, glad for some trivial thing that would ease the tension.

'Scram,' he said, saving a hand towards the door. 'The lesson's over for tonight.'

Outside in the soft, hot darkness, thinned in the open by the starlight, Kernow stopped in the dense shade of a full-leafed tree and stared out over the valley. At this hour it was a pool of shadow threaded tenuously by isolated strings of pale-gold street-lights; blue dots pin-pointed the road to Duntroon, crouched under the shadow of Ainslie, where every ridge was specked with the ruby lights that had been scattered freely over the flat expanse of the airport below. A cooling wind that had something of the fragrance of the lucerne flats below him brushed across his face and rustled in the leaves above him; his sight blurred so that each pin-point of light before him found a companion and swam unsteadily.

To buy some land! His hands clenched hard about the wads of notes they held; not the rich black soil of Poland, farmed and loved for hundreds of years by his father and his father's father, but the wild soil of this wild, wide country that would have to be tamed, and coerced, and then, with love, brought to yield. For me, and my sons, and my son's sons, he said passionately to the darkness and the silence and the moonlight. And here, in my hands, I hold it, the red soil.

He turned suddenly about and walked briskly across the red gravel slope to where he could see the roof of his hut glistening palely in the white light of the stars. Eastside, this Australian place that he had hated so much, had taken on a strange new beauty.

THE ONLY ONE WHO FORGOT

The black boy sat on a smooth rock jutting out of a deep clear pool in the reef, idly watching the flash and stab of gulls into a school of mackerel in the shallows. They scattered the water into flung diamonds as they struck, tormenting the air with their shrill, savage cries. Big boomers thundered far out on the edge of the reef, but at his feet the water slid hissing over the coarse sand, clucking and sucking at the holes. Never still, never silent. Behind him, at the other end of a gleaming white shell road, the little town slumbered already in the golden threat of midday heat, not quite alive, not altogether dead. It was all he had ever known, this rock, this beach, this sea, this little town. He was content, when his work at the hotel was done, to sit and watch the luggers come in and see the great clouds roll over the edge of the world.

He turned quickly at a sound behind him. It was gentle, furtive, like a goanna stirring in grass. A little girl stood on the sand, looking up at him. The bright white glare of the coral made her wrinkle her eyes and her nose, and her mouth was screwed into a tight red bud of conjecture.

'Hullo boy,' she said brightly. 'You see any ships?'

The black boy jumped lightly from his rock and stood beside her. Her skin, he saw, was pale gold, and soft gold curls bobbed on her shoulders beneath the brim of her golden straw hat.

Her eyes were blue — blue as perclums, he realised, suddenly. 'No,' he replied, gravely. 'No ships. Only luggers, sometimes.' He spoke the language of the hotel and the post office, unaccented. The language of Miss Bella and Bob Mayo, and Dan the mailman. It was the only kind he ever heard, apart from that of the occasional travellers who might stay overnight at the hotel. To anyone but the girl standing at his side, it would have sounded strangely out of place on his thick, plum-coloured lips.

'There's plenty of ships where I come from,' she said. She stooped and picked up a whorled shell. For a moment, forgetting him, she held it to her ear, and listened with wonder to the sigh of the wind, and the ghosts of tales the great waves had breathed into it. Then she dropped it. 'Down Perth, that is. Where'd you come from, boy?'

The black boy frowned. He didn't know, rightly, where he came from. He couldn't know. Nobody had thought to tell him. He had been brought back to the settlement one day, twelve years ago, by Dan the mailman. He had been deposited, a smelly little bundle of rags and bright eyes, on the floor of the kitchen at the Royal, the only pub in hundreds of miles of that barren nor-west coastline.

'Poor little cow,' Miss Bella had said, looking down at the piccaninny on the cool linoleum. 'What is it, Dan — a he, or a she?'

'A little buck. Found 'im bellerin' is head orf 'longside a bit of a swamp a few miles out. I dunno. 'Is mumma might'a got took with a 'gator, or somethin'. There wasn't no niggers around. So I brought 'im in. Couldn't leave 'im there.'

'No. A'course not. How old is he, Dan, d'you reckon?'

'Aw — I dunno.' The mailman removed his wide, stained felt hat, and scratched his head. ''Bout three, I guess. Give 'im some tucker, Bell.'

'What you going to do with him?' Miss Bella demanded, moving over to the cooler.

'Aw — I dunno,' the mailman said, again. ''E can live at the post office, 'til 'is mob comes in for 'im.'

'Well, I suppose that'll be alright. What you going to call him?'

Dan's eyes roved over the ceiling in search of inspiration. They lighted on a bottle on top of the dresser. 'Brandy!' he said, with a dry chuckle. 'That's a bonzer name. Brandy!'

'It'll do,' Miss Bella said. 'He won't be here long enough for it to stick, anyway.'

But she was wrong. No mob came looking for the piccaninny. He stayed on with the kindly Dan, graduating first to odd jobs round the post office and later, when he was old enough and strong enough, to wood chopping and bar cleaning at the Royal. Through the years his mind forgot, and his heart forgot, the thousand nomad lives that dreamed in his blood.

He frowned again, thinking about the puzzle of his origins. The little girl did not press her question, however. She probed a limpet off the rock with a sharp-edged shell, and made the universal approach of childhood. 'My name is Shelagh,' she said, engagingly. 'What's yours, boy?'

'Brandy,' the black boy said, readily.

Shelagh laughed, a high silvery sound. A gull which had been foraging nearby went sheering into the upper air. 'Brandy?' she cried. 'That's not a name! That's something you drink!'

'It's my name,' the boy insisted, without heat. 'You've come to live at the pub, haven't you? You're Mr Bob's little girl from Perth?'

'Yes. I've been to school there, but we've got holidays now. I only got here last Sat'd'y, and I've been down here at the beach every day. Where've you been, Brandy?'

The boy pointed toward the horizon. 'On a lugger,' he said. 'I go out, sometimes. I been out three days, this time.'

'Oh, are you a sailor?' Shelagh looked at him with renewed interest. 'Can you swim?'

Brandy experienced an irrepressible urge to impress the pretty child who had so suddenly appeared on the little strip of beach he had come to regard as peculiarly his own. 'Course,' he said. He lowered a hand, and helped her up onto the rock. As she settled down beside him, he unselfconsciously peeled off his jersey. Beneath it, the skin was lustrous black, glowing and hairless. Smooth, forming muscles rippled over his ribs and down his back as he raised his arms above his head to dive. He plunged into the water, and the girl watched him, breathless. In the clear pool she could see his dark body, strangely flexible and distorted, like a long, black fish snaking around the sandy bottom. Sometimes he disappeared wholly, only to float into view again from some shadowy little underwater cavern. Sometimes he would turn over on his back and send up a great wobbling bubble of air to break the surface in a fat plop. Then, all of a sudden, when she was least expecting it, his sleek head burst out into the sunshine, sending glittering drops in every direction. He shook it violently, smiling a broad, happy grin.

'Oh, Brandy! You are good!' Shelagh clapped her hands delightedly, her long curls dancing on her shoulders. Brandy laughed aloud. He turned like a seal in the water, and swam lazily back to drag himself out and lie beside her in the hot sunshine.

'You like perclums?' he inquired, diffidently. He put a hand into a pocket of his ragged shorts.

'Perclums?' she said, puzzling over the new word. 'I don't know. Why?'

He pulled several weed-furred shells from his pocket, and sat up. 'You look,' he commanded, placing one of them under her small nose. 'You see 'im? Little blue feller?' She could see it now, a tiny button of blue enamel closing the shellfish's front door. He placed his long fingernail under it, and flipped it into her lap. She squealed with pleasure.

'Oh, isn't it pretty! I could make a rosary out of them for Sister! Will you get me some more?' She looked at him, entreatingly. 'Please, Brandy!'

The black boy grinned, and disappeared noiselessly into the pool. He came up at long intervals to breathe, and then disappeared again. Shelagh could see him most of the time. She watched fascinated, clapping every time his black arm reached up to deposit a heap of the shells on the rock beside her. When she had a glowing pile of the little blue buttons, he crawled back onto the rock, and sat beside her. He watched her as she rolled them into her handkerchief, and placed them carefully on a ledge. When she looked up he said, casually, 'I know a bonzer cave. You like to see it, Shely?'

Together they picked their way across the exposed reef. To the little girl from Perth, it was all enchantment. Scarlet and green flags of seaweed floated lazily in shallow pools. Anemones spread their greedy plum-coloured lips on the still water, and sea-urchins drilled meticulously with their long scarlet spines. Tiny multi-coloured crabs scuttled in panic all around them, and shells of all colours and shapes lurked under the ledges, spotted and spiked, some with green pearly sheen on their insides, some with two beady eyes and two daintily curved claws poking out at the opening. The day was all brightness for the white girl and the black boy, the wind cool and salty, the sky a limitless blue, the sea a peacock's tail touching the sky's rim out beyond the thundering edge of the reef. Gulls screamed and wheeled, and great black divers sat like lacquered birds on the rocks, holding their wings to dry. The beach shimmered in the heat, and noontime quiet put its finger against the lips of the white town in the hollow behind the dunes.

When Shelagh got back to the hotel, Miss Bella was standing at the table in the great cool cavern of a kitchen, making bread. Bob Mayo, the owner, was standing beside her. As the child stepped in from the white glare of the yard, she almost shouted at her, 'Where you been, Shely. It's after lunch!'

'Down at the beach, Miss Bella.' Shelagh had no diffidence about saying it. She had been to the beach every day since her arrival from the south, and so far there had been no trouble about it. She skipped to the table, holding up the flags of crimson weed she had brought home with her. 'Look, Daddy. Look what ...'

'Who you been with?' the woman demanded. She peered intently at the child, blowing a strand of mousy hair from in front of her eyes.

'Brandy. He knows all the best places. He catches crabs and things for me. He showed me a cave.'

'A *cave?*' Miss Bella glared at Mayo. 'See, you fool!' She mouthed the words, rather than uttering them. She walked around the table to where the child stood, and the man followed her with his eyes. *I should have married Bell years ago, and gone south, he thought. For the kid's sake. I don't even know her, or what to say to her, or what to do for her.* Even as the thought occurred to him, though, he knew he could never live away from the hot little town and the booming surf that throbbed on its air night and day. From the gleaming miles of lonely beach that shimmered away into the heat haze, until sea and sand and sky all met in one shifting mirage of opals. He knew he could never forego the drovers and the cattlemen from the wild plains east of the township. The pearlers who anchored in the bay sometimes, to escape the cock-eyed-bobs that sprang up so suddenly on those treacherous coasts. The mad miners in from the desert with their earnest tales of lost reefs and forgotten gorges. *The gold's there, sticking out of the rock in bloody great lumps. By cripes, but, you got to watch the niggers!* In the flickering light of the hurricane lamps, they traced their rough maps on the bar, dipping their fingers in the beer slops: produced their little nuggets and tobacco-tins of gold dust, their round, white iridescent pearls. And far into the night talked and drank, while outside the surf drummed against the reef and great yellow stars stabbed the soft darkness in furious gushers that sprayed across the black sky. He knew he couldn't leave it, and live. *And breathe perhaps*, he told himself. *But not be alive.* He watched the woman as she stopped beside the child. She rubbed the dough off her hands, and picked up one of the shells.

'Put it to your ear!' Shelagh cried, excited and pleased to share her secret. 'You can hear the sea! Go on, Miss Bella!' Bella looked down into the shining eyes. She smiled gently. For a moment, she stood among the soft, brown shadows of the hotel kitchen, and listened to the sea.

'Duckie,' she said presently. 'I don't want you to go down to the beach again with Brandy. You can play here, at the pub. Or wait until he's busy, and go by yourself. Don't go down with him.'

Mayo shrugged uncomfortably. 'God Almighty, Bella!' he

protested. 'The boy's alright!'

Miss Bella glanced at him with sudden, impatient anger. His wife, a delicate, selfish, south-bred woman, had refused to live in the north. She had died giving birth to her unwanted only child, and had left her husband, her hotel and her daughter to the warm-hearted, north-born housekeeper. In any case, Bella had already been mistress of both the hotel and the husband for years, before and after the marriage. The easygoing north accepted the situation apparently without noticing it. It knew from long experience what became of men without women north of the twenty-sixth. Bella, herself, had almost forgotten that there had ever been any other claim but hers to Mayo and the pub. She had never even recognised any other claim to the motherless little girl she had helped to bring into the world and had immediately taken over. She was enraged by Mayo's obstinate refusal to see what she herself could see so very clearly — the danger to any little white girl who played alone on a deserted beach with a boy teetering for the last few moments on the edge of virile, black manhood.

'Do you hear me, Shelagh?' she demanded, turning again to the child. 'You're not to go to the beach again when Brandy's there.'

Shelagh stared from the man to the woman, revolt fighting puzzlement in her glance. 'Why, Miss Bella?' she asked, eventually. 'Brandy c'n swim, and everything. He gets me perclums.' Her hand flew to her lips as distress replaced the puzzlement in her eyes. 'Oh!'

'What is it' Miss Bella cried. 'What's the matter?' She dropped to her knees in front of the child. 'Oh, what?' She grasped Shelagh by the forearms, and peered anxiously into her face.

'My perclums.' The child pulled away from her a little, perturbed by her violent reaction to what seemed to be a fairly simple matter. She had left her perclums on the rock, and had suddenly thought of it. But Miss Bella acted as if she had done something. 'Brandy got them for me,' she said. 'He dived in the pool for them. And I left them on the rock, in my hankie.'

'Oh — blast your perclums!' Miss Bella didn't try to hide

the relief in her voice, but she avoided Mayo's triumphant glance as she got to her feet. 'You can get them another time, when Brandy's not there.'

'But why, Miss Bella? Why does it have to be when Brandy's not there?'

'Well ... he might hurt you,' Miss Bella said, lamely. *What the devil can I tell her*? she thought, crossly. *Make up some damn thing*! 'He might steal your purse, or something.' Mayo muttered inaudibly, shaking his head and shrugging his shoulders impatiently, but she ignored him. 'You can't always trust a black.'

Black? The child looked at her, and then at Mayo, uncomprehendingly. Brandy was Brandy. He dived off the rock and shook his head like a woolly dog in the water. He got perclums and caught crabs, and he had shown her the cave in the rocks. She wrinkled her brow and said, in a puzzled tone, 'But, Miss Bella. I don't *take* my purse to the *beach*!'

The woman lost her patience. 'Purse or no purse,' she cried sharply, 'you'll do as you're told, my lady. You *won't* go to the beach again with Brandy, d'you hear? And that's *final*! Take them shells off the table, and don't let me have to speak to you about it again. Now ... *get*. And wash your hands for your lunch!'

Shelagh ran from the kitchen almost in tears, and in silence the man and the woman watched her go. When she got to her room, she snivelled and whined to herself for a while, but eventually picked up the seashells again. For a moment before she went to the bathroom, she stood with one of them against her ear, and the enchantment of the morning flowed over her again with the imprisoned song of the waves.

It was dark and cool in the kitchen when she crept through it after her afternoon nap. The blinds were drawn and the meat-safe shrouded in net, and a few flies buzzed disconsolately in the folds of the curtains. Miss Bella was in her bedroom upstairs, having a lie-down, and her father was ... somewhere. She took her straw hat from the peg by the door and ran into the dozing yard. The few golden hours left to the day were limitless. Before tea, she felt, she would have time to go around the world. She wandered down to where a lonely pig lived in a sandstone sty behind the garage. Wrinkling her nose at the odour that surrounded him, she threw little stones at him until he charged the stout gate. She retired with a pleasurable thrill of danger. Back at the kitchen door, she knelt in the red dirt and gathered crimson berries fallen from the peppercorn tree. One of the goats lay snoozing in the cool sand under the tank-stand, its short tail twitching automatically at the flies. She pelted it with berries until, in disgust, it heaved itself up and trotted off toward the rubbish-heap. Having exhausted the entertainment potential of the hotel yard, she did what she had known, all along, she would do. There was no sound from the hotel, and the white road outside it was deserted. With a quick glance at the window of Miss Bella's room, she slipped out at the gate and ran down the road toward the beach.

The black boy was waiting for her when she got there, sitting on the rock beside the pool. When he saw her coming, he jumped lightly to the sand.

'Brandy,' she said, cocking her head as she stopped beside him. 'What's a black?' The question had been forming in her mind on the way down from the hotel, and childlike, she put it without preamble.

'I ... dunno, Miss Shely,' the boy said, uncertainly. He brightened. 'Look, Miss Shely — I got something for you.' He stooped and took a neat parcel from a ledge at the base of the rock, and handed it to her. 'You have a look.'

Shelagh unwrapped the parcel, and stood transfixed. It contained a small pearl-shell, the rough edges smoothed away, the lustrous sheen of its inside surface gleaming with all the sea's cool colours of green and blue. 'Oh, Brandy!' she breathed. 'It's lovely! I'll keep it 'til I die, promise I will. Did you make it?'

Brandy's soft brown eyes danced with pleasure. 'Yeah,' he said. 'I done it. I smoothed it off with one of Dan's files. You like it, eh?'

'It's beautiful! She wrapped it again, reverently. 'Miss Bella's going to like it, too.'

'I know,' Brandy said. 'I gave her a beaut, once, with a blister big as your thumb. I got it on the lugger.' He looked at her shyly. 'Miss Bella, she always looked after me, like my mother. I live at the pub sometimes, too, when Dan goes out the stations.'

The housekeeper's name invoked in Shelagh's mind the picture of Miss Bella in the kitchen at the hotel, listening to the shell. And what she had said, afterwards. 'Brandy,' she ventured, 'Miss Bella listened to the sea, in the shell. Then she was cross. She said I mustn't come down here, to play with you. It's silly, isn't it?'

The black boy wrinkled his heavy forehead again. His entire life to date had been an association with practical things — eating, sleeping, the love of Miss Bella and the affection of Dan and Bob Mayo; helping Dan with the mail, chopping wood at the pub, and, more lately, the easy working companionship of the men on the lugger. This new dimension of doubt introduced by the child's questions oppressed him. His eyes clouded as he tangled with it.

'W'y?' he demanded, eventually.

'She said you might take my purse, or something. That's silly, too, because I don't bring my purse down here. Do I?'

Brandy turned away from her and looked out at the sun-splintered sea. His eyes were more darkly clouded and his brow more deeply wrinkled, as he wrestled with this additional new consideration. Steal? Miss Bella said? When he spoke again, it was with an uncharacteristic, adult hardness. 'Miss Bella — w'y'd she say that? I don' steal.'

Shelagh stepped back a pace, her hand at her lips. 'You aren't cross now, too, are you Brandy?'

He turned and stared at her intently, his eyes clearing as the realisation of her presence blotted out what his mind had been trying to encompass. 'No, not cross, Miss Shely,' he said, after a while. 'We'll go and get your perclums, eh?' He smiled happily as she placed her hand in his, herself smiling into his face, and tugged him proprietorially toward the pool.

While the afternoon wore on and cooled, they pottered around the reef together, collecting shells and crabs and seaweed and any pretty thing that took the little girl's fancy. Brandy was tireless in pleasing her, his eyes shining as he watched her, fair head bent, peering into the wonders of some deep, clear pool, or squealing with excitement when an extra-large wave frothed in across the coral and spread its icy-cold lace about her knees like a bridal-train. It was while she was manoeuvering a tiny fish into the corner of a pool for capture by him that she looked up with sudden dismay.

'Oh, Brandy! I've got to go! It must be getting late, and Miss Bella'll be cross again!'

Brandy's eyes flickered instinctively toward the sun. It was well past halfway between meridian and the horizon. Miss Bella would have finished her lie-down, and would have had a sluice, and would be in the kitchen, getting ready for tea. And wondering where the child was.

'Orright,' he said cheerfully. 'We'll race to the road, eh?'

She gathered the shells and the seaweed and the pearl-shell in its parcel, and then took off toward the road with a squeal of excitement. He stood for a while, to let her get a good lead, and then followed. She had not gone far when she sprawled headlong. She sat up with a shrill cry of pain, and clutched at her knee. All about her, perclums lay on the sand in little blue specks, and the pearl-shell, shed of its wrapping, gleamed in the sunlight. For a moment, before it blackened on the burning sand, the red spurt of her blood showed almost indistinguishable from the bits of scarlet weed she had scattered in her fall. At first she whimpered, but when she saw the blood flow, she opened her mouth to its fullest extent and emitted a high, ululating howl of misery and fear.

Miss Bella, on the way down to the beach to search for her, heard it. She stood stock-still, almost smelling the wind, glaring in the direction of the sound. It was not the girl who was in her mind, but the black boy. His brown eyes and hair, his thick, dark lips, his satiny black skin. His strong boy's body, so soon to be a man's. She had nursed him and coddled him, had even loved him. But now — black boy and white girl! With a sob of terror, she began to run toward the beach.

Brandy hurried around the corner of the rocky shelf, holding a large crab by its two claws. It was an unusually big one, and he intended to take it to the pub for Miss Bella, for her supper. As he saw the blood, he dropped it, and knelt on the sand alongside the wailing child. 'Don' cry, Miss Shely,' he said, cheerfully. As, many a time, Miss Bella had said to him. 'It's only a little cut. Look!' He leant over her gingerly, and touched her knee with his black finger. The nail was long and filbert-shaped, the skin between the fingers a creamy brown. 'There,' he said softly. Beneath his broad nose the light fair hair curled on the little girl's sunburned neck. 'There,' he said again. The child turned to him, put her hands about his neck, and howled against his faded jersey. His own hands strayed helplessly in the air, and then came to rest on her shoulders. 'Don' you cry,' he said. 'It's all right, Miss Shely. Don' you cry.'

Miss Bella, ploughing down the soft track from the road, stopped when she saw them squatting in the sand. Her hand at her throat, she screamed, 'Shelagh!' and the gulls wheeling above the beach screamed back at her. The black boy watched her as she floundered through the heavy, shimmering sand, her black skirt above her flaccid calves, her bosom heaving desperately. She stopped a yard away from them. Her face was crimson, and a pulse beat wildly in her neck. 'You!' she flung at him, hoarsely. Hate and fear burnt in the word. She could see only the black boy. Behind him, the white sand sloped to the soft green shallows, the deep blue brooded against the inner edge of the reef and white flashed again where great combers crashed against the outer wall. She could see only him. Beyond, to the rim of the world and beyond, the vast, timeless sea. Salty wind and sunshine wrapped them all around, gulls like silver boomerangs swooped and soared, splashed and soared again. At the end of the white road the half-dozen buildings of the little township gleamed almost unbearably, golden-pink, in the late afternoon heat. She could see nothing but thick lips and brown hair and jutting forehead, the puzzled frown in the boy's brown eyes, his black hands on the girl's shoulders. 'You!' she spat at him, again. She grabbed the child by the hand, yanking her to her feet. 'Get home, Shelagh!'

Brandy clambered up from his knees. 'W'y, Miss Bella —'

She swung her open hand across his mouth, hard. The blood ran from his lips and he stood still, his fingers creeping slowly along his jaw toward it. The woman's eyes blazed.

'Nigger!' she cried, shrill with fear. 'Damn black nigger!'

The boy still did not move. He stood staring at her, puzzled, frightened, hurt. Slowly the tears swam into his eyes — not the soft and easy relief of childhood, but the hard, spare grief of his dawning manliness. At the sight of them, her hand fled to her lips. She seemed to shrink inside her black dress as she stood, for a moment, staring back at him with dilated eyes. Without another word, she turned and trudged across the burning sand toward the road, dragging the little girl by the hand.

The black boy's fingers touched his lips, at last. He felt his blood with them, lowered them, and stared dully at their smeared tips. At his feet, flies covered the blackened spots of sand where the girl's blood had already dried and hardened. All about him, the ghosts of a million years postured and moved, daubed with mud and feathers, gleaming with sacred kidney-fat, crying out to the unresponsive blood that pounded in his own heart.

Only he could not hear, did not see.

Only he had forgotten.

Tiny crabs scuttled across his bare toes, carrying off the weed he had dropped, investigating the larger crabs he had intended for Miss Bella. He did not move. He stood staring up the white road, to where Miss Bella and the little girl had disappeared in the direction of the pub.

SOWERS OF THE WIND

(Extract, Chapter 4)

Lane and Flannery, once they got away from the wharves, hitched a ride up to the centre of the city and walked along the ill-lit, ruinous main street, jostled by crowds of Japanese and American servicemen. Walking aimlessly, they found themselves half-way up a long, shallow incline, with the town spread below them.

The street was flanked by bombed-out buildings and vacant blocks, wells of utter, impenetrable blackness in the pale-gold glow shed by the rare street lamps. Passing a gaping doorway in a ruined shop, Flannery, who was walking on the inside of the footpath, felt a hand drop on to his arm. A voice said gently in his ear, '*Gozaimasu* — please. You, chocoletto, cigaretto? Biscuit-o?'

'Holy mackerel!' Flannery jumped aside. 'He scared hell out of me, the bastard!' He peered into the shadows. 'What d'you want, you flaming ape?'

The Japanese edged out, partly into the pale light, half bowing, with a greasy cloth cap held against his chest and his shaven head bobbing backwards and forwards like a mechanical toy on his narrow shoulders. A grimace that might have been of pain or of pleasure distorted his features, disclosing the great, square teeth of the cartoon Jap; he bobbed and hissed, drawing his breath inward between this teeth, and repeated his request,

'You, chocoletto, cigaretto?'

'What's he want?' Flannery peered in bewilderment at the Japanese, who had produced a tightly packed roll of dirty notes, and once again repeated his demand. 'Look at the wad of dough he's got!'

'Wants to give it to us,' Lane volunteered dryly. 'Let's roll him and shoot through with his purse.'

An American serviceman, who had been watching from the other side of the road, walked over to them, calling out as he came, 'Don' sell nothin' to that son of a bitch, Aussie — they don' pay nothin' like the real price. You come on up the hill with me if you got stuff to hock'.

Flannery looked at Lane with a grin. 'Come on, the game's on,' he said.

The American joined them and they walked on up the hill together. 'You got in just today?' he inquired. 'I see the ol' hooker come in, an' one of my buddies reckons there's Aussies on board. Where you at, now?'

'Down by the wharf,' Lane replied. 'For a while, anyway.'

'One hell of a place, bud. You got any yen?'

'Yen? No...'

'Well, how in hell you goin' to get yourself a goddamn' woman?' The American stopped and looked at them in genuine amazement. 'You got any chocolates or cigarettes, or any goddamn' thing?'

'I got some weed, but no smokes,' Flannery volunteered.

The American shrugged. 'I got plenty,' he said.

They had left the ruined part of the town and entered the residential section, where practically no damage had been done. As they walked, looking from side to side of the road, their nostrils assailed by the peculiar odours that floated out of dark alley-ways and ill-lit shop fronts, he kept up a running commentary on the town and the Japanese people generally.

'See all this?' He flung his hand back along the way they had come. The road was rising still, and what lay behind them was spread out like a sand-table map. Darkness had softened all the harshness of the ruin; all that was now apparent was that on one side of the road they had come there was a sea of darkness, and that on the other pin-points of light shone amongst the houses. 'Two raids. You see those factories and docks? Boy, do those sons of bitches hate fire! They sure hate to fry!'

'Me, too!' Flannery laughed, and Lane, looking back at the town, breathed, 'Cripes, two raids! They must have plastered the joint some.'

'Yeah. Incendiaries. That's why all the damage down town is on one side of the road. Only that stopped the whole goddamn' joint from going up.' The American paused reflectively. 'Say, you should see Tokyo. This place ain't nothin' — apart from its docks it's just a brothel town. Even the Japs admit that. Tokyo's the place where the bomber boys really went to town. Yes, sir!'

'Yeah, I know,' Mark said. 'I read it in the paper. But they plastered Tokyo for some time. They did all this in two raids.'

'Well, wait until you see Hiroshima, then. That got flattened with one goddamn' bomb. Holy cow, you should see it! I bet them yellow-bellies hate our guts!'

'What, even now?' There was surprise in Lane's voice. 'The war's over, and they brought it on themselves, anyway.'

The American stopped walking and regarded him in amazement. 'Say, what Sunday supplement do you guys read? If they done it to you, what would you do — welcome the bastards? If your wife and kids was fried, or your old man was killed overseas somewheres, would you glad-hand them when they walked in? Like hell! I on'y been here a few months, but my bet is that unless we make a good job of it this time we'll have to slap them down again some day, the yellow bastards.'

He's right, too, by hell, Mark thought. And here we are, batting the breeze in amongst them! We could all be dominoed and chucked into a sewer, and nobody'd be any wiser! He peered down a lane that slanted from the corner they were passing, at the dim and formless figures that bobbed about in the shadows. For a moment, in the half-light and the strangeness, the old familiar crinkle corrugated his spine.

'I see one ol' lady out Hiroshima,' the American continued,

'she must'a got caught in the fire, somehow. Both her hands was burnt off — just the stumps left. And kids covered with burns from head to foot, and their mothers just sittin' looking at them as they died. Hell, they got them all hidden away, now, or the poor bastards just died, but when I first went out there they was still wandering around the goddamn' streets, dopey like hop- heads, and sitting in the gutters, screeching like all hell. The Japs reckon there was one-hundred-fifty thousand killed there, that day. I dunno, but it must'a been one hell of a day. Yes, sir, I guess they hate us.'

They reached a bend in the main road, from which a network of dark alleys shot out in all directions. In front of them the main road continued up the sharpening incline, disappearing in a murky cutting about a quarter of a mile ahead; by common consent, they stopped walking, and Lane leant against a lamp-post. It was now late, but there were still a few Japanese walking up and down the hill.

'Say,' the American demanded suddenly, 'what you guys want to do? You want a woman?'

Flannery looked at Lane, who stared back blankly. Like everything else in the Army, this moment had advanced on them inescapably. A thousand forces had combined to draw them to just this place at just this time, had even provided the American. They had known that it would happen — some time; just as they had known that they would get into action — some time. They had discussed it a thousand times. Cripes, just wait till we get amongst the Jap sheilas! It was nice to talk about, to boast about, to anticipate, and then, suddenly, with no more than a few months of warning, that in a moment had dwindled to a split second, they were faced with the decision.

Then, when it was action, they had merely begun to dodge bullets; now all they had to do was to say, 'Yes, my oath!' Or did they? The American was regarding them with a quizzical smile as they stared into one another's faces.

'Well, I don't know,' Lane said uncertainly, at length. 'We got no dough, you know.'

'Hell, I got plenty!' The American took three notes from his pocket and thrust them impulsively into Mark's belt. 'There's three hundred yen — I sold some stuff tonight. Go buy yourself a girl!'

'We can't take your dough,' Flannery protested.

'Jeez, forget it! I tell you, I got more of the goddamn' stuff'n Henry Ford.' He looked at them narrowly. 'Say, what's up with you guys — don't you want a woman? They ain't nothin' to be scared of.'

Flannery returned his stare. 'We aren't afraid of anything, mate.'

'Well, for Chris' sakes what's holdin' you?'

'We don't want to get jacked up, that's what.' Lane spoke the thought that had been in his mind and Flannery's. 'We got no blue-light outfit with us.'

'Hell, they fed you that hogwash, too? Look, I been here for a while. I came from Tokyo. Up there the brass reckoned they took a hundred dames off the street and ninety-five of 'em was clapped up. Well, that's all bull. Every day I have a different woman, and I ain't jacked up!'

Flannery looked at Lane again, and the American stared in bewilderment at them both.

'Well, for Chris' sakes, I'll get one for you. One each! Jeez, all you gotta do is ask!'

They were standing under one of the futile street lights that cast no more than a sickly glow, and that for a few yards only. They could see three vague figures approaching on the footpath, and the American caught at Lane's arm.

'Look, here's three dames now. I had plenty, but I guess another won't hurt me.' They all turned, and the three Japanese girls who were walking arm in arm on the footpath stopped uncertainly. They walked out into the road to give the three men a wide berth.

'Playin' hard to get!' The American winked at Flannery and Lane, and walking unhurriedly out into the road, grasped the nearest of the three girls by the arms. She looked up into his face as though hypnotized, and her two companions clattered on their wooden sandals to the side of the road to watch apprehensively. Flannery felt vaguely uneasy.

'Hullo, baby!' the American said to the girl in his grasp. 'You, *suki-suki?*'

She struggled weakly. '*Suki-suki*, no. Me, no!'

The other two started to moan softly and to chatter to each other, wringing their hands in distress. They did not take their eyes off the pair in the roadway.

'Ar, come on, baby!' The man thrust his body against the girl's. 'You *suki-suki*, fifty yen. *Go-juyen!*'

The girl stopped struggling and hung on his arms, limply. She still whimpered brokenly. '*Suki-suki*, no! Me, no. Please, no *suki-suki*!'

He released her with a sharp oath, and she ran to the side of the road where she cowered behind Lane, sobbing. Presently her two companions joined her, and Flannery could hear them comforting her behind his back.

He felt the blood rush to his face as the uneasiness he had felt before crystallized and suddenly burst over him in a rash of scalding shame. Holy Christ, he thought, the Japs have been doing this for years amongst conquered women, and here I am at it! Sick with disgust, he turned to look at the girl.

In the dim light her tear-blurred eyes looked back at him, half fearfully, and her thick lips trembled in her flat brown face. He almost smiled ... the Yank was not choosy, even in the dark.

'You, okay,' he said, gently. '*Suki-suki*, no.'

'Drew a blank, eh?' Lane said cheerfully, as the American walked back to where they stood. The three girls watched him uncertainly, huddled together. 'I don't think we'd better worry this bunch any more, do you?'

The American looked regretfully at the girls. 'Hell, no!' he muttered. 'Let them go. I didn't mean to scare the hell outa them — they must be the only good girls in this goddamn town, and I had to pick on them!' He leaned over Flannery's shoulder and pulled out a roll of notes, extracting one of a hundred yen. 'Here, Susie,' he said with a laugh. '*Suki-suki*, no, okay?'

His brown, wedge-shaped face, broad at the temples and

narrow at the jaw, was wreathed in a disarming smile, his even white teeth gleaming in the dim light. The girls smiled tremulously back at him; they all looked at the money, shaking their heads, but he tucked it into the broad sash of the one he had accosted.

'Here,' he laughed, 'go buy yourself a goddamn' chastity belt!'

The three girls clattered off into the shadows. They glanced over their shoulders as they went, even giggling a little as they got farther away.

'You know,' the American said reflectively, 'we should follow those dames. We c'd have 'em now for the asking. They got the green-backs, an' they know we ain't goin' to throw them on the road. Gentle 'em up a bit, an' you can have any dame, no matter who.' He looked at Flannery, his eyebrows raised in unmistakable query, and when the other shook his head, smiling, said briskly, 'Well, let's go — plenty more broads up the hill!'

'No, I don't think so, thanks,' Flannery said, turning to Lane. 'You want to go on, Sandy?'

'Not me, china. We better be getting back to the billets. It'll be pretty late by the time we get in, as it is.'

'Well, just as you like.' The American grinned. 'But one day, holy cow, will you beef about the chances you passed up!' He walked a few paces up the hill and turned round again. 'So long — on your way down town keep on the roadway.'

'Why?'

'It'll be safest. It's gettin' late, and some slap-happy Jap might pick you off.'

He started to walk away again, and Mark called out, 'Where are you going now?'

The American looked over his shoulder, briefly. 'Get me a bed for the night, I guess. With someone in it!'

They stood and watched his back, broad at the shoulders and narrow at the hips, disappear up the hill. His voice floated back to them as he hailed a passing Japanese. When they turned and walked down the hill their footsteps echoed loudly in the deserted street.

'What a funny beggar!' Lane mused aloud. 'Off he goes, just like that, by himself. I wouldn't be game, right up here!'

'He'd go anywhere after what he's looking for, I reckon!' Flannery laughed. 'He's like a dog on a hot scent!'

'They're all born with hot pants, those Yanks,' Lane said, and they walked on in silence through the ruined city.

The billets were deep in darkness and silence when they crept slowly up the stairs, their boots scraping on the concrete steps. The dormitory was freezingly cold, and the darkness was filled with the rustling of men twisting and turning in their sleep beneath their meagre coverings, trying to keep warm. They gasped as they took off their tunics and greatcoats, and Lane whispered, 'Cripes, I'm not going to undress, Mark — a man'd die!'

'Me, too.' Flannery dropped his boots to the floor with a subdued clunk. 'Go on, get in and warm it up a bit!'

They had just settled down in the creaking stretcher when the beam of a torch flashed on them, and they both raised their heads.

'Hullo!' A soft voice spoke from the door. 'Cuddlepot and Snugglepie! Where have you brave warriors been?' It was Salom, and he came and stood beside their bed.

'Up town,' Flannery said shortly.

'Didn't you hear about the order, no leave tonight?'

'I heard. The war's over. Listen, Sally, before you go, will you pull that coat up round our necks? What're you doin' up at this time, anyway?'

'Orderly stooge.' Salom put his torch on the floor and pulled the coat up, tucking it in firmly. 'And what did you do tonight — anything?' His voice had taken on a silky caressing note.

'Nothing,' Mark said, shortly.

'Nothing?'

'You heard — you ain't got rag ears. Now what about letting us get some sleep?'

Salom picked up his torch and walked away without reply. When his footsteps had died away in the corridor outside, Flannery whispered to Lane, 'He gives me the willies sometimes.

I don't know what to make of the animal.'

'I do,' Lane replied flatly. 'He's a hock. Now, quit your bleating and go to sleep!'

THE MAGNOLIA-TREE

The steep incline flattened out into a small shelf about a quarter of an acre in extent, cut in half by a hot stream that had gushed from the flank of the volcano farther up the valley. Murphy, at the end of the line, was the last to reach it, and shrugged the pack from his shoulders with a sigh. Behind them the flat coastal plain spread like a green sea, a woolly sea that washed in motionless waves at the feet of the hills and surged in a dense flood up the ravines that seamed all the country around the burning mountain.

'This'll do us, eh, Jim?' he suggested to the fair man who stood watching him.

'Uh-huh. Good as we'll get.'

'Okay.'

Murphy turned to a big kanaka.

'Work'im fire, Lukwa,' he said quietly, pointing to a patch of dried grass. 'Long harp.'

'Yes, Masta.'

'I'll get some tucker out,' the fair man volunteered, stooping over his pack.

'What we got?' Murphy inquired. He was a big, dark man, with corded arms and heavy shoulders, and legs like small trees.

'Roast duck,' the other replied, and laughed. 'Bully — but we got plenty of it.'

'Then take it out of your own pack, Jim,' Murphy said. 'We been using mine all along, and you'll find yourself carrying all the kai soon.'

'Broad shoulders,' the fair man shrugged. 'Hurry the coon with the fire.'

Murphy looked up the valley, at the volcano that from where he stood seemed to block the eastern end of it. The setting sun shone hotly on it as it rose, the bare, golden mass of it, from the jungle that clawed at its sides. The higher slopes were too hot for vegetation, and cotton-wool dabs of smoke clung among the ragged gullies. High above it towered an immense plume of pearly smoke, all washed with warm pink where the last rays of light cascaded over its bulging sides.

Behind it stretched mile after mile of lonely purple hills and twilit jungle that withdrew through mist and rain beyond the horizon. Unconsciously, Murphy sighed, and turned to watch the kanakas.

Two of them had cleared a patch in the coarse, hummocky grass and erected over it a framework of slender saplings, held together by strips of kunda-vine. They covered it with a dense mat of ginger leaves, enough to keep out the rain of one night, and spread a layer of ferns on the ground in its shelter.

Murphy grinned to himself. Once you couldn't sleep without clean sheets and a pillow, and now you curled up like a grub on the ground and slept like a top. Life, like death, a great leveller.

The fair man was dishing out the heated bully-beef into two dixies; Murphy squatted on his haunches and began to eat.

'Our leafy's ready, Jim,' he said. 'They're good coons, all right.'

'Yeah, they're all right.'

The other's face was impassive, his voice impersonal. He seemed to be without interest in what was going on around him, his whole attention fastened on the meat in his dish. Another might have resented it, but Murphy had known him too long, and was used to it. Yet it seemed sometimes that he could remember a time when it had been different, and at times, as now, he tried to crystallise the memory into something definite.

When they had finished eating, they sat in the deepening twilight and smoked, talking softly about the kanakas, the island, the days behind them and the days ahead. By sunset of the next day, they hoped to make the bare slopes above them, now hidden in a thin mist of rain and dusk.

'Jim,' Murphy said suddenly, 'did you notice the volcano, at sunset?'

The fair man didn't answer him immediately. He looked at him closely and then said:

'No, not particularly. Why?'

'Oh, I dunno. It was so ... well, pretty.' Murphy rolled himself another cigarette, and shielded his face in his hat as he lit it.

'That's all right, if you go for it, I suppose,' the other replied casually. 'I don't.'

If you go for it, Murphy thought; and suddenly, for no reason at all, he remembered the magnolia-tree. Poor old Jim!

'Jim,' he asked softly, 'remember the magnolia-tree?'

A long time ago, those hot summer nights when he used to ride around the Bateses' on his bike after tea to beg Jim off for a swim. Jim's mother was a funny woman — her house was always spotlessly clean; and after she had polished the floors she used to spread newspapers over them so they wouldn't get marked again in a hurry. None of the youngsters, who flocked into the Murphy home like a cloud of starlings, liked to go inside the Bates' place; even Murph, Jim's best friend, never felt comfortable there. It seemed that they were jealous of him. When he asked if Jim might come out, Mrs Bates would screw up her eyes and say, 'Well, he was out last night, down the beach...'

Mr Bates who always sat away from the table reading, would stop and listen. He never lowered his paper, but you could feel his attention on the conversation, and when his wife had said yes or no, he would rustle the pages and go on with his reading. Jim always had to wheedle: 'Aw, go on, Mum — let's!' as though he were asking for the world; and she'd look at him for a moment and then at Murph, squirming uncomfortably by the door.

'Well, all right, then,' she would usually say, 'you can go. But I don't know what you got a home for, I really don't. See you're back by nine o'clock ...'

They never waited to hear more, but ran off before she changed her mind — she had never actually done it, but they always felt that she might. Murph breathed easier as he left the house; but he never got over the embarrassment that he felt in the kitchen of Jim's home, begging for such a little thing. A swim after tea on a hot night, which his own easy-going parents took for granted.

It was always the same performance, as if they wanted to keep Jim to themselves all the time. He was afraid to ask them for permission to go out, frightened that they might somehow divine that what he found outside his home meant more in a way than what lay inside it. He always said to Murph: 'You ask her, Murph — she'll let me, then!'

All the evening, they skylarked in the warm river water, under the floodlight on a pole at the end of the jetty. Inside the circle of light the water was clear and green like the glass of a green bottle; in the dark, outside the circle it was black. You swam through it wreathed in pale fire, and could see where the fish and crabs darted around the piles under the jetty. Deep down cold flames writhed among the rocks on the bottom.

The girls joined in the rough and tumble; and there was one night when Murph, flinging his arms around one of them to pull her into the water, her hard little body, cool in the clinging cotton bathers, felt it like cold fire against his side. In the midst of all the splashing and the noise, he stopped dead still. The shrill cries of the girls, the laughter and the cool caress of the water, the mysterious green fires in the dark, were not enough. A summer night like this held something more, something new. He knew it suddenly and certainly; it made him feel sad and lonely, and yet filled with a strange and exultant power.

As the hot summer nights of that year slipped by, Murph sensed that most of the others knew it too, an intangible thread that carried a curious current from one to the other. Lying on the sand after their swim, on the cool sand that was yet warm underneath and smelled of salt water and seaweed, they laughed and gossiped, smoked tentative cigarettes, some of them, and watched the golden lights of the prawn-fishers bobbing in the shallows, but found it hard to look into each others' faces. They were chary of giving away a secret they learned all at the same time, waiting, half-afraid, for the thing, whatever it was, to happen.

One night, Murph and Jim left the others under the light at the land end of the jetty and wheeled their bikes up a quiet street where the darkness lay in deep pools between the lights. The music of the hurdy-gurdy on the beach pursued them faintly as they went and the whole of the avenue was deserted.

'Gee, Jim,' Murph said suddenly, sniffing like a setter, 'cop the smell!' It was a bitter-sweet perfume, and it hung on the air like the scent of orange-blossoms, a hundred times intensified.

'Yes, a magnolia-tree,' Jim said quietly, but with a curious sort of satisfaction in his voice. 'There's not many of them around,' he added, confidingly, 'but I know where there's another.' They pedalled a few yards in silence, and he said suddenly, 'Look, there it is, the magnolia-tree.'

Murph looked where he pointed; it was a dark, glossy tree, smooth leaves streaked with moonlight, and it was starred with great luminous white flowers, chalices of scent and dew and darkness.

'Magnolias,' Jim said again, softly. As he stood in the dark he saw a moon-silvered terrace and shadowy trees, and white arms that were somehow mixed up with the dreamy songs they had been singing on the beach earlier that night. He listened, and the remembered music teased the warm air and beat in throbbing waves against his heart. 'Aren't they lovely — like pale, lovely girls.'

Before Murph knew what he was going to do, he leaned his bike against the fence and shinned up the tree, which hung low over the footpath. He was gone only a few moments; Murph, waiting below, could hear him rustling as he clambered around in the boughs above, and then he dropped lightly to the path with an armful of exquisite blooms.

'Look ... smell!' he said, but buried his own face among the waxen petals.

The other boy stood uneasily by and looked up and down the street. Heck, the old girl who owned the joint might come out, and then there'd be a blue — she was a crabby old sort. Besides, a man was growing up, and you didn't go racing around the streets with bundles of flowers like, well, like a sissy. Someone might come along and see them, someone they knew.

Almost as the thought crossed his mind, a cyclist pedalled up the avenue from the beach, a big lout who was in their class at school. 'Gawd, be on the pansies!' he called out in an assumed falsetto voice. 'Give's a kiss for a flower, Cecil!'

He was swallowed in the darkness before the sound of his voice had dripped out of the air; Murph turned to Jim, who stood staring after the bike as though he had been smacked in the face. The magnolias lay at his feet, spoiled in the red dust. Murph picked up his bike.

'Come on, Jim,' he said, 'it's getting late.'

'Murph — ' the other boy said, and stopped. He wheeled his bike out on to the road, and pedalled off in silence. When they got to the Bateses', it was all in darkness, and they stopped at the front gate, noiselessly.

'Good-night, Jim,' Murph whispered. 'See you tomorrow.'

'Murph, do you think that too?' Jim demanded.

'Think what?'

'Ar — stop kidding. You know what. You heard the gawk on the bike!'

Murph knew what Jim meant all right, but he didn't know what to say. He had never seen anyone look quite like Jim had, then, the hurt and the bewilderment. He fiddled with the bell on the handlebar and muttered: 'Aw, I dunno. You don't want to take any notice of those silly cows. They don't understand, sort of ...'

'Well, if they don't understand, then let them mind their own bloody business!' Jim blurted. 'Mum, and Dad, and everyone!'

He pushed open the side gate, ran down the path and was

lost in the shadowy garden.

'You remember that,' Jim said, in a strained voice. 'You're a funny cove!'

Murph looked at his cigarette. It had gone out.

'Give us a light,' he muttered.

All around them the secret noises of the jungle whispered unceasingly, mingling with the soft murmur of the river, and a thousand phosphorous eyes watched unblinkingly from the darkness.

'Yes, I remember it, and that's why I can't set you about the volcano. You've changed a bit since then, china.'

'Haven't we all!' the other laughed shortly. 'I learned my lesson early, that's all. Remember that pet magpie you used to have, and when the wild birds found it out in the paddock, how they picked Christ out of the poor thing? Well, that's how it is. You can't be any different from the mob unless you're rich or able to bat them down. I'm neither, so I toe the line. In the long run, you collect less hurt.'

'That's bull — you don't have to.' Murphy stood up and stretched. 'You don't get nowhere, buckling under.'

The other merely shrugged, with a funny, tight little grin, and Murph, watching him, knew that he had been talking through his hat. He didn't even believe it himself. Unless you strung along with the mob, and kept your nose wiped, you got a thin time of it — unless, as Jim had said, you could stand up to the lot of them. And that took a lot of doing. People generally seemed to band together like primitives to harry any poor cow that stood out of the ruck, seemed frightened of him, almost. Life, like death, a great leveller.

'Think I'll hit the hay.' He stretched again, and yawned. 'Coming?'

Jim stubbed his cigarette in the damp leaves.

'Yeah, no sense in sitting here.'

He stood up and for a moment laid his hand on the other's shoulder.

'Don't take any notice of what I said, china. It'll be all right, you'll find.'

He meant it, too ... it was just a matter of keeping your nose wiped, keeping your thoughts to yourself and never laying yourself open to ridicule. You could have a lot of happiness in a quiet way. You rubbed along.

'Yeah, it'll be all right, all right!' Murph said — the old formula. 'But you don't have to wear a front for me, Jim.'

'No Murph, I guess not.' *(It's all I can say, even if it means adding pretence to pretence.)* 'Coming?'

Together, they crawled into the leafy shelter. The night remained, full of beauty, cool, ageless. A soft glow showed where the kanakas crouched close over their tiny blaze, and the fireflies trailed their crazy tinsel web among the dark trees. Far up the valley, the volcano strained up out of the jungle, clothing itself exquisitely in the first cold light of the rising moon.

LOOKING AFTER BERT

The house was quiet, as it always was at that time of day, suspended between the little activities of getting up and breakfasting and cleaning, and the decision of what to have for lunch: almost audibly thinking about its past, a visitor had remarked once with tight humour, and congratulating itself on the security of its immutable future as the home — cage, coffin — of monied Miss Harriet Moon.

That same Miss Moon now sat, insulated from the bleak and sleety day outside by drawn curtains, and glowing mallee-roots in the deep fire-place of the dining room. It was a habit she had got into soon after her mother's death, when the house seemed bigger and quieter than she could stand, of using the dining room rather than the sitting room during the morning — it meant they had to light only one fire, and from where she had placed her chair she could easily take part in the conversation addressed to her from time to time by her cook-housekeeper, Mrs Bohun, of whom occasionally she caught glimpses through the half-opened door into the kitchen.

Right up to Mrs Moon's death it had been kept closed, except for the passage in and out of persons, the end results of Mrs Bohun's labours having been passed with nice ceremony through a servery hatch into the sphere of a maid now departed. But with her mother's death, Harriet Moon had felt self-conscious about keeping up such a degree of state for one — herself — and had decreed the permanent closing of the hatch. In the silent house the opened door into the kitchen had given her a contact with at least one human activity, and there were times when the garrulous old woman was entertaining; even when she was not, she was company.

After staring for some days at the closed hatch, Harriet Moon had fallen back on the memory of art classes attended as a matter of course at her expensive school, and for a while afterwards, and had covered the dining-room side with a painting of a receding coastline washed by seas of a wonderful blue, and had draped across it tiny muslin curtains: so that when she half- closed her eyes, and stared hard at it, as she now did, she could almost believe herself looking through the window of some clifftop house at a coast she had either imagined or heard about, and certainly had yearned to visit, ever since she had laid the first magic patch of blue on the smooth wood of the old servery hatch to create it.

In the big room, it was the only thing unchanged since the dinnertime two years before when Mrs Moon had dropped her fork with a frightening clatter onto her plate and leaned forward over the table, her lips in a ludicrous twist as though she were incredibly about to shoot some ribald remark towards the sideboard and its photograph of her dead husband — whom she had rejoined while her daughter and the maid watched her united in terror, before the clatter of her fallen fork had died on the startled air.

Harriet Moon had sometimes considered doing over, if not the entire house, then at least this room in which she spent so much of her time. But in the years before her death, even when it seemed to Harriet that nothing would ever destroy her, Mrs Moon had said several times, as though carefully arranging surveillance over her daughter's activities when she herself would no longer be able to do it: 'Look after Bert and Mrs Bohun when I'm gone, Harriet — and don't change the house. I want to feel that if I come back — and who knows? — I'll find everything as I left it.'

So Harriet Moon quailed when it came to the point of moving against the faded prints, the illuminated addresses from a score of lodges and charitable institutions, the framed invitation to a ball in honour of the Duke and Duchess of York, the dusty pawa shell recalling a visit to New Zealand — the china and silver and plaster and brass nick-nacks which her mother had so prized, while forgetting for at least the last twenty years of her life that she owned them. And in any case, what could she do with it all? Harriet Moon had argued with herself a hundred times. Stack it away in a spare room already stuffed with mementos of other lives, just to clear the walls for whatever she herself might collect in the lonely years before a dinnertime when she too might drop her fork, and twist sideways to leer at the vacant spot on the sideboard ... where no photograph of a husband of her's would ever have stood?

'Brains aren't so good, nowadays,' said Mrs Bohun from the kitchen, breaking a silence of at least fifteen minutes' duration. 'They used to clean them once. Now they just send them all higgledy-piggledy, any old how. Times have changed.'

So that's what we're having for lunch, Harriet thought, pulling her mind back from the coast of her own imaginings. Brains. For a moment she wanted to say: Yes — you, for instance. You wouldn't have *dreamed* of chatting to Mother through the kitchen door. The door wouldn't even have been *opened*!

'Of course things have changed,' she replied automatically, looking at the half-opened door. 'But wash them well and put plenty of breadcrumbs with them, just the same. I'm not that keen on them.'

'They're good for you — they give them to people in hospitals. And your mother always had them for lunch, Thursdays.'

'My mother hasn't had them Thursdays for more than two years, now,' Harriet Moon remarked crisply, feeling, as always, the warm satisfaction which accompanied any small breach in the carefully preserved edifice of Mrs Moon's immortality.

'Boy!' Mrs Bohun cooed unexpectedly in sugary tones. 'Mother's boy! Did 'e eat up all 'is dinny-bones?' Harriet heard the clink of something laid on the table, and the shuffle of the old woman's bunioned feet on the black-and-white lino of the kitchen, and then Mrs Bohun's slatey-grey, smooth head appeared around the edge of the door. In her normal manner — she squeaked and dropped her aitches only when addressing the late Mrs Moon's relict budgerigar — she said: 'Shall I let him out, Miss Harriet? Won't hurt him to stretch his little wings.'

'If you clean up after him,' Harriet Moon said.

'Who ever *does*, except me?' Mrs Bohun's head bobbed out of sight, and Harriet Moon heard the thin rattle of the cage-door being slid up. A moment later a tiny blue-green bird flicked through the doorway, circled the room on wildly fluttering wings, and landed neatly among the tumblers and salad bowls on the polished jarrah top of the sideboard. He cocked a claw behind one ear, scratched himself thoughtfully, and said in a voice shrill and minutely crepitating like the whispering of an old, worn gramaphone record: '*Let's a-a-a-all go down the Strand!*'

''Ave a banana,' Harriet Moon said, automatically.

The late Mrs Moon had been an accomplished pianist, of course, and on Sunday afternoons had played and sang, roguishly even into her sixties, the ditties of her girlhood: and, if there were people in to tea, would always close her performance by saying with a perplexed smile: 'I don't know why Harriet won't play. I've tried with her, heaven knows. Music's my life!' The budgerigar, now nearly six years old, had acquired a remarkable command of words and phrases, and would entertain the visitors while Harriet Moon lurked awkwardly by the window, hating it and herself and her mother, who would say: 'Look — even Bert can sing!' smiling winningly at her daughter through the visitors, who would smile with her and cluck their commisseration.

Now the budgerigar clicked across the polished wood to the oval mirror to exchange greetings with the unattainable other self which appeared for him, every morning, glittering blue-green among the glittering crystal and glasswater. He nibbled at the reflected beak, cocked his head, strutted and talked gibberish, laughed on a high, hysterical note, and finally rolled onto his back to wave his twig legs in an ecstasy of self-importance.

'Isn't he a caution!' said Mrs Bohun, who had stationed herself at the doorway to watch his morning performance. 'Bert! Did 'e like the ole side board? Bert!'

Hearing her voice the bird stopped waving its claws and looked at her. It rolled over and stood up, stared stonily at Harriet Moon, and suddenly bobbed, like a worshipper genuflecting with both knees. When it stood erect again, there was a tiny spiral of ordure on the polished wood beneath its tail. This it examined, turning around and eyeing it knowingly before once more resuming its play.

'There — I told you so,' Harriet Moon said, hopelessly. 'The dirty little beast.'

'It's only natural,' said Mrs Bohun.

'It would be just as natural in his cage.'

'No. It's got something to do with flying, I've been told.' Mrs Bohun lifted the corner of her apron and removed the little speck. 'They sit around in the cage and nothing happens. When they get out, and fly, and work their wings it moves their little insides, or something. I ...' she stopped speaking and peered intently at the curtained window at the other end of the room. 'There's a car just pulled up at the gate.' She padded over to the window and ever so carefully moved one of the drapes aside. 'One of those big swanky cars, too. A Rolls-Royce.'

'For heaven's sake, stop eavesdropping,' Harriet Moon commanded. 'The car might have just stopped there ... for anything.'

'I'm not eavesdropping, I'm looking,' Mrs Bohun replied, without heat, as though speaking to an impertinent child. 'And the woman's getting out. Fur coat.' There was a moment of silent inspection. 'She's opened our gate.'

'Then go to the door, instead of lurking there like a Bolshevik!'

'Well, who ever does answer the door, but me?' the old woman demanded, dropping the edge of the curtain. She spoke with the humorous half-insolence of the favoured old retainer. Her late employer had left her well provided for anyway, and the three days a week she did for the daughter were purely as she had confided to one of her familiars at the Old Folks' Centre and Library, to keep Miss Harriet on her toes.

'I'll go into the drawing room,' Harriet Moon volunteered, half rising.

'No. Stay there,' Mrs Bohun said, again in the same peremptory fashion. 'It's warmer.' She smoothed her unwrinkled hair and brushed her spotless apron over her belly and disappeared into the hallway.

The woman who preceded her into the dining room a few moments later was old and tiny and beautiful. She stood poised like a doll in the doorway, a half-inquiring smile on her red mouth.

'Please forgive this intrusion,' she said. Her voice was light and musical, and beautifully produced. 'I was on my way to morning tea with the Shaw-Smiths, and got lost. I shouldn't have driven myself, it's so long since I was home, here. But ...' she smiled fully, and spread her tiny gloved hands to solicit forgiveness of her stupidity. She was exquisitely dressed, Harriet Moon noticed, with a confection of deep purple velvet violets on her mist-grey hair, and a deep purple dress showing at the opened front of her grey squirrel coat. 'When I realised I was really lost, I just stopped at the first house which looked as if it might have a telephone and ... well, here I am. May I please ring the Shaw-Smiths and explain why I haven't arrived?'

'Of course,' Harriet Moon said, readily. The Shaw-Smiths were an old-money family who lived in a huge Italianate mansion two or three miles away among the avenues and crescents on the south side of the river, and anyone going to morning-tea with them, and especially anyone driving her own Rolls-Royce, must be someone. But this woman obviously was someone. Even the elegant suede boots on her tiny feet, opened halfway to the instep, showed a squirrel lining, and the faintest perfume which preceded her into the room — carnations, violets, guelder-roses? — reminded Harriet Moon of summer evenings in a garden she had never even seen.

'You're very kind,' the woman said.

'Not at all,' Harriet Moon responded formally. 'Perhaps my housekeeper could ring up for you?'

Mrs Bohun had been standing slightly back in the hallway, calmly taking in the detail of the woman's dress and appearance — possibly for some future anecdote at the Old Folks' Centre and Library. The woman turned a wide smile on her.

'If you would ...'

'Then do, please, Mrs Bohun.' Harriet Moon said. 'Say that ...'

'Miriam Bonaccor,' the woman said, dividing the intelligence nicely between Harriet Moon and her servant. 'Mrs Miriam Bonaccor. Would you just explain that I've lost my way, and will call on them later?'

Mrs Bohun nodded, and stumped off in the direction of the lobby where the phone was, leaving Harriet Moon and her visitor alone in the gleaming, fire-warmed room.

'It's a terrible day out,' Harriet Moon said. 'Perhaps you'll stay for a few minutes, and warm yourself? My name is Harriet Moon.'

'You're most kind,' Miriam Bonaccor walked into the room and shrugged off her coat, which she draped casually over the back of a chair. She took off her gloves and stood warming her hands at the fire. 'What a lovely room,' she remarked, looking around her, and then turning to Harriet: 'Quite an old house?'

'It was my grandmother's, then my mother's and then ... mine.'

'Your parents are dead?'

'For years,' Harriet Moon said. 'Would you care for a cup of tea?'

'You really are most kind.'

'I'll have Mrs Bohun make it when she finishes your phone call.'

'Thank you, indeed.'

Miriam Bonaccor walked back to the chair on which she had dropped her coat, and sat down. She looked around the room once again, slowly, taking in each piece of furniture and decoration as her glance rested on it. When she saw the servery hatch she paused for some time. Then she swung to face Harriet Moon.

'The little painting there — the trompe d'oeil by the door. Who painted it?'

'I did,' Harriet Moon said, deprecatingly.

'Then you've been abroad?'

'No. I learned a little at school, here, and then at art classes, afterwards. It's the first I'd done in — oh, years.'

'I didn't mean that,' said Miriam Bonaccor, returning her glance to the painting. 'I mean ... the scene. Where did you see that?'

'I didn't see it. I did it out of my head.'

'My dear — that's a stretch of coast on the Cote d'Azur.' She stood up and walked to the hatch, placing the point of a finger on a white fleck, half house, half smudge, poised like a swallow's nest on the cliff above the sea. 'That is my home.'

Harriet Moon felt a curious rippling sensation, not entirely pleasant, at the base of her neck where it joined her shoulders.

'Coastlines — bits of them, anyway — are much the same anywhere,' she said. She was surprised that it sounded more like a question than a flat denial, as she had intended of whatever the other woman was driving at.

'Perhaps,' Miriam Bonaccor said, 'but not this bit. I know it too well.' With her back to Harriet, she placed a finger on the painting and traced a line a couple of inches off the paint at the left-hand lower corner. 'Just here there is a villa owned by a retired French opera singer — terrible old woman who drinks abominably, but very interesting and wicked. When I open my place — I have lived there for two months every year for the past three years — I dine with her quite often. We sit on her terrace, and ...' the point of her finger trailed back on to the paint, coming to rest again on the white smudge: '... this is the view I see. Have seen, a hundred times.' She turned to Harriet. 'You see, my dear — I *know*.'

'It can only be coincidence, of course,' Harriet Moon said.

'Coincidence, of course.' Miriam Banaccor arched her slender brows. 'What else?' She walked back to her chair and sat down, still looking at Harriet with a quizzically amused expression. 'But my dear, what is coincidence? Merely a remarkable occurrence of events, perhaps — but ... what brings it about?'

She spoke lightly, though with a curious intensity, as if she had access to realms of knowledge and experience Harriet Moon had never even dreamed of, and in the silence which followed her words the younger woman felt once again on the skin of her neck the shivering premonition of a door she had never opened to a room of whose existence she had never known.

Miriam Bonaccor returned her gaze to the painting and said almost sharply, 'Why have you never travelled? You could afford to, obviously?'

'I don't know, now,' Harriet Moon said. 'I always wanted to — I don't know where, but maybe to sail up the Nile to Luxor, to see Samarkand ... but Mother didn't ever suggest going anywhere. She was always so occupied. And ...'

Her words trailed into silence, and she sat staring at her hands. You what? What did you do in all those years, by God, *a quarter of a century*, while Mother was too busy to think of going to Samarkand?

'Nothing, really,' she said aloud, and Miriam Bonaccor looked with gentle pity at the side of her face.

'And what kept your mother so busy?' she asked. 'How did she spend her life?'

'In all sorts of ways,' Harriet Moon said guardedly, without looking up. 'Most of it, I suppose, in doing good.'

The door from the hallway opened and Mrs Bohun entered, closing it behind her. 'I told them you were lost and would get in touch with them later,' she announced.

'Thank you,' said Miriam Bonaccor.

'I told them where you were, too.' The old woman inclined her head towards Harriet Moon. 'They asked me to thank you.'

'Mrs Bonaccor is staying for a cup of tea,' Harriet Moon said. 'Will you make it?'

'With lemon, please?' Miriam Bonaccor added, winningly.

The old woman hobbled into the kitchen, closing the door behind her, and Miriam Bonaccor picked up the conversation as though it had never been interrupted.

'For whom did she do good?'

'Well ... for everybody she could, I suppose.'

'It's a very relative term,' Miriam Bonaccor said — not tartly, as Harriet Moon had expected, but smilingly, and the mood in her glowed warmly, like a candle, across the little space between them. 'It depends upon whom it is being done for, and why. In most cases it is a form of arrogance exercised on people who either don't have the intelligence to realise what is happening to them, or whose exquisite lower-class reticence will not permit them to tell the do-gooder what she should do.'

'Such as?'

'Go and jump in the lake,' Miriam Bonaccor said, with such unexpected vulgarity that Harriet Moon smiled with her. 'Of course, you must not get the notion that I am against good.' She smiled archly, and spread her elegantly ringed fingers to the blaze, regarding with blatant satisfaction the multiplied twinkle of diamond, ruby and emerald. 'I've spent most of my life doing good, too ... but to myself.'

'You make no bones about it.'

'Why should I? As a result, I can afford several cars, and a nice home — *three of them* — and travel, and interesting friends, and to be precise, all that makes life worth while.'

Miriam Bonaccor paused, staring at the servery hatch and the blue sea which washed soundlessly below her home on the Cote d'Azur — one of her three houses, Harriet Moon thought, watching her, and felt a gnawing sense of envy almost of injury, that she herself had missed all this strange woman had experienced merely, it seemed, through utter selfishness.

'Are you, or more pertinently, have you ever *been*, married?' Miriam Bonaccor asked, suddenly, without turning around.

Harriet Moon was completely unprepared for the personal question, but the budgerigar saved her the embarrassment of answering.

'*Let's a-a-all go down the Strand!*' he carolled scratchily from the top of the sideboard, and immediately attracted the attention of both women to himself. Conscious of his audience, he scratched behind one ear and intoned wolfishly: *''Ave a bana-a- na!*'

Miriam Bonaccor, looking at him coolly, said: 'Talking birds. One's self writ strange. They're ... malevolent.'

'Bert's harmless,' Harriet Moon said. 'Mother had a lot of them, at different times, but he was her special pet. She reared him from the egg, almost.'

'There's a place for animals,' Miriam Bonaccor said, as though the other had not spoken. 'For birds, in the bush. For dogs, in Chinamen's stews. And for cats, in the alleys where they belong. Otherwise they take over houses — and people.'

The tiny bird, which had been watching her as she spoke — watching her malevolently, Harriet Moon noticed, with an inward smile — suddenly launched itself from its gleaming red platform and landed expertly on the crown of her hat, blue-green among the clustered violets. She seemed to shrink a little, although she sat immobile.

'Take it off,' she commanded.

'It's a trick Mother taught him. She used to put a piece of apple in her hair, for visitors.' Harriet Moon got up and walked over to Miriam Bonaccor. She took the bird, cupping the whole of his sleek, hard little body in her hand. For a moment she tightened her grasp on him, and he glared hatred at her from his golden eyes. Miriam Bonaccor sat still, cold and silent as stone, until she released him. 'I'll put him back in his cage.'

On her way to the kitchen, Harriet Moon mused: So the world isn't quite her oyster. Sometimes when she lifts the shell, she finds something that isn't a pearl. A budgerigar, for instance. The thought gave her some comfort, as though chance had placed in her hand a weapon to combat this stranger's otherwise overwhelming superiority. As she slid the door of the cage upwards, the bird twisted his head and nipped her savagely at the tender edge of her fingernail. She almost threw him through the aperture, hating him again.

'A cuckoo in the nest, if ever I saw one,' Mrs Bohun hissed at her back, her eyes turned furtively to the closed door.

'Hush,' said Harriet Moon.

'Hush, nothing. What did she come here for?'

'To get out of the rain, I imagine,' Harriet Moon whispered drily. 'What else?'

'That I'd like to know. I've seen her sort before. Her and her Shaw-Smiths!'

'Don't be ridiculous!' said Harriet Moon.

The copper kettle bubbled on the gas jet. The old woman filled the pot she had placed near it on a silver tray, with cups and saucers, a sugar-bowl, a dish of sliced lemon, and four little pink cakes.

'Lemon!' she muttered scathingly. 'She's found out you've got money. She'll talk you into putting it into something — oil shares. I'm going down to the shop for some things. You be careful while I'm away. Don't you do anything.'

'Don't be ridiculous,' Harriet Moon whispered again. 'Here, I'll take the tea in. You may go.'

When she returned to the dining room, the stranger had completely regained her composure. She sat, leaning slightly forward, staring dreamily into the fire. As Harriet Moon put the tray down on the small table, and lowered herself into the chair beside it, she said: 'Then ... *are* you married?' — once again as though nothing had interrupted their previous conversation.

'I'm not married, and I never have been,' Harriet Moon said.

'A pity.'

'Then you are? Of course ... *Mrs* Bonaccor ...'

'I have been,' Miriam Bonaccor said. 'Four times. Right now I am — to use a theatrical term — resting.'

'One might suspect you would need to.' Harriet Moon remarked tartly. This new revelation of this woman's fecundity for living aroused in her a block of resentful thoughts — not, she was surprised to realise, against Miriam Bonaccor, but against something she could materialise in her mind only as life, things, chances, and what they had all added up to for Harriet Moon. Four times this woman had walked into the bedroom of a new life with a man she loved. Four times, a different man. While I ...

'Perhaps,' Miriam Bonaccor said, breaking in on her thoughts. 'But should one marry — like the pelican — for life? Can you imagine how exhausting it would be to sit through a whole play without intermission? Or a football match? Or an afternoon at the races, without occasional visits to the lounge?' She laughed, completely restored to her good humour and self satisfaction. 'I will *not* be bored ... although I must admit that all of my ... intermissions ... have not been at my own behest. Two of my husbands died — but both, fortunately, leaving me a little better placed to ...' she smiled beguilingly at Harriet Moon, inviting her to be a partner in the elegant conceit she intended: '... to obtain tickets for another performance?'

Harriet Moon sat staring with dull resentment at the crowded wall in front of her. Far from sharing Mrs Bonaccor's tinkling laughter, she had hardly even heard the words which evoked it. For the first time in years she was compelled, by this woman's empty-headed chatter, to examine her life and to compare it with that of somebody else, and the comparison stunned her. While I have sat here guarding this houseful of rubbish and birds and old women, and feeding Bert and gossiping with Mrs Bohun, this woman has been living in a way I can hardly speculate on, with drunken opera singers and houses and jewels, and traveled up the Nile to the temples of Karnak. She has listened to a muezzin in the twilight, with a husband's hand at her breast. While I ...

'I was in love once,' she said, still staring at the wall. 'When I was nineteen. And he was in love with me — I know it. David was his name. I met him at the art class. He was a mechanic. I told Mother, and she said I should bring him home one night for supper, after the class. He wore boots ... you know ... and his nails were not quite clean. How could they be? He was a mechanic. But the backs of his hands were smooth, and the veins on them ... I wanted to touch them and feel his blood running under my fingertips. Mother made fun of him — oh, delicately! — and when next I went to class, he was not there. Nor the next time, nor the next. So then I stopped going.' She turned to Miriam Bonaccor. 'I had almost forgotten. I think I *had* forgotten. And now you must come, with your talk of travels, and your friends, and your marriages. Why did you? Why did you have to come here, to my house?'

'My dear.' Miriam Bonaccor said. She made no attempt to comfort, but sat with her hands folded in her lap, looking at

Harriet Moon. 'Perhaps it is because of all that I did come — because coincidence, perhaps, is a word we use only because we cannot, or are frightened to think of another. For some time now I have been looking for a companion — indeed, I was intending to ask the advice of Mrs Shaw-Smith about it. I want a woman — a lady — to travel with me. Not as a servant, but as a friend ... although, of course, I should pay all expenses. I am going to Egypt, to sail up the Nile ... no, truly,' she insisted, as Harriet Moon raised her glance disbelievingly. 'I have already made the reservation for next month. I could show you my ticket. I have done it before, but in one trip — in many, even — one never sees all of it; and I love it so. Will you come with me?'

'What — forever?' Harriet Moon said. The three syllables, hard and sharp on her lips, felt like a sentence she had already passed under, and as she looked at the woman her glance was filled with disquiet.

'Of course not,' Miriam Bonaccor said instantly, even a little sharply. I am not one of those women who trail endlessly about the world with a good-looking ... companion ... young enough to be my daughter. I need you — there are things you can do for me. In time I will marry again, and no longer need you. But when I no longer need you, I assure you you will no longer need me, unless you are a fool — and I don't think you are. Will you come?'

'... next month?'

'No — now.'

'*Now?*' Harriet Moon cried. Her heart leapt to her throat and hung there like a grape. 'Why now?'

'If you wait any longer — if I go away today without you — you will never go,' Miriam Bonaccor said. 'And there are other reasons. You painted my home, when you had never even seen it. And I ... I came to this place, of all the homes in the city.'

'But ... that's it. This house!' Harriet Moon gestured distractedly around the room at the silver and crystal, pictures and ornaments, carpets and furniture: the doors she had always walked through and the windows through which she had spied upon the world now unrolled like a carpet before her feet, terrifyingly, by this terrifying woman. 'I can't just ... leave ... all this!'

'Things,' Miriam Bonaccor said, dismissing them.

'But *my* things!'

'Your housekeeper will see to them. They won't disintegrate just because you're not here looking at them.'

Why can't I just say no? Harriet Moon wondered. Through the half-opened door to the kitchen, her glance caught the twinkle of the budgerigar's gold-painted cage.

'Then ... Bert?' she said, almost with triumph. 'I can't leave him. He was Mother's pet. She asked me to look after him.'

'And your Mrs Bohun, too?' Miriam Bonaccor surmised, implacably. 'Her too? The world is cluttered with old maids keeping such promises to corpses.' She shrugged. 'You loved your mother so much?'

'No ... I didn't.' Harriet Moon said. The panic died down in her, and she stood up and walked to the sideboard. 'I really didn't like her at all — ever. Nor she, me. I was just another of her things. If it had been possible, she would have had me stuffed and mounted, I think, and nailed to the wall with the pawa shell. Mrs Bohun would have dusted me.' She turned to Miriam Bonaccor. 'I never liked her,' she said simply, 'and then I hated her. I still do. But she made me promise.'

'My dear,' Miriam Bonaccor said. 'Your mother is dead.'

The sleet scratched at the window, and in the flickering of the crumbled incandescent heap of coals in the fireplace the blue seas of the servery hatch seemed to move, restlessly, against their rocks.

'Of course she is,' Harriet Moon said, finally. 'It's two years since she had brains for Thursday lunch.'

'I beg your pardon?'

'Nothing ...'

'Then ...?' Miriam Bonaccor said.

'In a moment.'

Harriet Moon left the sideboard and walked over to where

her handbag hung over the back of a chair with the heavy coat she had worn on her morning walk. When only twelve years of age, she had been commanded by a swimming teacher to dive from a low tower which, then, had seemed Kosciusko-high. She had fidgeted and whined, pressing herself against the handrail behind her until the shame of her classmates' urging had sent her finally, headlong, into the space above the glass-green water in which — even at that moment — she had had time to see the hard gold shafts of sunlight slanting down into the dark and had been filled instantly with a wonderful exhilaration of adventure transcending all terror. She had never felt it again until now, and her hand trembled on the little gold elephant-clasp of her bag. Her cheque-book, pocket-book and keys, the little chamois ring-necked bag for loose change — everything was there, she thought, like a portmanteau packed for flight.

'In a moment,' she said again.

She walked into the kitchen, slid up the door of the budgerigar's cage and extracted him, cupping the whole of his sleek, hard little body in her hand, familiarly. He looked up at her, winking his eyes and working his bill, but made no sound. Unhurriedly she turned to the gas-stove, flipped on the largest jet, and held his head directly in its hissing flow. He wriggled and squeaked, trying to look at her, but she held him tight. In a while, just as the fumes were beginning to nauseate her, he wriggled no more. He shuddered, minutely, and relaxed against her palm.

She laid him gently on the edge of the sink. She looked at him for a moment, and stroked his blue-green plumage. 'Poor Bert,' she said, softly.

When she returned to the living room, Miriam Bonaccor stood up and looked at her questioningly.

'Then ...?'

Harriet Moon took up her handbag and coat.

'I'm ready, now,' she said.

WONG CHU AND THE QUEEN'S LETTER BOX

You mightn't think there'd be a very strong connection between an old Chinese market gardener and a pillarbox owned by the Queen of England — but there was: a long and intimate, and in many ways a romantic one, too.

Both the pillarbox and the Chinaman first knew South Perth as a rushy riverside retreat of cow-paddocks and market gardens and bush, where the settlers along the river's bank had their own jetties and flat-bottomed boats for travelling to and from Perth, and horses leaned thoughtfully over every second fence along the one main road through the suburb.

Both were associated, for nearly an entire biblical lifetime, in the same quiet little coign of it; saw it grow, saw gravel give way to bitumen and roadside trees to electric light poles, saw the bun give way to the bingle and the bingle to the wig, the cart to the car and the backyard grapevine to the telephone. Both became so much a part of it as not to be missed until they departed, which they did within a few months of each other.

The pillarbox used to stand on the corner of Suburban Road and River Street — now Mill Point Road and Douglas Avenue — where youngsters who are now grandparents used to turn down, still munching on the morning toast, to take the ferry to town and their first jobs.

I don't know when it was put there, but it bore a florrid 'VR' and the date 1857, so it might well have begun its long office only about 30 years after the first settlers ventured up the swan-haunted river.

A solid single-towered little castle of reaction, it was in some ways not unlike the dumpy queen-empress who owned it, and under the shield of whose power it took delivery of letters to be sent all over a world which then existed almost solely as an appendage to her Empire.

It was six-sided, about five feet high, and it was painted that wonderful imperial shade of red common to pillarboxes, fire brigades and the jacket of Guardsmen. On top it had a Germanic sort of spike like the one which used to surmount the Kaiser's helmet — perhaps not as sharp, but sufficiently so to make the box completely unsatisfactory for sitting on top of ... I know, because I used to try, and so did several generations of South Perth children before and after me. Thinking about it inevitably brings back the childhood it presided over, a period now as remote and strange and in a way as unbelievable as life on a quasar.

Mill Point Road was then a ribbon of red gravel flanked by twin ribbons of deep, red dust between a double line of the loveliest trees ... planes and kurrajongs, gums and cape lilacs, lillipillis from which, on the way home from school, we stoned the tiny, tart 'Chinese apples', moreton bay figs trimmed meticulously to the shape of opened umbrellas that, nevertheless, kept out far less rain than the straggly old gums.

It was the spine of a suburb which then didn't stretch as far as Fremantle Road — there was still a lot of almost virgin bush even beyond Angelo Street. Our home was on it, and most of my childhood centred between that home and 'the shops' where the pillarbox was — Mr Rogers the butcher and Mr Faddy the grocer and post office; there was hardly a day when I did not pass the box on my way to get a reel of white cotton forty for my mother or a twist of hundreds-and-thousands for myself, climb on it or wait at the base while my Lion or Towser or Barney ceremoniously completed the lustrations which, stoically, it bore from a thousand generations of South Perth dogs.

Why, when I look back on my childhood in South Perth is it always summer? I see the urchin who was myself, with other urchins, chuffing happily through the roadside dust past the pillarbox being either trains or flocks of sheep, as the mood takes us, but either way enveloped in a red cloud that eddies up to the dense summer foliage above us. Or I stand transported, every time, as Colonel Le Souef in his open carriage flashes past, at 15 miles an hour behind four of the zoo's dinky little shetland ponies: The council watering cart sloshes through the burning afternoon, and we spin like drought-maddened frogs in its spray: Scarecrow 'blackies' and their stick-insect children, whose tangled black hair and blazing black eyes I can still see, all these long years after they have gone to their dreaming, trudge past our front gate hawking their clothes-props through the streets of the quiet riverside suburb which they used to own. From far off the tinkling bell of the tiny ice-cream cart calls, no louder than the sobbing of doves in the trees by our side fence, but more imperative than the voice of God ... and throughout the long summer evenings in the shadows of the shop verandah, the laughing and chiaking and softly winking cigarettes of the dread 'corner boys' affronts the righteous. 'D'you want to grow up to be a *corner boy*?' my Mother threatens me again, over some old misdemeanour: And although nothing could enchant we more than an invitation into that raffish circle — there is a jockey and a fisherman among them — I can hardly tell her so.

The pillarbox saw it all and heard it all, through childhoods long before mine and long after, meanwhile taking into its stolid care letters written by South Perth parents and lovers and children and wives to men fighting in the Boer War, The Great War and the World War, in Korea and Malaya and Vietnam ... and, no doubt, because he worked in a garden just down the road, it received whatever Wong Chu sent back to his family and friends in China during the 60-odd years he lived in South Perth.

Looking back, it seems there never was a time in my childhood when no Chinamen padded along the shady, oyster-shell footpaths of our neighbourhood, waved grinning from the big, hooded carts, appeared at the back door with fruit and vegetables — lome beauties were our favourite apples — sat quietly in the ferry or stood quietly in the shops, a part yet apart in the friendly everyone-knows-everyone affairs of the suburb.

They lived and worked, maybe as many as 50 or 60 of them all told — on the broad strip of superb black soil which fringed the river, behind a dark belt of trees and rushes, almost without a break from close to Mend Street to the edge of Victoria Park.

The gardens, those of 'our' Chinamen, anyway, were as much our playground as the river or our own backyards. Then, of course, we didn't know how beautiful they were, with their patchwork green carrot-tops and pale green lettuce and milky green cauliflower in season, the blood-red of beetroot and the purple of egg plant, and the gold-flecked lakes of melons and pumpkin at the damper, lower end of the garden. Armoured gilgies dozed beside their holes in the square wells scattered among the beds for watering and dipping the vegetables, and in the slow moving waterways by which the run-off of a score of bubbling springs converged on a mysterious underground tunnel leading to the river, bright constellations of red goldfish exploded in all directions as we took after them with — had we but known it — utterly harmless 'spears' from the thicket of bamboos down by the river.

Wong Chu — 'Charlie' like all the others — worked in the garden below my home. A small, bird-boned man with flesh as brown and hard as sheoak wood, he wore the clothes common to all 'Charlies' — a rough working shirt and dark blue cotton trousers which folded over at the waist like a sarong; never boots or shoes in the garden, and only, in the worst of weather, the big 'umbrella' hats of their homeland ... they seemed to prefer instead the Australian-style tucked-in cornsack in which bobbing about their gardens with another sack tied apron-wise around the waist, they looked like an industrious company of monks, or perhaps dwarfs.

Generally they slept in galvanised iron huts at the drier, top end of the garden, having in the middle of the cultivation an open-fronted shed in which the cart was housed and gardening implements stored along with great bunches of seedheads of most of the vegetables they grew; often they cooked and ate in these sheds too. We were fairly free of the garden shacks, but rarely ventured into the sleeping quarters. There were about those, curious shifting shadows, pungent scents and unexpected shapes which evoked all the strangeness and menace of that vast, distant and ancient China where they ate puppydogs and drowned baby girls in the yellow rivers. In their recesses, our friends' everyday eyes were darker and more oblique, their dark hair more uncompromisingly dark and lank. They smoked long hubble-bubble pipes of bamboo, in the little spouts of which they ignited — with a long taper — tiny pellets which we all were then certain was opium, but which, before I grew up, I had realised was only Champion Flake Cut from Mr Faddy's irreproachable coffee-smelling shop. In those sheds, moreover, they conducted orgies ... everyone knew *that*. Most Saturday evenings they dressed in stiff blue serge suits and unaccustomed black shoes and went into town ... to play fantan down in James Street: everyone knew that, too. They rarely came home until Sunday morning, and when they did they were often followed at an interval by white ladies; up from the ferry, past the fluttering disapproval of Jubilee Street front-room lace curtains and so to those mysterious galvanised-iron living quarters. And orgies.

But if those ladies were somewhat less than kin and more than kind, who is now to blame Wong Chu and Sun Kwong Wah and Ah Kim and all those hardworking, lonely Charlies separated by long years and half the wide world from the much more satisfying loves they had known in their villages in distant Yunna, or Kwangsi, or Shantung? They were up and working long before the first ferry — then the criterion for early rising around our way — and the fire-flies went to bed before them. The gardens were turned over spadeful by spadeful for every new crop, and were fertilised by great heaps of straw and manure brought from the stable up on the dry ground. Planting, weeding and harvesting was all done by hand, and in the musky summer evenings of frog-croak and bittern-cry from the swamp by the river you could trace the passage of the softly effulgent cascades from their huge watering-cans — one on each end of a yoke across the shoulder — as they wove backward and forward over the parched beds. Nobody worked harder in South Perth, few were more law-abiding, and none was kinder to the flocks of grasshopper kids — who in the fond belief that they were unobserved as they crept through the rushes at the bottom of the garden — stole their melons and harassed the goldfish in their ponds.

I have two very clear recollections of old Wong Chu. One was of the day when, having caught several dozen crabs from the now unimaginable bounty of the river, we gave most of them to him. He appeared utterly staggered by the gift; he stared around the shed, obviously looking for something to give in return, and finally thrust on us two enormous cauliflowers fresh from the garden. The other time was when he returned from his trip to China, I think in about 1924 — I was about 10 years old. Before going he had promised he would bring back a present for me. He did — six magical Chinese kites of featherlight bamboo and flimsy red and green rice-paper, in the shape of some legendary Chinese bird. As you set them on the air they floated off: If I close my eyes, I can feel them in my hands now, and feel too beneath my bare feet the cool damp path of black soil on which, when he gave them to me, we stood in the middle of his now vanished garden.

Suddenly both Wong Chu and the pillarbox are gone. One day late last year some men came with shovels and a truck and a bulldozer and before you could say knife a century and more of South Perth history had been obliterated ... to be replaced by a hideous functional one-legged red box like a disgruntled oomfah bird with whatever head it might possess tucked under a wing inscribed, not with the lovely florid monogram of a great Queen, but with a legend in white, mean paint suggesting when the citizens of this diminished day might deposit their mail in the expectation that it will be delivered between strikes.

Not long after the pillarbox disappeared, I was not a bit surprised when a friend, whose family had been looking after old Wong's affairs for twenty years, told me, without preamble: 'Old Wong's going back to China.'

I had been seeing the old chap, a few times a week, ambling down Jubilee Street to the shop — to the shop which long ago had replaced Mr Faddy's burnt-out emporium, along the street on which, those far-off Sunday mornings, the ladies had walked behind him up from the ferry. I don't think he ever connected me with the larrikins who snatched his melons, but he would always pause and say: 'Welly ni' day!': Or, squinting up at the sky, knowingly: 'Maybe lain, eh?'

All the years while we played by the river, outgrew our childhood, left school and found jobs, went to war and came back, got married or went roaming, grew to middle-age and beyond ... all those years the pillarbox stood on the corner and Wong Chu worked among his vegetables ... in the finish, with all the other Charlies gone and the gardens destroyed, on a little plot at the end of my street, in his old shack, with his old horse for company until that died, too.

And now both he and the pillarbox are gone, I don't know where the pillarbox is, but the old man is in Hong Kong among the family he had not seen for half a century. I hope he is happy. I hope that Kwan-yin will send a great big celestial dragon with flaming eyes and scales of jade to watch over him, as long as he lives.

NO MORE THAN YOU CAN AFFORD

Tom Logan looked up from a long, concentrated stare at the carpet and found his wife's eyes on him, over the top of the morning paper she had been reading. Tired, and just far enough above the blur of print for him to see also the shallow mauve troughs of weariness below them. The hazy preoccupation of his mind could hardly have been called thinking; a vaguely mutinous realisation that as he stared at the carpet in his living-room on the old, familiar earth, the men whose white-toothed, crew-cut pictures he had just seen on the turned page of the paper his wife held were, even then, shuffling around like immense grubs on the dusty, frozen, unimaginable surface of the moon. Those men were of roughly his own age, and physical make-up and mental ability. But while they probed gingerly at what lay outside the wall, in preparation for whatever forays might be made in their wake, he, Tom Logan, had done nothing at all but to establish a firm base for himself inside the palisade, to marry and beget children in the immemorial pattern. Of Joe Blow, the yardman at the pub and, if you wanted to take it a bit further, he thought, with a wry grin, of Joe Blow's dog. Not a comforting reflection.

In answer to the unspoken inquiry in his wife's eyes, he lied. He gestured toward the light-and-shadow fleck on the pale umber pile, where the mid-morning sun fell on it through cream lace curtains deprived, for the time being, of their anodized gold venetian protection.

'Remarkably like a camel,' he said, and grinned.

On the previous evening they had lain on the living-room floor, she propped up with cushions, he sprawled like a black starfish on his back, and had listened to most of a recording of Hamlet which he had bought her for her birthday a month or so before.

'Or shaped like a weasel,' Nesta said. She strung along with him tiredly. She was well into the eighth month of pregnancy — her fifth in the fourteen years of their married life. As usual, she had been having a hard time of it. Her ankles, ordinarily no more than a little thicker than normal, were gross, the skin stretched tightly and shiny over apparently boneless trunks of lardy flesh, and she was up and down all night to the beautiful old flowered jerry which her mother had resurrected from some family glory-hole when she had first begun to complain about what she and Tom referred to as the Great Ord River Irrigation Scheme. He could joke with her about her condition — could make himself joke with her — but as always he was repelled by it. Inclined to blame her, even without wanting to, for getting into it. Resentful of the hiatus it caused in their physical lives and social activities.

'Did you stay till the bitter end?' she asked. 'Last Night?'

'No, Ness. I packed up soon after you. You were asleep when I came in, though.' His eyes dropped to the carpet again as he spoke. He said, 'What's all this about wall-to-wall? They say it like a sneer these days. It looks pretty good to me.'

'Who says it like a sneer these days?'

'Julie Syme, for one. And if she's saying it, so's the world. She hasn't had an original idea since she decided to latch onto Joe.'

'When did you see Julie Syme?' Nesta said, suspiciously. 'And how in the name of God did the talk get around to wall-to-wall carpet?'

'I didn't see her, and the talk didn't, etc. I haven't seen her, let alone spoken to her, for — God ten years or more. Tony

Shaw was talking about her at the club, Wednesday afternoon. Joe had been punishing his ear about her. Joe's youngest sister's getting married, and she was choosing the carpet. According to Joe, Julie told the kid wall-to-wall was for the bookmakers, or something like that. Made the kid howl. You can't blame Joe, even if what they say is true.'

'What *who* says is true? And what do they say?'

'Tony Shaw, in the club bar, Wednesday. Joe was there, nineteenth-holing on in fine style. The fourth day in a row, Tony said. And when Nancy Reynolds left, Tony said: Watch this! And Joe took off after her like a bitch in heat — her the bitch, not Joe. Tony says they've been playing boys-and-girls for a month or more. And apparently Julie's the only one doesn't know about it.'

'I hope for Joe's sake he's not banking on that!' Nesta raised her eyebrows derisively. 'You damn men! I thought you went to the club to play golf. I can just see you all huddled around in the locker-room, talking about who's sleeping with who.'

'An engrossing subject — especially in my line of business. Today's golf partner might be tomorrow's client. It pays to keep the ear to the ground.'

'And write all the names on the walls, like they do in men's johns?'

'It's nothing to what you see in ladies',' Tom said.

'When were you ever in a ladies' lavatory?'

'Oh — tons of times. Not lately though. At Uni. The bloke I used to take English tutes from, there was only a ladies' on his floor. The gents' was down one flight of stairs. So we used to keep nit for each other, and duck in.'

'What if there was someone in residence?'

Tom laughed. 'We used to check first. We'd sing out: Anyone in there? And if there was, we'd just bake it. I believe the girls used to do the same in the gents' on the floor below.'

'Carefree campus days!' Nesta said. 'Good name for a popular song!' There was a sneer in her caustic tone, but her eyes as she looked at him betrayed her, as they always would. They held a nostalgia for something she had never had, and a little spite because she never *had* had it. Not because her parents had not been able to afford it, or because she lacked the intelligence to go after it, but because in the privileged enclave of her set at the time the 'University mob' had still been considered at the best far too earnest, and at the worst too damn pushy. She was one of the old-family clique, five generations from some middle-class British go-getter with a bit of capital, good connections and a lot of cheek who had arrived early — although not in chains — and had so prospered that his grandson had been able to select a spot for himself among the circumscribed gentry of the moribund little capital already stagnating beside its delightful, dreaming river. The family fortunes and position had been established first on farm-lands in the south of the State, but more spectacularly, afterward, on a livery stable in the city. The tight-lipped acumen of Nesta's grandfather, and her father's luck, had midwived the change from horses and buggies to the biggest car agency in the city, and later had added service stations. In the process the image of the city tribe of Summerfords had become somewhat tarnished by its deep immersion in trade, but there remained still the unexpended treasure of more-or-less ancestral lands and homes at several dismal whistle-stops in the south where, a century-and-a-half before, family properties had been established. In the wake of straying cattle who usually found water on some good soak or river, or simply where the exhausted, dusty woman in the bullock dray had been unwilling, or unable, to drag the bellowing children an inch further. Nesta had taken Tom to visit one of these storied pioneer-homesteads on their honeymoon. Not really knowing what to expect, he had pulled up at a ruinous but still sturdy two-storey farmhouse with the shingles still intact under the iron roof, although falling apart rapidly around some nice old cedar furniture and exquisite joinery in the local Swan River mahogany, and a dreadful barn of a kitchen where blizzards of blow-flies yearned over the encrusted dogs' bowls on the floor, or butted hopefully at the sides of an ancient meatsafe suspended by a chain from a jarrah beam — but hand-adzed — in the ceiling. And all presided over by a grimy harridan in a man's felt hat, whose grandfather had built the house, and whose mad sixty-year-old maiden daughter — whom they didn't ever get to meet at all — hovered like an uneasy draught among the tattered lace curtains at an upstairs window all the time they drank their afternoon tea, gingerly, from chipped Rockingham cups in the rank garden below. Nesta had begun agitating to leave almost as soon as they arrived, and had remained unusually silent throughout the entire visit; apparently it had been a long time since she had visited Great-Aunt Hollie's. Tom had then been a successful young lawyer obviously on the way up. He had never known, nor cared, where any of his grandparents had been born. As a consequence, during the courting he had gone somewhat in awe of his plump, proper, loving girl's name and background, her forebears in the State's legislature and mentioned frequently in its meagre records of exploration and practical extermination of the blacks. He had felt much better about things after the visit to Aunt Hollie's. Even while driving back to the capital on that day, he had permitted himself the great pleasure of admitting to himself what really he had known for quite a long time — that whatever virtues of virility and resilience and courage had driven the early Summerfords across those miles of sentinel, malignant bush to found the heritage, all had deteriorated, by the time it reached Nesta's father, into a mere squalid acquisitiveness and a sterile pride in name and bank account. And that her mother, never-forgetful great-grand-daughter of a pioneer Greenough horse-breeder whose stock had been the talk of Imperial messes in India a hundred years before, now had the look, the smell and the texture of an old bank-note. It was something that occupied his random thought for some time afterward. He found it curious that while any number of great European families had flowered in presence and prestige through the centuries, and in some cases still dominated the stages set for them by their ancestors long before Western Australia was ever heard of, most of the founding families of his own community had dwindled into poverty of either estate or blood, or both, in less than two. They had inbred fiercely, of course, tucked way down in their outrageous nether end of the world. With nothing but cousins, servants, convicts and aborigines to choose from, it was inevitable — although none at all of the alternatives had been entirely passed over. He never brought the matter up with Nesta, even while sometimes intending to. In the earlier years of their marriage he had desisted from delicacy, inadvertently passing-up the only time at which she might have laughed, or at least might have discussed it objectively. But all of a sudden it seemed, with no mellowing middle-age to their association, she had begun with tragic prematureness to look vaguely like her mother and to sound acutely like her father. He had known for some time now that he would never bring it up unless to hurt her or to best her in one of their increasingly frequent brawls: *For Christ's sake, your old man's grandfather was a gin-jockey, wasn't he?* Or: *Just as well you married a peasant, isn't it? Or the kids might have been fucking albinos?* This probability, even the accusations, had occurred to him long before this morning when he sat in the living-room with her, making an effort, and conscious that she too was making an effort, to behave as though no fourteen corrosive years had passed since that visit to Great-Aunt-Hollie's.

'I'll say, carefree,' he agreed.

'Did you ever sleep with her? Then?' Nesta's diffident tone informed him, as explicitly as words might have done, that she had been waiting, perhaps for years, for the proper occasion to put that question. Without seeming to want overmuch to know. 'With Julie, I mean.'

'No, I didn't sleep with her, ever,' he said, earnestly. And then, with a sudden, purposeful change to gutter coarseness, because her terrible delicacy enraged him, as ever, 'We didn't often do it where we could sleep. But I screwed her plenty. Parks, beaches. A few times in the lecture rooms. Like corned beef at the boarding-house, those days. Always on. Until she woke up that she was giving away something she could get a good price for.'

'Oh no!' Ordinarily Nesta would have reprimanded him primly for his crudeness. Now she stared back at him, her eyes glittering against their mauve drapes even though her lips formed the conventional sounds of disapproval. 'Not for *money!* Did she?'

'Christ, no! Not that I ever heard about, anyway. I certainly never paid her. She was after a rich ... '

'Little pitchers,' Nesta said pointedly. When he turned his head, it was to see Nella, his elder daughter, standing in the doorway. At twelve, she had her mother's long, coltish legs but his own dark good looks, refined in her case to a rather conventional black-hair-and-blue-eyes, clear-skinned Celtic loveliness which, he hoped, she would grow further into, rather than out of, as she grew older. His own sister, a beauty at fifteen, had been just another desperately winsome Australian-Irish brunette at twenty-five. Already, particularly when he had been drinking, he had begun to hate the young man who would take his darling away from him, who perhaps even now in some other house in the very same suburb was beginning to feel the urges which would culminate in the dreadful abduction of his daughter away from this house to a bed and to raptures in a world which Tom Logan would orbit like a sputnik, permitted to land on it only when he got the appropriate signal from the controllers.

'Hi lovey,' he said. 'Where you off to?'

She touched the deep blue of her Girl Guide uniform skirt and smiled at him adoringly. She had a snowy white lanyard clipped to her shoulder with a silver whistle dangling from it, just between her already forming breasts. The upper sleeve of her right arm was covered with brilliant flashes for cooking and bushcraft, map-reading and sewing and first-aid and half-a-dozen more of the subjects she had been immersed in, it seemed to him, since she had begun to walk. 'Get with it, buster,' she said, breezily, 'Do I look as if I'm going skating?'

'How would I know? You darn kids wear anything anywhere these days. Jeans to Government House, bikinis to the supermarket.' He smiled at her. 'You okay for dough?'

'Uh-huh. Thanks, Daddy.' She turned to her mother, aging five years in a second. It was something that intrigued him: that while with him she was still the schoolgirl, with Nesta she seemed almost a contemporary. 'Mummy — I've waited long enough for Bernie to ring. If ...'

'Hey!' Tom interrupted. His heart had fluttered, almost as if a moth had got trapped in his shirt-front and had begun to bumble about. 'Who's this Bernie character? Why haven't I heard about him before?'

'*Bernice Cohen*, smartie!' Nella said, articulating every syllable with glasslike purity. She smiled comspiratorially at her mother. 'Boys! Who *wants* them!' To Tom, she said, with a resumption of the glassy, adult-to-child tone, 'She's new at school, and she's my *girl*-friend.'

'Plenty of dough?' Tom said. He rubbed his hands and stroked his nose suggestively.

'Oh daddy!'

'Come and give us a smooch then.'

The door had hardly closed behind the swish of her blue skirt when Nesta got back to Julie Syme.

'You were saying, about Julie?'

'Oh — Christ, it wasn't important. I was just going to observe that she got what she was after, and quit. She didn't go to the Uni for a degree. She was after a husband in a certain bracket, and she got him. It could have been anyone, but it was Joe.'

'What about you?' Nesta said, and he knew she had arrived at the nub of her inquiry. 'Couldn't it have been you?'

'Maybe — for a while. But Joe outranked me. All those ancestral acres. And the old family home down Dardanup. Like your Aunt Hollie's.'

Nesta ignored the dig. 'Well,' she said breathlessly. 'You've got your damn nerve. Telling me I got you on the rebound after *that* hot-pants bitch ditched you for Joe Syme! Just like that!'

'For God's sake, Ness! You asked me. And it was five years before I met you. And she didn't get me, she got Joe.'

'*And* a nice lift, too,' Nesta said, spitefully. 'What was her father? Manager of some little chaff-and-grain store out in East Widgiemooltha?'

'Three Springs,' Tom corrected her.

'Wherever. Precious little wall-to-wall those days, and now it's not good enough for her!'

'Maybe she's just matured,' Tom suggested. He counted up to ten, the tip of his tongue pressed against the back of his front teeth. It was Nesta at her worst, looking more like her mother and sounding more like her pudding-faced old man than he would have thought possible. What the hell if Julie had turned it on? It was a long time since women had been branded for doing it. Now they put it out as casually as they had their hair set. A damned sight more casually, a lot of them. You had to make an appointment to have your hair done. Julie had just happened to be a trail-blazer on the way to the Nirvana of the pill. On today's standards, she would be considered about as square as the base of the Great Pyramid.

Thinking about the Julie Mason he had not thought about for years, Tom Logan found himself thinking also, with a breath-taking immediacy and far more clearly than he could recall the last time he had made love to Nesta, of what he and that Julie had done in the parks and the lecture rooms he had mentioned: even in the biggest of the parks, it had seemed, just the two of them, with maybe a moon or a mopoke to share it. His heart jumped as his memory led him to one particular lecture room, on one particular afternoon, twilit, quiet except for shouts from the quadrangle below the windows and a slammed door, somewhere, all still and warm with the grassy exhalations of early summer days. Her breath, sweet as a cow's, her hair, the taste of her lipstick, the moist greasy texture of her closed eyelids as he stared at them in the deepening shadows and the quiet. Once more, after only two days that had seemed like the Long Vac, the swooning pressure of her breasts against his body.

'Which brings us back to where we started,' he said crisply. He still stared at the carpet between his feet. He knew that if he didn't return immediately to their customary trapline of domestic banalities, he just might reveal something of what he had been thinking: of what had been simmering beneath his consciousness for months past and was at that moment threatening to lip the crater. 'What's so terrible about wall-to-wall, all of a sudden?'

'Fashion,' Nesta said, delicately adjusting her own pace to his. She was far more aware than he realised of what he thought he had kept hidden, but in many ways she was not yet ready for a show-down. She was a relatively uncomplicated woman, fond and mulish. In the fifteen years of her association with Tom Logan she had seen him change from follower to leader, bit by bit, and had lacked either the will or the wit to stay a jump ahead, or even to keep level. From aspiring to her world, as he had seemed to during their engagement, he had soon come to regard it as a sort of toyland for grown-up children — or un-grown-up adults. And he had made no secret of his opinion of it, and the people who shared it with her. The pictures, the records, the books and whatever he bought her for her birthdays and their anniversaries were far beyond her comprehension in any but their simplest aspects. They were really for himself, and she knew it. As he rose in his profession, and among the people related to it, she pursued a perfectly horizontal line of development. Inevitably each year drove a wider wedge between them, until the children were their only point of contact outside the bedroom. It was one of the reasons why she continued to let herself fall pregnant, long after most of the wives of her set had sworn off babies and had even begun to laugh at her for what they called her old-fashioned sense of duty. In the matter of contraception, as in most things, she had no strong opinions one way or another, but she calculated that she would need Tom for at least another ten years. By that time she would be nearly forty, anyway, and the child about to be born would be well-established, and Tom would be in a position financially to make the kind of settlement she had in mind. Then, she planned, she would lead him on to disclose what he really thought, and wanted, and even muttered about, wildly, sometimes, in his sleep.

'Fashion?' he echoed her.

'They talk you into wall-to-wall,' she explained. 'Then, when everybody's got it, they start a whispering campaign against it. Non-U. July Syme's just the kind would fall for it.'

'Like minis,' Tom said. He ignored her crack, to edge further into the shallows, and safety. 'Now it's all maxis, and you can't sure as hell let down a mini into a maxi!'

'You seem to know a lot about it?'

'I've got a good model to study.' Tom looked directly at her and smiled. Dark, eyes blue as a girl's with shiny, long lashes, but masculine as a rooster. All she had ever wanted in a man: and suddenly, as she stared back at him, she was suffused with panic to realise that however coldly she might plan for a future without him, he was all she would ever want. Seeing the realisation naked in her eyes, he softened into fondness for her. 'By hell I wanted you last night,' he said. 'When he was on about the thing to lay between a maid's legs. You know?'

'A bit impracticable at this stage?'

'Oh — I don't know. Old wives' tales are that the husband should. Right up and into the ninth month. Feeds the baby, they reckon.'

'Good God! I can't imagine how!' Nesta's tone was waspish with the sort of prissy distaste that drove him wild. 'I'll stick to the formula, thank you,' she went on. '*And* after the event.'

Tom's glance had dropped to the carpet again while she had been speaking. He jerked it up again, at the very end of the leash he had fastened on his hot Irish temper, when he realised what he thought was the implication behind her words. 'Christ!' he said. 'I wasn't trying to ...'

'It's the McMorrow auction today,' Nesta interrupted him. She was speaking to him from behind the paper which she had raised to her face again. 'Why don't you go?'

Tom stared in angry frustration at the back of the paper — the same photographs of the men then walking around on the moon. He wanted to pull it away from in front of her eyes and see what she was really thinking about. Instead, he took out his anger on her suggestion. 'McMorrow?' he said, witheringly. 'That old queen?'

'Was he?' Nesta said, without lowering the paper. 'I didn't know. But I'd always thought he was some sort of nut, I must say.'

'That settles him then. Once you called a bloke a queen, and that was the end for him. Now it makes no impression — everyone's doing it. If you really want to stop the traffic, you've got to say he's some sort of nut. To imply just the right degree of decadence. Something with ducks, like.'

'He was a distant cousin of mine,' Nesta said, with a hint of reproof. She still hadn't lowered the paper.

'Oh, hell! *Old-family* old queen, then. It makes all the difference! But I'd still keep it dark if I were you.'

Nesta rustled the paper. 'Anyway. It says: 'Gentleman's residence, four bedrooms, four bathrooms ...' Dah, dah, dah. Here it is. 'Quantity genuine Georgian silver, flatware. English and French antique china. Carpets and rugs, Aubusson and Turkish."' She lowered the paper at last, and looked at him inquiringly. 'You might be able to pick up a couple of nice rugs, and get rid of this wall-to-wall drag. Like Julie Syme. Why don't you go?'

'Where are the kids?' Tom demanded irritably. Stung again by her needless reference to Julie, and by the suspicion that the name he had even more thoughtlessly made about himself and its owner, had already been installed as a staple of Nesta's conversation with him for a long time to come. 'I only get one morning at home a week,' he went on aggrievedly, 'and they all shoot off like rockets into the wide blue yonder. As if they couldn't damn well stand the sight of me.'

'*You* have to go to golf every Sunday morning, of course,' Nesta said caustically.

'Do *they* have to go out every *Saturday* morning?'

'Nella's at Guides — you know that. They're arranging a fete for World Health. Terry and Joe are at cricket. They go every Saturday morning. You enrolled them — or had you forgotten? And Maudie's at the Learn to Swim classes at Crawley. She will be, every Saturday morning, for the next four weeks.'

'Huh. Will they be home for lunch?'

'Yes — all of them. One-ish. So why don't you go down to McMorrow's?'

For the first time Tom really considered the suggestion. The old McMorrow place was on the way to the club anyway. If there were nothing worthwhile stopping there for, he could push on and spend a couple of hours chewing the fat with the Saturday morning regulars at the bar. 'The silver might interest me,' he admitted. 'As an investment. It's sky-rocketing. They just can't get it. What time does the thing begin?'

'Eleven. You'll be a bit late, most likely miss the first few lots, but ...'

'Why don't you throw something on and come along?' He knew she would refuse, and knew also that if he had thought for a moment that she would agree, he would never have made the suggestion. 'It'd take your mind off things.'

'Good God! And have that hobble-de-hoy mob looking me over, and wondering when?' Nesta dropped the paper and presented him with the vinegary face of distaste which he particularly detested, and which he certainly could not recall having seen before they were married. The cat-crap-under-the-nose-bit, he called it, a disgust he could neither understand nor condone in her.

'Or who,' he cracked, before he could stop himself.

Another wife after such long familiarity might have cracked right back at him with the butcher or the baker or the candle-stick maker. But not Nesta. Her fine, arched eyebrows levitated sharply, and she permitted herself to stare back at him for a moment, the dull fire of acute dislike, almost of hatred, glowing in her tired eyes. 'You really are a bastard,' she said.

The auction was already in progress when Tom arrived at the McMorrow place where it perched high on a bluff overlooking one of the most expansive — and expensive — panoramas of the river. The double-storey new wing in mid-Thirties stucco-and-tile neo-Californian-Spanish loomed incongruously above the lovely proportions of the 125-year-old single-storey settler's homestead under whose white-painted iron roof, Tom had been told, the original shingles were still sound and dry and ready to serve as when the first McMorrow — the first antipodean McMorrow, that is — had placed them there with his own hands.

There were cars parked for hundreds of yards on both sides of the street in the shade of huge, ancient gum-trees, and the driveway was crammed. As Tom got out of his old black Riley he was almost stepped on by the shining brown riding-boots of the man who had pulled in behind him in a Silver Wraith Rolls. He looked up. It was Charlie Dougherty, an ex-bricklayer who, after the war, had started out with nothing but his deferred pay. By the time he was forty, or so Tom had been told, he could sign his name to a cheque for two million — and before the change-over to decimal currency.

'Hi there Chas,' Tom greeted him. 'Don't trample me to death with those damn great plates of meat. Where'd you hitch the nag?'

'Bloody bunrush,' Charlie Dougherty said. He elbowed Tom in the ribs. 'The old poofter certainly did his boyfriends proud, eh? Four bloody bathrooms! Antique silver, Turkish carpets! Fuck me!' He was sporting narrow cream moleskins with his riding-boots, a tan hacking-jacket and a Paisley silk cravat tucked into his daffodil silk shirt. His cheeks were still hard as grano, and the nails of one of his thumbs and the middle finger of his left hand were irretrievably, undisguisably, gnarled and busted among their manicured and tinted fellows.

'What're you after then?' Tom asked. 'Or did you just come along to snoop in the halls of vice?'

'Christ! Seen plenty 'a them! You should'a been in Singapore with us last time. In one'a those massage joints. I asked this Jap sheila if she'd give me a French job, and strewth! Almost before I'd got my fly unzipped ...' They had turned in at the gateway. 'Doll wants me to get some of the silver. You know how they get. Ruby glass. Then spinning-wheels. Knick-knacks, fucking cedar chairs. The lot. Now it's silver, and every cupboard in the joint's crammed already.'

'What you get today won't fill any cupboards for you,' Tom said. 'You're going to have to fight for it, if it's the silver you want.'

'What? Nesta too?'

'No. Me.'

'Christ.' Charlie Dougherty grinned at him speculatively. 'You didn't used to visit here when the old chap was around, did you?'

As they walked up the driveway together, the old garden enfolded them serenely, quiet, with trellises of out-moded roses no longer sold at the nurseries, elephant's-ears and huge clumps of pampas grass that had weathered the years of disfavour to find themselves, along with kerosene-lamps and buggy-wheels, once again high in public esteem. Over it all the steady drone of the auctioneer's voice evoking for just one more morning every single pollen-weary bee that had ever plundered its sun-muzzy oleanders and camellias and drooping golden wattles throughout a hundred summers. As they reached the french-windows leading from the wide, cool verandah into the ground-floor living-room, he was displaying a large porcelain bowl decorated in a riot of blue, magenta and gold.

'This superb piece, ladies and gentlemen,' he intoned, sensuously stroking the bulging sides of the tureen as he spoke. 'Davenport Iron, early nineteenth century. Part of an incomplete service I am under instructions to sell, piece-meal. You'll observe the gorgeous chinoiserie of the pattern? Peonies, phoenixes, the little temple? See? Tucked away among the verdure? A collector's piece, ladies and gentlemen, even divorced from the remainder of the service.' He rotated it again, adoring it, for a moment forgetting the monied peasants who would purchase it. And would probably put plastic roses in it. 'What can we say for it, to start if off? Fifty dollars?'

The bidding was launched by a woman deep in the press around the fireplace, almost at right-angles to where Tom was standing. Charlie Dougherty commented from the side of his mouth, 'Some po, eh?'

'It's magnificent,' Tom said. 'Not just the look of it, but ... how in hell does it survive? Think! A hundred-and-fifty years ago, those big, fat, fox-hunting squires were milling around it, swilling their punch out of it. They're gone, long ago, but it's still here.' He stared at the bowl, poised high above the heads of the crowd, like a monstrance in the reverent hands of the auctioneer. 'I bet there's some technique they don't know about yet,' he said, 'would bring up their fingerprints on it.'

'Sorry to stop you in full gallop, cock,' Charlie Dougherty said. 'But it's a soup tureen, not a punch bowl. Doll's got a stack of 'em.'

'Well, their soup then. But I'm going after it.'

'And I'm going over there to talk to Mollie Love. See you later.'

While they had been speaking, the bidding on the tureen had reached eighty-two dollars and when Tom moved in, the woman by the fireplace had the bid. Within a minute or two it had resolved itself into a contest between their alternate nods, the woman finally taking it out for one-hundred-and-fifteen dollars.

'To the lady by the fireplace,' the auctioneer announced, happily. He had not expected the lot to reach one hundred. 'But don't go away Mr Logan. There's the rest of the service yet.' He turned to the fireplace, smiling archly. 'If Mrs Syme will let you get off with it, that is.'

Surprised to undergraduate breathlessness, Tom craned around the bulk of the woman next to him. Between the shifting heads of the score of other people between them, he watched Julie Syme threading her way toward him. She seemed to have altered little since their last meeting, which had been at a club ball a couple of years after his marriage to Nesta: and in fact not much more since he had known her as Julie Mason. She moved with a world of assurance the bursary girl from Three Springs could never have known — but Joe's money would have seen to that. And to the clothes. The perennial slacks, sweater and sneakers Tom remembered from their association had given way to what he recognised as a Chanel suit, black with white braid, and a coral-and-diamond cluster over the right collar-bone. The thick, wavy, sun-bleached hair, so sweet-smelling. Her make-up was a suggestion, unlike the dogmatic psychedelic statements favoured by every other woman in the room. Her bust was high and firm under the cheeky little jacket, her legs slender and smooth below the knee-length skirt, her feet narrow and trim in their spindle-heeled black patent leather shoes. She was suddenly beside him.

'It's ...' they both said together. And then laughed. She finished the sentence for both of them. 'Been a long time.'

'Sure has,' Tom agreed. 'We might as well live at the North and South Poles as at the opposite ends of little old Perth. For all we see of each other.'

'Well ... there's no real reason, is there?' She shrugged, and with one hand fondled the jewel at her shoulder. 'Strange, though, you should bid against me for that piece. Did you come for it?'

'No. Just took a fancy for it. I'm sorry. I must have cost you twenty or thirty bucks.'

'Give the cat another canary! What did you come for?'

'Heard you were here.'

'Go on,' she said, and smiled.

'The silver. Providing it doesn't go sky-high.'

'Console yourself. You've saved a packet. About twenty people came just for that, and they put it up first. The Horrockses from Bunbury bought the lot. They got themselves some family portraits last time they were in Melbourne, and now they're shopping for the rest of the ancestral deal.'

'Still the bitchy little bitch, eh?' Tom grinned at her, and she wrinkled her nose at him. Tom said, 'You know, you've scarcely altered at all? It's fantastic.' He stared at her again, a long look which became far more searching than he had intended. She returned it steadily, without embarrassment. Watching her, he recalled that whenever Nesta might be paid any similar sort of compliment, she would bridle and curtsey and would finish up by producing, as though it were a pearl of repartee, any of half-a-dozen banalities she seemed always to have at the tip of her tongue to suit any occasion. He took a deep breath and broke their locked gaze by turning to the podium. 'Are you going to buy the rest of the set? If you are, you can have the tureen at your first bid.'

'Thanks. But it's too pricey by far.'

'Then since the silver's gone, I think I'll go too. Pick up the kids on the way.' He held out his hand. 'It's been nice seeing you again, Julie. I mean it.'

'I'll walk out with you,' Julie Syme said. As she passed in front of him to the door and he caught the warm scent of her body and her hair, he was appalled to feel again, across the otherwise unbridgeable gulf between him and his student days, the insolent, lazy uncurling of desire in the pit of his stomach. The garden still slumbered, but more deeply now in the greater heat and hush of almost noon. The thick curtain of wisteria over the verandah drowned out the voices from inside the house. Long folds of gum-leaves dripped low to the browning lawns, and several children ran in and out of them in silent exaltation, their mouths opened soundlessly in their ecstatic faces, their brown limbs glittering among the glittering leaves. The throbbing of doves high above reminded Tom Logan of something he couldn't materialise in his mind, something about his own childhood that suffused him with a gentle sadness. Julie laid a hand on his sleeve, and they stopped beside a huge camellia bush covered with plain, old-fashioned pink blossoms.

'It's sad,' she said. 'Such a lovely old home, with such long associations. And now ... before you can say knife — twenty-storey flats.'

'And twenty families get the view instead of one,' Tom said. 'In any case, what can you do with a place like this, these days?'

'Live in it?'

'Sure. If you're old Walter McMorrow. With the McMorrow bank balance.'

'Did you ever meet him?'

'Christ, no,' Tom said.

'Don't say it like that. You didn't know him.'

'Did you?'

'We used to come here. A few times, after we were married. He was a wonderful host. Civilised. Before his sister died, they used to entertain quite a lot.'

'He used to entertain a lot after his sister died. Hear tell.'

'Hear tell. I heard tell enough in there today. It was the main topic of conversation. And conjecture. You can imagine how it was handled.' She picked one of the camellias and held it to her face. He saw that her hands were still slender and brown, the nails warm and pink and filed close, no flaky cuticles or ragged lacquer. The hands in which she used to take him, and hold him, without self-consciousness and mawkishness. Reverently, with love, he thought suddenly, looking at them. As the auctioneer had held the soup tureen. 'Love,' she said. 'That's all he wanted, really. I hope he got it. Somehow.' She glanced at him. 'Do you ever think of the old days, Tom?'

'No. Not really.'

'No. I guess not.'

'It's a long time ago, Julie.'

'So long?'

'That's a lie, of course.' He knew he should not say it, but said it, anyway. 'But only just. I thought about it today. An hour ago. I thought about that afternoon. Late afternoon, it was, in 'C' Lecture Room, in the Arts building. You said you'd be there, and I came over, after cricket practice.' He laughed, and without embarrassment, smiled into her inquiring eyes. 'I was thinking how easily we could cram it all in, those days. Study, cricket practice, parties. Love. And bob up for more. Do you remember the day?'

'No. We're ... looking at different sets of pictures. I remember a lot, though.'

'You think of it a lot, then?' he asked, and felt the ancient serpent stir again in his groin.

'Off and on. Right now, I'm remembering a winter night in the boat-shed. Cold as charity. Those wet boards!' She shuddered elaborately, but smiled at him. 'Funny. You remember summer, I remember winter. We must have been a steady old couple. A year, anyway.'

'It looks as if people are beginning to come out,' Tom said. 'Maybe it's breaking up in there?'

'You said a funny thing, a moment ago. Love. Study, cricket practice, parties and love. Did you love me, or was it just the screwing you meant?'

'No,' he said. 'I meant love. I loved you.'

'But not marrying love. Not ...' She paused, and looked at him with transparent, unassailable honesty. 'Not respect? I was too easy?'

'If a man suggested that to me, I'd flatten him,' Tom said. 'You believe me?' She nodded, and he went on, 'I don't think I thought of respect, then. It was all of a piece, whatever it was that I felt. I respect you now. I mean, I now respect the person you were then.'

'No kid?'

'You were honest. You didn't try to trap me, or to ride me. And it wasn't just all screw-screw-screw, Julie. We had fun. Remember?'

'I got engaged to Joe,' Julie said. 'You and I'd been out the night before. Down to City Beach, in Colin Forest's car. And I got engaged next day. I thought you'd raise blue murder.'

He shrugged. 'We were intelligent people. Like in the song. No tears, no fuss, hooray for us.'

'Yes. Intelligent.' She nodded, in agreement with what he had said, or with some thought of her own. Watching her, he couldn't tell. 'After all, that's what I went to the Uni for, in the first place. A husband with money. I wasn't about to go back to Three Springs. You knew that?'

'I guess.'

'You canny lawman! I shopped around a bit, and you knew that too, didn't you?'

'Some of it.'

'Then why do you think I picked on Joe?'

'You loved him.'

'Spoken like a true Aust gent.' She inclined her head, noncommittally. 'I married him, anyway. And now ... I'm going to divorce him.' He raised his eyebrows, and she shook her head with a touch of impatience. 'Oh, come on! You must know about it? It's all over the place. Out at the club — Tony Shaw would know, for certain. He and Joe are thick as thieves.'

'Nobody's mentioned divorce to me. Tony said Joe had been sleeping around, though.'

'Six times a week and twice on Sundays,' she said. 'And I guess you think I've been too. To compensate?'

'I told you, Julie. I never thought about it at all.'

'I haven't,' she said. 'Not one god-forsaken time. Because of his mother, if you'll believe me. I started off hating the old girl. Joe took me home a couple of times. To the town house. She could see how things were between us. Bed-wise, I mean. So on the third visit she said, very gaily, girl-to-girl: 'Of course you wouldn't think of *marrying* Joe. He's such a rake-helly young man for a nice girl like you'. She laughed. 'A rough translation would be: 'Stick with the chaff-and-grain, kid. You're okay as a hack, but you wouldn't do as a brood-mare.' So of course I was more determined than ever to marry Joe. And he wasn't such a bad sort in those days, either. Icicles formed on the ceiling when we were *married*, I can assure you. I decided early on she'd never have the chance of saying 'I told you so' to me. After a year or two I got to know her, and she got to know me. They're not all inbred morons, Tom. Joe's behaviour before our marriage, and afterward, it crucified the old girl. When the kids came along, she moved more and more into my camp. We're good friends now. I'm as glad for her sake as I am for my own that I didn't do what she expected me to do. And what I expected to do, myself, if you want the truth. I've been what you might call an exemplary wife and mother — though I says it meself what didn't ought to.'

'How does Joe's mother feel about the divorce?' Tom asked.

'Advised me to go after it. Began advising me years ago.'

'Then why did you hang on so long?'

'The kids,' she said, simply. 'But they're grown now. Both of them. The girl was married this year. The boy ... he's a lot like Joe. He can look after himself.'

'But ... a daughter, married? We're about the same age, aren't we?'

'I started seven or eight years before you. Remember? How old is your eldest?'

'Twelve,' Tom said. He was assailed with a sudden panic. Seven or eight years. If Julie's daughter could get married at twenty, so could Nella. He had less time in possession than he had already had. Julie had dropped the ruined camellia. She stood with her hands motionless at her sides, looking straight into his eyes.

'I'll level with you, Tom,' she said. 'You're the one I loved, use any definition you like. The only one I ever loved, ever will love, I think.'

'Then why did you do it?' Tom shouted at her, in a whisper she could only just hear. The question he had been too proud to ask then, and which had rattled around in his head, from time to time, ever since. 'Why, why? Why *Joe*? Jesus, only the night before ...'

'You never asked me,' Julie said, coolly. 'It had been a year, and you never said a word.' She reached out and took his hands. For a moment, she was so close to him that he could see plainly the grey in her fair hair, and the tiny lines at the corners of her eyes. She had the same clean scent, and her hands were firm and cool. 'We loused it up then, Tom,' she said. 'But I'm going to be available again soon. Do you want to?'

The still warmth of the garden was the still warmth of the lecture room which he had remembered but she had forgotten. His heart kicked viciously against the side of his chest. After a moment he began to shake his head in time to its suffocating beat.

'But I can't, Julie,' he said. 'My kids are still kids. And we've got another coming.'

She let his hands drop. 'I see your point,' she said, gravely. She turned away from his gaze and looked at the house. 'People are starting to come out. Goodbye, Tom.'

When he got home, Nesta was still sitting in the living-room in her house-coat. There was a smell of lunch cooking, and the television was still on. Maud, his younger daughter, was squatting in front of it, her dark hair still damp from her swim. When he came in, she scrambled to her feet and ran to him.

'Daddy! I *dived* today. Off the *third* step!'

Nesta looked expectantly at his empty hands, and then into

his face. 'You didn't see anything you liked?'

'Nothing I could afford,' Tom Logan said.

THE OLD WATERFRONT, MACAU

The seafront footpath is the backyard — or the front yard, it is difficult to tell — of a row of timber, plastic sheet and tar-paper hutches which straddle out over the shallows on the usual assortment of spastic supports. In this way, there is a gradual merging of land-based activities with the wonderful water-borne existence of the boat-people ... a breed apart, proud and independent, among the thousand splinter divisions of the Chinese nation. It is difficult to discern where one stops and the other begins, since every shack has tied to it, at a suicidal sort of ladder descending to the water, a pencil-slim dinghy or pot-bellied sampan that serves as gad-about, guest-room, or auxiliary kitchen, and sometimes even as chicken-run and dog-kennel. Beyond this row of boat-houses or house-boats, there is a sort of Tom-Tiddler's-ground, a public thoroughfare, a little Grand Canal of open water on which there is an unending shuttle-service of small craft between junk and shore and shore and junk, operated usually by beldams too old to do anything else, sometimes by young wives with babies pick-a-back, out to swell the family income; and sometimes even by children who are, perhaps, on the late shift at school.

On the seaward (or rather, since we are in the harbour) on the Chinese-shore side of this watery avenue, are the junk moorings. This is incontestably the territory of the boat-people, and a most fascinating, ever-changing, agelessly unchanging spectacle it is: if you were to see nothing else in Macau, it would be worth your having made the visit.

There is little enough to choose between the filth of the sidewalk and the filth of the water — except that the latter will be swilled out come the turn of the tide — but even at its noisiest and most noisesome, the boat-city exists in a sort of archaic dignity and authority ... which, in all probability, derives from the rhythms of two-thousand years of living in just this way and, even, perhaps, in just this spot. Watching the junks depart and return, depart and return, an ancient village which disintegrates and reforms daily in the same place, dumping its rubbish over the side after every meal and every clean-up, I have often speculated upon the fabulous midden which must exist in the preserving mud beneath it, and have wondered why no branch of archaeological investigation has ever thought to mount a dig (or perhaps, a drag) there, to uncover the record of its existence since the first few boats nosed into this cosy anchorage, so close to the fecund fishing grounds of the estuary, but close also to all the very necessary things that only the despised land can produce.

The junk village is like a scene by Breughel, in which everyone disposed about the canvas is doing something — either funny, useful, traditional or obscene. It is a show-stopper at any time, the sort of thing you can stand and watch for a whole morning, and not realise that a whole morning has gone by. I go down often at dawn, to watch it stir and rub its eyes before plunging into the free-for-all of the day.

In the first grey light, it is like any other village — except that, almost imperceptibly, it rocks. It is, for once, relatively quiet: no noise at all, except the bark of an early-rising dog, the wail of a baby, and, near at hand, the creak of some old hull as it shifts in its sleep. And overall, but so much a part of the pattern as to be un-noticed after the first few seconds, the chug-chug of diesel motors as, one after another, like cows let out to graze after milking, the junks glide down harbour to the bay, and the estuary, and the open sea.

The first light touches the hills of China, just over there, and a moment later drips gold on the highest masts of the forest. All of a sudden, life begins to stir. Here and there, as if by pre-arranged signal, wavering blue smoke spirals up from cooking fires. Men and boys appear, drowsily, and relieve themselves over the side. In the sampans closest to the seawall, you can see brightly-coloured cotton quilts thrown back, as children roll off them onto the deck. Dogs appear, yawning and wagging their tails, and sniff at their bowls in anticipation of breakfast; chickens tethered in a sampan ruffle and scratch, and their gorgeous lord, also tethered, stretches his neck and greets the day like any other rooster, anywhere. The waft of incense takes over, as renewed joss-sticks mix their pale eddies with the aromas of cooking and salt-water and refuse. Young women roll back the roofs of canvas, plastic and tar-paper which every night transform working boats into bedrooms for families. One old lady in a sampan close to the wall dips her false teeth in the water alongside and scrubs them vigorously ... as well she might! ... before replacing them; other old ladies totter and creak around, yet amazingly sure-footed in the tiny craft, doing the small morning tasks of their lot. Other old ladies who work the morning ferry service pole back and forth between the thicket of boats and the landing-steps. A flock of school-children disembark in smart blue school-blazers and a crescendo of squeals, and scamper along the little kerbside eatery by A-Ma's temple for breakfast bowls of watery noodles, rice and soup. The first basketfull of cockles is dumped into a steaming cauldron on the footpath. Young women with children at heel, and in slings on their backs, chivvy their broods in and out of the ferrying sampans like mother quail. One unbelievably smart young man (mustard-coloured suit, pink shirt and massive mauve tie: he does not sit down during the trip) leaps up the steps and beetles off among the cockle-cookers, the first pedicab drivers, the garbage collectors and the children already playing stone-scissors-paper on the sidewalk, the chickens the dogs the cats the fish and the coiled-up, drying snakes, to an office in that other world, up-town. There is a growing concatenation of cars, and the first crackers of the day — or maybe the last of the night, it isn't possible to tell — hasten the departure of any lingering demons. The sun is well up. Communist flags flutter bloody and brave at the mastheads, and in bunches and cascades elsewhere, on almost every junk. Another day has begun on the old waterfront in Macau.

GREEN GROW THE RUSHES

The de Blore place stood on a high ridge of sandstone, looking out over the river to the city on the other side. Its enormous weatherboard and lacy-iron pile used up sufficient space and material for the twenty 1975-type family-kennel 'units' which, in fact, now occupy the site. Framed and shadowed by huge old trees, with pergolas of wisteria and bignonia, it overshadowed the low-lying riverside paddocks where we lived, topographically and socially only a rung or two above the multi-coloured swathe of vegetable gardens the industrious Chinese left-overs from early gold-rushes had established on the crescent of deep, rich black soil built up by a million years of flood deposits on the southern bank of the river. It offered us a two-sided message — for our elders, what they had missed out on, and for us, what we might attain to: it was in its heyday at a time when youngsters still planned to attain to something other than retirement and the pension.

I used to go up there with my father. He was a piano-tuner, come down in life — as my mother used to remind him whenever the opportunity presented itself. Although now I wonder if she was reminding him, or informing us, that there had been a time when things had been better. Not that he didn't make a reasonable living for those days, even though it was early in the Depression. It seemed as if every second person then had a piano of some sort, and of course, every piano needed tuning now and then. He had his daily bit of business, and there were the occasional dances and wedding breakfasts and twenty-first birthday parties in the Mechanics Institute Hall. Also, he played Saturday nights at the old Bijou, that incredible old fleapit where, nevertheless, overture and entr'acte were studiously observed, and sometimes after interval, a visiting tenor would sing *Roses in Picardy* and *A Wandering Minstrel*. With one thing and another, my father made ends meet, and without my mother going out to work. Wood stove, outside copper for the washing, four kids and part responsibility for the vegetable garden must have kept her from wondering what she might have been if she hadn't fallen for my father's winning Irish ways. I don't recall ever having been hungry, other than just-home-from-school emptiness we filled immediately with bread-and-jam or bread-and-dripping, so undermining our health that I near the end of five decades without ever having seen the inside of any but a military hospital — and what I was in there for was certainly not brought on by any diet deficiency.

My father used to take me up to the de Blore place to recite. It earned me the envy of every youngster in the district — not that I could recite, but that it got me access to what was in a way the enchanted castle of our immediate neighbourhood. Old de Blore bestrode our affairs like a great, pot-bellied colossus. He was legendary around the large country town that Perth then was, and for a couple of thousand miles north of it, as a first-in drover and now station-owner, who had physically battled the blacks for their territory. He had spear-wounds in his back to prove it, some said. He had been a prospector and a mine promoter, a pearler and a camel-master and god-only-knows-what else — and had made money at all of them. A big part of the legend, for us, was that aborigines from his stations were employed in his house, his garden and his stables. Since Mrs de Blore had died years before in a cyclone in Broome, perhaps even before I was born, there was quite a lot of conjecture, which I didn't understand at the time, as to his relationship with the aboriginal women. They worked exclusively in the house, and seemed happy enough, but the moment they became aware of the presence of outsiders — my father and me, for instance — they would simply disappear: or if they didn't disappear, they would hang their heads so that their curly brown hair made a curtain before their faces, and you could see their eyes glinting at you from behind. I never saw the men who worked in the stables. The gardeners always seemed to be standing around only half-visible in flecked sunlight under the trees, or ever so slowly dragging rakes or barrows across the lawns and among the roses. Sometimes, in their moleskin trousers and huge felt hats, they squatted in groups on the paths, smoking stick-thin roll-your-own cigarettes, retracted so deeply between their grasshopper thighs that their bottoms rested on the gravel. They never seemed to speak, or perhaps they did so by signs, and their eyes as they watched us up to the house were veiled as with the smoke of bushfires, secret and — to me, anyway — frightening. I was always glad to make the security of the side verandah, crowding my father's heels as we went up the steps to where old de Blore sat in the afternoons. Even then I sensed there were many who had trouble not spitting whenever the old man's name was mentioned, and I had heard him described variously as a tight-fisted old bugger and a damned black-birder and a bloody old gin-jockey, all without being meant to be overheard, and without really understanding what I heard. To me, then, he was just another adult phenomenon. I was far more impressed by the horses he used to drive, in his landau, on his way to what my father called 'shivoos' in Perth, than by the possibility that he might in some curious way be married to one or more of his black gins — which was the way I understood it from talk suddenly curtailed whenever I came within range of it at home. *Old de Blore.* Whale-fat, turkey-red, bull-voiced, perclum-blue eyes swimming in pits of raw meat. I didn't learn until years later that he had suffered with the sandy-blight early-on, up north. I just thought he was mad as a meat-axe, and he frightened the stuffing out of me sometimes, even when he laughed.

A fat, red-headed, jug-eared, freckled composite of memory

and old snap-shots stares back at me from the bathroom mirror in which little Dinny Walsh so assiduously slicks down his mop with Sunshine soap for his appearance on the de Blore's side verandah. I must have been a smarmy little brute. I could 'take-off' people, and I was always the King or the Ogre or the Child Jesus, or whatever it might be, in the school concert every year. Although my Dad was Irish, and hadn't come out to Australia until he was a grown man, he went wild for Banjo Paterson and Will Ogilvie and all that push for horse-and-stirrup singers, and of course, I was the minstrel boy. I think I must have been the only youngster extant who could say the whole of *The Man from Snowy River* by heart — with actions, and what the nuns called 'expression'. I wonder that people didn't just throw up at me.

My father had a horse-and-cart which he made use of to combine a delivery-round with his piano-tuning, taking things into town, bringing things out, dropping things here-and-there about the suburb. It used to nark my mother, and I could never understand why he kept on with it. I know now, of course. Making ends meet. In those days, fathers did all sorts of curious things to eke out the 'sustenance' from the government. The father of one of my school-mates had a clearing contract on a bit of land destined to become a football-field. He blew off nearly every finger of boths hands, one or two at a time, and in comparison with many other families, he breezed through the Depression on the insurance money. In his own way, my father blew off *his* fingers rattling around the suburb behind his gentle old Ginger, because I know, now, that it hurt him like hell. His past was of a piece with the names of Lake Way and Nannine and Peak Hill, which were the first words I recall hearing, in casual conversation between my father and my mother, and in long afternoons of old-times talk between them and Sunday visitors in blue-serge and massive gold-nugget brooches. The aluminium nose-peg of a camel was one of my first playthings, yet it was not until I had grown up that I connected them with a time when he, too, had been a sort of legend around the Murchison goldfields, a camel-master at the same time as old de Blore, and chasing the same kind of business.

What with one thing and another, we would be up at the de Blore place every few weeks. When my father had done what he had to do — he was also handy with clocks — old de Blore would settle himself on a big cane chair on the verandah, overlooking the river, and would roar: 'Come on, now, Dinny Walsh! What are you going to say today?' I always had something ready, because he would give me a sixpence and an apple or an orange to go with it. Apples and oranges came in halves at our place, and sixpence was my Bijou money, Saturday nights, or fish-and-chips when I went to the beach, swimming, Sunday afternoons. I had got to know that his favourite was that one, *The Bush Christening.* On the outer Barcoo where the churches are few and men of religion are scanty ... I think I could say it right through, now, if I put my mind to it. I would stand about four feet away from him, but still in the range of the blast of his breath — rum or whiskey, to this day I don't know which. He would always begin roaring with laughter even before I had begun. Then, I didn't know why, except to think that I was a gun entertainer. Now I do know. What a poor, pompous little shit I must have looked. Heels together and toes out, as the nuns had drummed into me. Bow, with my right hand flat on my paunch, my left clenched in the small of my back — the nun's training again. And off I'd go. Now, fifty years after, the scene has become formalised in my memory as some sort of Byzantine composition of brittle, coloured glass, in a way not unlike the 'tableau' the nuns crammed into every break-up concert, willy-nilly. The smallest and fairest (non Anglei sunt, sed angeli) in crepe-paper wings and white angels' shifts, scared witless on borrowed pedestals and staring down in adoration at somebody's sleepy-doll in somebody else's wicker washing-basket. Old de Blore in his huge wicker basket, my father and me; the ferns in bailer shells about the polished floor of the verandah, the sleeping river, the low, mauve skyline of the city. I can even remember, vividly, the white centres to the heavenly-blue flowers of a plant called 'wandering Jew' that spilled over the sides of the hanging baskets. I never think of it, now, without burning for the way I exulted in my degradation, the way I so willingly sat up and balanced the biscuit on my nose for that brutal old bastard.

Sometimes I used to see Miss Honour. Miss Honour de Blore. Even now, just to say the name makes my heart turn over. I loved her with the hopeless love of ten for seventeen. I don't think I even knew it was love. All I realised was that what I felt for her was different from what I felt for the Virgin Mary. Honour de Blore was all but inaccessible, whereas the Mother of God was there every day on the shelf above the blackboard, in the blue-and-gold mantle whose protection we sought in the gabbled Oh-Mary-my-mother-I-place-myself-under-thy-mantle last prayer of the day, before we set out to rob the Chinamen's fig trees on the way home from school. And Honour de Blore almost always wore white, but soft, and so that you could see right through it to the pink or blue underdress she wore, with embroidery on it. She was dark, with deep blue eyes. She had long hair, and she did it pulled back loosely, red-brown and wavy, into a huge black ribbon bow, stiff as cardboard, that sat there as if an outsize butterfly had alighted on the nape of her neck. Sometimes, as we arrived, she stood in the doorway leading into their entrance hall, with the stained glass glowing blue and red and green and gold all around her. Further down the hall there was a white plaster arch with carving on it and crimson velvet curtains held back in the loops of gold cord with tassels, and on either side hung Chinese vases full of pampas grasses from their garden. Sometimes, when we had made our way past the black gardeners down the side path to the steps leading up onto the verandah, she would come out, would lean her back against the rail to watch us, the blue of the river behind her. Usually, with her white dress, she wore a narrow black patent-leather belt, and almost always she had stuck a red rose or a red geranium in it. Right below her, it seemed you could see the dark green swathe of rushes beside the river, on the far side of the Chinamen's gardens. *Come down the rushes*, we would say, when we were little nippers, and we would play explorer or pirate, or would fish for gilgies in the springs. *Come down the rushes*, we'd say later on, when we were in the district football team, and picking up girls at the edges of the dances in the Mechanics Institute Hall, with my own father, like as not, pounding out the *Pride of Erin* or the *Jazz Waltz* inside. Come down the rushes.

The only time I ever saw Miss Honour away from old de Blore's was down there. It was a grey-satin evening the colour of a mullet's belly, when the electric signs in the city across the water bled blue and green and gold in wavering lines almost to where we stood on the southern bank. Three of us had been down crabbing in the shallows. We were walking home along a raised mud dyke between two of the Chinamen's irrigation ditches, in the cool, swamp-smelling last light of shrilling frogs and night-herons booming in the sheoaks which then fringed the river on our side. We were cold in our sodden shirts and shorts, and were laden down with our catch and our nets. In single file, like the Chinamen, we were lurching along the path when the Jim or the Jack or the Joe in front said, in a breathless and surprised sort of way: 'Uh ... good evening, Miss de Blore.' I was last in line, and for a moment I thought he was having us on. We used to talk about her, and about meeting her, and getting fresh with her, in the ways of boys just beginning to feel their oats. In the way, maybe, boys living around Windsor Castle might talk about the unattainable occupants whom they only see, but never get to speak to. But as we drew level, I could see it was she, all right, in one of those luminous white dresses and a scarf around her shoulders. She said: 'Hello, Dinnie!' even though it was two or three years since I had been up there to recite for them, but she didn't pause for so much as a second. Almost immediately, she was out of sight in the brown shadows, and when we had gone some distance in the other direction, the one in the lead said what we had all been thinking, I guess. 'I wonder what the hell she's doing down here, this time of night?' The one in the middle said, with a giggle: 'I never saw any bloke lurking around!' Being last in line, I had the privilege of the last comment, and I know they would have accepted it without question. 'Don't be bloody silly about blokes!' I said. 'Miss Honour.'

Time passes, and usually it demonstrates just how wrong you can be.

That was the summer I got my Junior, which was the big deal in those days. Rather miraculously for the times, I got a job also. In the Post Office, for which I suspect I had to thank the influence of old de Blore — at my father's request, of course. Within a year, I was sent to a country centre in the south of the State.

The 'post office Johnny' I replaced had doubled as sports reporter for the local paper, and I was offered the job. I found I had a flair for it, and before long I was submitting pars about all sorts of things, and having them accepted. Then I got an offer to string for one of the Perth dailies, and finished up drifting into journalism. The war lifted the lid of the oyster for me, and when it was over, I began working my way round, looking for the pearl. The trail led me half-a-dozen times in and out of Hong Kong, so that before I knew it had happened, that bright jewel had sunk its proboscis into my veins like a true anopheles, and had infected me for life. Only less a disease with me was Macau, and on my last visit, about five years ago, I settled for living there and commuting to and from Hong Kong by hydrofoil. I had a small suite at the old Hotel Belvedere, a Charles Adams pile of flaking stucco and blocked drains crowning a rocky bluff that does sentry over a wide, junk-haunted expanse of the Pearl River estuary. There, of all places in the world, I met Honour de Blore for the first time since she had walked away from me that summer evening in the Chinamen's garden in South Perth, the luminous white of her dress drifing like a moth toward the river bank and the rushes.

I met her one Sunday morning in the flush of spring, when every foot on the hillside below the hotel seemed covered with greenery, and every spray of greenery seemed covered with blossom, and every blossom seemed covered with butterflies, in the Chinese manner: for don't forget it, in Macau you are in China, for all that several centuries of Portuguese rule have scattered the mouldering facades of beautifully-iced churches and convents all across the high ridge overlooking the Baia do Praia Grande. I had been sitting out on the little bit of the terrace which the busy coconut-fibre brooms of the *farwongs* still managed, somehow, to keep at bay the encroaching tide of rubbish, the by-product of the gross over-population which threatens to sink that exquisite little promontory of the Flowery Kingdom under the waters of the Pearl. The spring was still morning-cool, so I had my back to the warming rock wall. At the other end of the terrace, perhaps forty feet from me, a very well put-together woman was leaning her elbows on the balustrade, her chin in her hands, staring out towards where the misty Ladrone Islands sailed, unseen, like ghosts of robber junks on the amethyst water. Is it because of what I now know that I can say I suspected from the moment I walked out onto the terrace, and saw her there, that it might be Honour de Blore? In any case, I had been willing her to turn around and put me out of my doubt — which she did, eventually, and stared straight back at me, her eyes narrowed in the bright sunlight. Then she walked over to me. There was no hesitation, no coyness.

'Dinny Walsh', she said. 'You're a long way from South Perth.'

'Honour de Blore', I said, standing up. 'So are you.'

We stared at each other for — I don't know. Maybe five seconds. I have no idea what she saw. Like most people, I believe, I hold some sort of appreciation of what I look like. It probably flatters me to myself. It hasn't changed for years, anyway. What I saw was a woman still beautiful, her brown hair heavily streaked with grey, but suiting her, her face lined, but gently. Eyes calm among their crows'-feet. Or resigned? Again, I don't know. Whether naturally, or by some artful dodge, her figure seemed hardly changed at all, although perhaps a little heavier. She was dressed with that deceptively simple elegance that cripples bank accounts, in a long-sleeved blouse of some sheer white stuff tucked into a full-bottomed skirt, knee-high, of some sheer black stuff. At collar, wrists, waist and hem, deep bands of Chinese brocade on which the design had been picked-out with seed-pearls and semi-precious stones. After two marriages to extravagant women, I have a pretty lively appreciation of the look, and the cost, of good clothes. It occurred to me at the time that it was costing someone plenty to dress Honour de Blore. It was I who broke the silence.

'Then — what are you doing here?' I said. Maybe, in the twilight of my male chauvinism, as though she couldn't possibly have as much right as I to be rolling around the world, or as much competence to keep herself while she was doing it. She must have read me correctly, for she said, simply: 'I am Li Po. In Hong Kong, of course. Not here.'

As she spoke the words 'Li-Po', the name Hetty Chia flashed through my mind, like the kingfisher's wing that glitters in so much Chinese poetry. I could not even pause to wonder why. I lost it immediately, in my surprise at what she had just said. There are only two Li Pos worth talking about. She couldn't be the Tang Dynasty poet who drowned himself first in wine, and then in a lake, trying to embrace the reflected moon. So she must have meant the high fashion house — not the biggest in Hong Kong, but certainly the most exclusive, with half the world's jet-set clothes-horses on its waiting list. It was above any chatty preoccupation with the right moment to reveal or conceal the knee, or liberate or confine the bust. It meant simply supreme elegance, and its signature was, in fact, the opulent embroidery I had been staring at, and to which my attention returned as Honour de Blore said the name. She caught the direction of my glance, and shook one of the glittering cuffs.

'I'm my own best advertisement,' she said, smiling. 'As a matter of fact, it's why I'm over here this weekend.' She waved to the tangle of pink-tile roofs below us, the teeming cock-lofts crowding crooked lanes from which hundreds of years of European commerce had not been able to remove the ingrained obstinacy of their Chineseness. 'There must be three or four hundred women going blind, down there, embroidering this kind of thing for me. I used to get it done in Hong Kong, but ... you know. Trade unions. They're not so particular here.' She smiled, and shrugged. 'Still the oppressors of the workers, us de Blores. Once, it was the blacks we diddled. Now it's the ... the Chows.' She emphasised the word, long discarded, I imagine, except among Australians, in a way that whisked me straight back to my boyhood in South Perth, and my mother saying: *Go down the Chows and get me...*

At the same moment, I recalled why the name Hetty Chia had jumped into my mind a moment ago: from a conversation half-heard, during a previous visit to Hong Kong, at a sunset cocktail party in one of those crazy towers of splintered glass that rear like jewelled chopsticks on the perilous dark slopes of the Peak. During the sort of sudden silence when one surreptitiously looks at the clock to see if it is quarter-to anything, someone close behind me had said. 'Hetty Chia was to have come, tonight.' Someone else, very English, had said. 'She owns Li Po, doesn't she? Remarkable flair. Different from most Australians.' And somebody else, very Australian, very ocker, said. 'I'll say different! She married a Chow. What price the White Australia policy now?'

I stared at Honour de Blore. 'But, if you own Li Po...'

She looked back at me, with an amused smile. I think she must have read me again, or perhaps she was just used to it. She said: 'I really can't be Honour de Blore, eh?'

'You are Hetty Chia?'

'For business purposes. Hetty was my mother's name, so I borrowed it. Honour Chia is a bit awkward — and in any case, the Hetty sort of name is in, in the rag trade. I prefer plain Mrs Chia, but of course, nobody will use it.' She gestured toward the bench. 'But please sit down, Dinny. And I will, too.' She sat, as gracefully as I should have expected, and tucked her high-heeled shoes becomingly beneath the bench. As I lowered myself beside her, she said, again with that amused smile: 'You most likely would have known my husband.'

'Chia?' I spent a moment or two thinking back to Chinese I had met at her level, in Hong Kong and elsewhere. 'Maybe,' I said at length. 'But I'm afraid I can't recall.'

'It was a long time ago,' Honour de Blore said. She was no longer smiling. 'Chia Kuan Yu. You would have called him Charlie.'

One of those enormous black, blue-splashed Macau butterflies landed on the warm rock above her head, and hung there, voluptuously pulsing its wings to the rhythms of that shimmering spring morning. I saw instead a black ribbon bow on a girl's neck, and her leaning against the lacy-iron balcony on the side verandah at old de Blore's place. Behind her and below her, blue-clad figures of Chinamen weeding, tying, hoeing, watering among the vegetables they cultivated in exquisite order to the very edge of the dark swathe of rushes by the river. And any one of them would have glanced up at a call of *Hey, Charlie*! They had names — Sun Kwon Wah, Sook Lee, Yeang Lo Chee. Chia Kuan Yu. But we had called them all, indiscriminately, Charlie.

'Jesus Christ!' I said.

Honour de Blore ignored my exclamation. 'My father used to do all their business for them,' she said. 'They were always up at the house about something or other — leases, bad debts, letters they couldn't understand. You know the sort of thing. He had always done the same thing for our station blacks, so I guess it was second nature to him. I used to meet them all, on and off. It is how I met Chia. It was the only way I *could* have met him. He hadn't been in our country very long. It was something about his indenture and he came up about it. One of the older men brought him. He was young, and beautifully built. A light sort of build, but very strong. Good-looking. And exquisitely courteous. And about my age.' She laughed, unaffectedly. 'As a matter of fact, he was the sort of bloke, if he had been a pale-face my father would have made good and certain that he didn't get within spitting distance of me. As it was, I think he believed I couldn't actually see a Chinese market-gardener as a man, let alone as a man I might fall in love with. I'm sure he would have had just as much expectation of my falling for one of our abo stockmen.' She paused for a moment, and stared at her hands, lying serenly in her lap. 'Isn't it strange? Everything against it except that it *would* happen. Class, colour, religion, language, money. Even probability. Most of all, that. It was so *improbable*.' She looked up at me. It was her damned, uncompromising honesty and lack of side that got me. 'The very next evening I went for a walk down to the river, on that raised path through the garden. The night you met me. The first time I had ever done it. And I met him down there, of course. I knew he would be there. And I suppose he knew that I knew.'

'And friendship ripened into love, and love into marriage?' I couldn't keep a touch of — what? Disbelief? — out of my tone. She ignored it, and immediately set me right back on my butt.

'Something like that — although we had no time for first steps,' she said. She even smiled. 'It might be more accurate to say love ripened into intimacy, and intimacy into conception. Because that's how it happened.'

Now, of course, something like that would be a breeze. Things were different, then. While she was speaking, half my mind had been remembering about an Australian woman, a friend of my parents, who had married a Chinese much older than herself, a respectable, moderately wealthy sort of bloke who otherwise would have been considered a fabulous catch for this particular suburban belle, in Perth particularly. At my local-football-team level, the comment was all about the legendary sexual prowess of the Chinese, and how she must have heard about it. The only adult comment I ever heard was my mother's tight-lipped observation to my father, when she thought I wasn't around. *They might at least have observed a thought for the unfortunate children!* I don't know what that woman's life was like behind her own door, but it must have been sheer hell outside. She was immediately, completely ostracised, of course, but she was hounded as well, with the kind of Christian brutality you encounter only, still, in Australian middle-class xenophobes. I felt a sort of horror that Honour de Blore might have been subjected to anything like it. I also could not credit that old de Blore could have let it happen.

'But what about your father?' I said, following up the thought. 'Surely to God he didn't ... well, didn't go along with the deal?'

'There was no orange-blossom festival at the old homestead,

if that's what you mean.' She gave me a wry smile. 'When I knew I was pregnant, I told him. He nearly shed his skin. *Him* — with a tribe of half-caste kids on every one of his stations. And still sleeping two or three nights a week with one or another of the abo housemaids. Then I told him who the father was. He didn't even answer me. He never spoke to me again.

'You mean, literally?' My mind was full of that mad, red face, those eyes that had glittered at me from their pits of suffering flesh. 'Never again, not one word?'

'Literally, never again, not one word. And he disinherited me, into the bargain.'

'So what did you do?'

'Chia and I got married. I bought him out of his indenture, and we came back here to live.'

'But all of that must have cost you plenty?' I said. I couldn't see the apprentice market gardener having the kind of money implied, so she must have footed the bill. 'How did you manage, if your father had cut you off?'

'My mother left me a packet when she died,' Honour de Blore said. 'And the house — it was hers. So was all the money, for that matter. It was she who gave him his start.' She glanced at me, quizzically. 'You know she was drowned, don't you? In a willy-willy, up at Broome?'

'We used to hear it talked about, when we were kids.'

'I bet you did. But you heard wrong. She committed suicide. She just followed the tide out, one morning. And didn't turn back when it did.'

'What do you mean — followed the tide out?' I said.

'You've been to Broome?'

'Lots of times.'

'Then you know how far the tide goes out on that coast. Miles, in some places — and you've got to be damn careful when it turns. But not her. She was born there. She didn't get back because she didn't mean to.'

'Who told you? Who told you it wasn't in a willy-willy at all?'

'He did. My father. When I was fifteen.'

'Then — why didn't you put him in?'

'My word against his.' She shrugged. 'He said that if I passed it on to anyone, he'd have me committed. And he would have. I can hear him now. *You'll be in a strait-jacket before your next period's due.*'

'Jesus,' I said. 'And I always thought you had it made. I used to look into your hallway, and the stained glass, and the velvet curtains. And the gardeners, and the ponies in the stables. And you, with a red rose in your belt. Jesus Christ.'

'I think, now, he was mad,' Honour de Blore said. 'When you get older, you piece things together out of what you heard, and saw, when you were a child. And didn't undertand. For instance ... do you know why he used to pay you to recite?'

I had been listening to her, but looking down the roadway, where a skinny little woman was pulling the tiny Chinese pineapples she carried in two baskets at either end of a pole across her shoulder. If Honour de Blore hadn't been there, I would have run down the steps and bought a couple. They were the sweetest things I've ever eaten. The word 'recite' brought me back. For a split second I was on that side verandah bowing and smarming my way through some bit of ballad, with actions and expressions. Old de Blore roaring in his huge wickerwork chair, my father never saying a word at the top of the steps leading down to the garden. I swear, I could smell the huge creamy trumpet lily that overhung the end of the verandah. 'Well — why?' I said. And I knew as I spoke that what she would tell me would kill me. 'I thought it was because I amused him, or something.'

'He hated your father for some reason. They were running camel-teams in opposition, once. Lake Way to Sandstone, with mining machinery. Did you know?'

'I didn't then, but I do now.' I felt again in my hand the cool, sharp edges of the aluminium nose-peg I had played with as a child. With it, my father had directed a camel across that blood-red never-never long before the days of walkie-talkies and surfaced roads — on the great, high-wheeled, lumbering waggon behind his team, perhaps, a choice load he had snatched from under old de Blore's nose. Young de Blore then, of course. 'Did they have a run-in?' I said.

'Probably. Whatever it was, he knew it crucified your father to have to watch you being a good dog for *him*. Wagging your tail for the sixpence, or the apple, or whatever it pleased him to throw at you.'

I managed a laugh, but I don't think I had ever felt my heart closer to breaking. Not for me. For that poor, funny, pompous little bugger old de Blore paid to make a goat of himself in front of his father. 'I suppose you used to have a good laugh, too, when I'd gone?' I said, lightly.

'I thought you were so good,' Honour de Blore said, so gently that I knew she was well aware of how I felt. 'I really did look forward to your coming up with your father. You believe me?'

A very proper amah in black satin trousers and a white linen jacket led two little Chinese girls out onto the terrace. There was one of those vermillion-painted shrines against the balustrade, and they made a beeline for it. The amah lit the joss-sticks, and with immense solemnity and self-importance, the little girls stuck them in the tray of sand at the base of the shrine. They stood back, their hands closed together in front of their noses, as we do. The one who was facing me went crosseyed, trying to peer around the church-roof of her fingers. 'What was your kid?' I asked Honour de Blore. 'A boy, or a girl?'

'A girl,' she said.

'I suppose she'd be married, now?' I said. 'Does she live here, in Hong Kong?'

She didn't answer me immediately. The little girls had finished their devotions, and were now, just as solemnly, playing stone-scissors-paper. She watched them for a moment, and then looked out over the estuary, her face away from mine. Fairly obviously, she was commanding her composure, so I waited for her to speak. When she did, it was quite matter-of-factly, as if she were discussing some acquaintance. She looked straight at me.

'When I first came here, with Chia, I bought a place out in the New Territories — out beyond Sha Tin,' she said. 'You could, then. Dirt cheap. And so beautiful. I still live there.'

She seemed to want to steer clear from talk of her child, so I said the first thing that came into my mind. 'And your husband, too?'

'The Japs killed him, when they took over,' she said. 'We stayed in the house, and when they came, he went to the door. They must have thought he was a house-boy, or something. They bayonetted him, there in the hall. I saw them do it. They shunted me off to the compound, out at Repulse Bay. I stayed there for the duration. When I got out, after the war, I couldn't trace my little girl. You see — she looked quite Chinese. She would just have got caught up with the mob. I know the amah took her, and hid her — and then the amah was killed.' She glanced away, briefly, to the tumbling roof-tops of the slums, crowding the Belvedere's high stone wall. 'For all I know, she could be down there. She could be one of the women going blind, doing embroidery for me.' There was nothing I could say, and it seemed she had said all she wanted to say, because she turned again to me and closed the past, like a book finished. 'So I became Li Po.'

'Just like that.'

'You go so far, and it's all against you. Then ... it's as though they'd had their fun. You can't put a foot wrong.' She shrugged. 'But it really doesn't matter, any more.'

'Why Li Po?' I asked for no reason other than it would push our conversation further along in the direction she seemed to want it to take, away from her husband and her child. To say nothing of all she had been through before she had ever got so far. 'Was he such a hot dress-maker?'

I think she knew what I was up to, because she followed my lead without missing a beat. 'Why not?' she said. 'When he writes things like: The dragon roars, stopping the thunder, and bamboo rustles, breeze-driven, in the courtyard?'

I gave her the two lines leading into her quotation: *The fierce sun scorches, blazing, then black clouds come, pouring rain from above.* I had done a lot of reading in ancient Chinese poetry, mainly because some of it is among the most beautiful ever written. As the best of everything Chinese is among the best of all time. She glanced at me, in real surprise.

'We're a long way from *The Bush Christening*,' she said, smiling.

'We're a long way from where I used to say it.'

'Indeed. I guess South Perth has changed a lot?'

'There's a twenty-storey block of dinky little flats where your old home was,' I said. It seemed to say as much as could be said about what had happened to that dreamy river-bank where, in my memory, it is always summer.

'I know,' Honour de Blore said, 'I own them.'

I was incredulous. 'You mean, it was you had that beautiful old place bulldozed?'

'He wouldn't die, until I did,' she said, simply. She stood up, and walked over to the balustrade, and leaned against it, as she had been when I had first seen her, that morning. Looking out across the estuary. I felt it in my bones that she was leaning against another verandah rail, looking across another stretch of water — and when she spoke, I knew I was right. 'I wonder who walks who down the rushes, these days?'

'There's no rushes,' I said, and felt some satisfaction, to pay her back for the house. 'They bulldozed them, too. For a carpark.'

She glanced briefly at her watch, then walked back to me. 'I've got an appointment, Dinny. It's been good to see you again.' She was above all that banal nonsense about let's lunch one day, soon, or don't forget next time you're up this way. I was thankful for it.

'Are you ever coming home?' I asked.

'You can't.' She held out her hand, palm upward, a curious gesture as if she could see in it what they had put in pickle for her in the years ahead. Or in syrup. 'You'll find out one of these days, maybe. It's like the gins used to say, up on the station, when I'd tell them it was time they stopped going walkabout. *No-more, Missus*.'

She took my hand, shook it, dropped it, smiled at me once more, and walked away toward the steps leading down to the roadway. She did pause there for a moment, though, and glanced back at me. A big mok-min-fah tree was spreading the first of its mushy, blood-red blossoms just above her head, a famous Macau cure for tummy-trouble. By the time I was back in Australia, they would be a blood-red carpet on the terrace, and the locals would be coming from far and near to gather them.

O, MOON OF MULLAMULLA

The moon was just rising, red-gold, when Mortlock pulled up at the main gate of Mullamulla. It was a beautiful night for the visiting poetess. A couple of hours after sundown, the sky was still a deep, royal blue, paddocks pale with the luminous silver of dried grass, thickets of standing trees hovering above them here and there like rainclouds. He cut his engine for a moment to savour the stillness. It was not stillness, anyway, but an absolute harmony of swamp night sounds, frogs, crickets, rustle of undergrowth, occasional birdcall contented and sleepy. Somehow, nevertheless, it all added up to a deep, restful silence.

The entrance to Mullamulla was through a magnificent grove of paperbarks, the biggest Mortlock could recall having seen anywhere in the south of the State. The Winters' private road in from the highway ran along the crest of a natural sand ridge, the ragged white boles of the trees rearing up on either side, almost locking their foliage overhead. In the spring, still, the verges were pink with the little puff-ball wildflowers which had given their name to the place. Mortlock unlatched the white-painted gate and swung it back against the solid white-painted strainers. An apple-pie white-painted fence took off from it at a sharp angle on both sides, like the wings of a north-coast aboriginal fishtrap. The soles of his shoes clanked on the solid steel bars of the cattle-trap, and he thought, with a smile: *Good old Charles! Cattle-trap and gate! He'd put up a bloody drawbridge, if he could!* Still, it was an example of the thoroughness, the superlative farming and real love of the land that had enabled five generations of Winters to hang onto Mullamulla, when time and taxes had caught up with so many, the early Mortlocks among them, who had started off at the same time with just as much going for them. Four men were permanently employed and housed on the property with their families — as their fathers and grand-fathers had been; the dynastic habit did not begin and end with the owners. Three thousand acres of rolling sand-plain, with good stretches of timber and half-a-dozen lakes and swamps teeming with wild-fowl and other game. At least two thousand acres of improved pastures, and dams galore. Stout fences, good roads, first class sheds with equipment of the best and most modern. One of the most well-thought of merino studs in Australia, and a newly installed beef cattle stud edging up the ladder at no snail's pace. And all within thirty miles of the capital. A developer's dream, Mortlock mused, standing on the cattle-trap with his hand on the gate, listening to the night sounds which some developer would — one day, for certain — banish forever under desirable brick-and-tile. And all held together simply because Winter after Winter had grown up with the place, had learned to know it and to respect it, paddock by paddock, lake by lake, hill, swamp and gravelly outcrop. Had worked with it rather than on it, to make it the superb machine and lovely artifact and — of course — million-dollar asset it was.

Except young Charlie, Mortlock thought, as he walked back to his car. *Charles the Sixth. The heir. His great-great-great-grand-daddy must be turning over in his grave like a bloody rotisserie.*

The visiting potentate, as Mortlock had come to think of her, was not being entertained at the main homestead. Well, fair enough. She was young Charlie's kettle of fish. The barbecue was being staged at the old overseer's cottage, several hundred yards inside the gate. When Mortlock turned in to it, there were already a score or more of cars pulled up under the towering double row of pines some long-dead Winter had planted, and had watered and guarded from the stock until they could fend for themselves. Three fires had been lit, and the glow from them flickered beautifully among the lower branches, without really penetrating the shadows below. Two of them were spanned by lengths of railway line resting on logs at either end, with plates of quarter-inch steel laid across them. Between the fires, there was a solid timber bench loaded with trays of sausages and steaks from Mullamulla culls, bowls of salad, assorted sauce bottles, piles of cut and buttered bread, cutlery and paper plates and napkins. On the third fire, off to one side, a large stainless steel urn bubbled. A second bench, beside it, bore a huge enamel teapot and mugs on the same heroic scale, obviously on secondment from the Mullamulla shearing shed, and cartons of milk, tea and instant coffee in jars, and china bowls of sugar. Beside it, also, stood Charles Winter, a tall, round-shouldered, rather pot-bellied man with abundant pepper-and-salt hair and the beaked-nose, mildly pop-eyed look of the cartoon English lord. There was no real friendship between him and Mortlock, and whenever they met, Mortlock made the same mental observation: that whereas it had taken twenty generations to evolve that look in Britain, it had surfaced after only five in Australia. *Must be the inbreeding early on, before the convicts came!* he thought, again, as he walked toward Winter. *Damn lucky I escaped it!*

'Hello, Charles!' he said. He gestured toward the tables. 'Still doing the loaves and fishes act?'

'Pro forma,' Charles Winter said. His voice was recognisably, and pleasantly, Australian. 'We've got it down to a fine art.' He did not quite like Mortlock, feeling for him the mild distaste which the class-proud, class-conscious, class-responsible feel for the dropout from their class. The Mortlocks had relinquished their holdings, taken up only a few years after Mullamulla, through a combination of bad management and indifferent land, and a consequent disinterest on the part of the three generations which had held it. Mortlock had been able to bounce back among the landed gentry simply through a shrewd prescience as to when to buy and when to sell during the nickel boom of the Sixties. He had been able to buy back most of the old family land, and to instal as manager a graduate of Muresk Agricultural College who very soon began to run the property at a profit: all of which seemed somehow unfair to dedicated farmer Winter, who entertained for him, but never indicated it, something of the sentiments the ant is supposed to entertain for the grasshopper. He ran his protuberant blue eyes over Mortlock's trim shape, still easily contained in a body-shirt and slacks outfit designed for a man at least twenty years younger. 'You don't get much older.'

'Don't try to,' Mortlock said. He was, nevertheless, as always, gratified by the compliment. When people said to him, as they often did: *Well, I wouldn't have put you much past thirty-five!* he always replied: 'Go on! I'm damn near fifty!' When, in fact, he was only forty-six. He glanced around the expanse of dry couch lawn in front of the little cottage. 'Where's the visiting potentate?'

'Mollie Wilcannia?' Charles Winter laughed. 'That's good. The visiting potentate. I never thought of it that way.'

'Some sort of a poet, isn't she?'

'Like I'm some sort of a bloody cow-cocky!' Winter liked to ocker it up occasionally to relieve the strain of being, at all times, the Winter of Mullamulla. 'She had a skinny little book published a couple of years ago in Sydney. Some fly-by-night Commo outfit, more interested in stirring than they are in abo poets.'

'How the hell did you get hold of it?' Mortlock asked. 'I didn't think poetry of any kind was your bit.'

'Young Charlie had it. He showed it to me. Rubbish.'

'Not all of it, apparently. I heard some reviewer on about it. He read one piece, she's sitting in a creek-bed listening to what the old people are saying to her. That was good.'

'Well, yes,' Winter admitted. 'When she was talking about her own experience.'

'And before someone steered her onto what the noble savage

suffered at our hands!'

'Before the Canberra mob latched onto her as some sort of Judas-goat to lead them into this new world the poor bloody tax-payer's being milked to set up for them!' Winter turned and stared with sudden, prim, Mullamulla disapproval at where most of the guests were gathered under one of the pines. Laughter and chatter and the clink of bottles on glasses bounced out of it, against the movement of cigarette ends in the gloom. 'That's her, over there. Holding court with the local yammagees,' he observed sourly. 'The Canberra mob could have done better for their money, I think.'

'They don't have much to choose from, I guess,' Mortlock said. 'Look ... here's Bonnie Francis.' A dumpy, fair-haired woman of somewhat middle-age had just walked into the firelight from the direction of the parked cars. She was wearing a white linen trouser suit with a belted safari jacket and two vivid purple scarves, one knotted at her throat and the other around her hair. Mortlock hailed her, and she picked her way cautiously toward them, as though over a dangerous stretch of reef. 'What's up with your feet?' he demanded, as she pulled up alongside them. 'Broken a fetlock?'

'It's these damn platform soles,' she said. 'I'm scared of falling off them.'

'Then why wear them?'

'Us oldies got to stay with it!' Bonnie Francis glanced with an oblique grin at the still hard and flat male breasts outlined by his skin-tight shirt. 'You in your body-stocking, me in my platform soles.' She turned to Charles Winter. 'Hello, Charles. As I always says ... you got a glorious place here.'

'*And* sanctified by six generations of uninterrupted possession of the spoils!' Mortlock said.

'Oh, shush!' Bonnie Francis said. 'On a night like this! That moon!'

'We arrange it for special guests,' Charles Winter said.

'Including, tonight, representatives of the original owners, and a wise woman from the east to read the auguries,' Mortlock said, to Bonnie Francis. 'You know what it's all for, tonight, don't you?'

'Well ... This aboriginal poet?'

'That's only a blind. Charles is going to give Mullamulla back to the boongs.'

'Yes,' Charles Winter said. 'When you give back yours.'

'The hell! We gave ours back long ago!'

'A nice euphemism for goofing out,' Bonnie Francis observed. 'Still, you've got most of Milong back again.'

'That's what I mean,' Winter said.

'I earned that by the sweat of my chinny-chin-chin,' Mortlock protested. 'I bought it with good, hard-earned nickel-shares. You got Mullamulla from your old man, Charles. And he got it from his, and so on — right back to when it was reefed off the poor bloody blacks.'

'It was Crown Land,' Winter said, equably. 'We didn't hunt anybody off it. I mean great-great-great-Grandfather Charles didn't. He actually paid the Crown for it.'

'And who was wearing the Crown that picked up the loot?' Bonnie Francis demanded.

'Bloody old Vic,' Mortlock said, knowing it would offend Winter's well-known Royalist loyalties.

'I bet it wasn't old King Billie of the Bibbulmun!' Bonnie Francis looked out of the circle of firelight at the shadowy trees and the silvered paddocks, the lake of darkness that was the paper-bark swamp down by the road. 'Poor beggars. I never come here, but I think ... lakes, bush, duck, kangaroos. What a heaven it must have been for them!'

'Don't you think it might be just as much a heaven for us?' Charles Winter said. 'And what do you think they'd do if they were to get it back?' He paused a moment, and added, pointedly: 'Presuming we could find somebody has any right to it?'

'They'd live on it, like they always did,' Bonnie Francis said. 'Like they were intended to.'

'By whom?' There was a touch of humour in his agreeable voice. 'And what makes you think they even *want* to live on it, Bonnie?'

'Of course they would!'

'Then pardon me for disagreeing with you.' Winter's tone took on a hard edge, as though, suddenly, he had grown tired of humouring her vagaries. 'You've got rocks in your head if you think they want to do anything but what they're doing right now. What they've become used to doing — what *we've* made them used to doing. Made them regard as their right. Sitting around in parks sucking bombo. Having sob-sisters from the Welfare outfit running them, hand and foot. Bitching about how hard they're treated ... but just offer one of them a job that's likely to raise a sweat! I saw a very funny cartoon, once, very funny, but very pointed. And very damn appropriate to what we're talking about now. These two dogs are running along either side of a wire fence, snarling blue murder at each other through the wire. You know how they do? Well, they come to a break in the fence, and if they want to, they can get at each other. Not on your life! They take off again, on the other side of the break, snarling their heads off like before. That's how it would be with the abos — nine out of ten, at any rate. Give 'em a break in the fence, and they wouldn't want to go through it.' His sudden vehemence had taken the other two by surprise, and it showed in their faces. He grinned, sheepishly. Suddenly, once again, he was charming, urbane Charles Winter, of Mullamulla. 'Hobby-horse,' he said, by way of explanation. 'Sorry.'

'Darling!' Bonnie Francis laid a hand on his arm. 'We were only pulling your leg!'

'I get brassed off, sometimes, people telling me what I should do,' Winter said. 'I think about it myself, believe me. Quite a lot.' He grinned at them, and gestured around the clearing. 'For instance. I could have forbidden Charlie to have this shivoo here, tonight. It's still my property.' He shrugged. 'He'll do what he wants with it when I'm gone — and Marcia. If I go first, she won't have any crazy shenanigans when he takes over.' He referred to his wife, who had been a most expensively- educated, widely-travelled, beautiful but brainless 'society- girl'. In return for becoming chatelaine of Mullamulla, she had delivered a handsome *dot* from another of the old landed families which, also, had managed to hang onto their property. In their case, however, principally by using a relatively modest pastoral fortune to found the city's first credit company. It was, in fact, one of a succession of dynastic alliances which had helped the hardworking Winters to weather the storm until the very growth and prosperity of the State had rendered Mullamulla's farming and stud operations impervious to anything but another, even more monumental, depression than that of the Thirties. Marcia Winter was not in evidence anywhere around the barbecue fires, and Bonnie Francis grasped the legitimate excuse to give another direction to what had become rather an embarrassing conversation. She turned away from Charles Winter, and appeared to search for his wife.

'I don't see Marcia,' she said.

'Don't be Uncle Willy,' Charles Winter said. He quite purposefully affected the ocker again in order to cover still further the subject which Bonnie Francis had just shoved decently beneath the carpet. 'It's not entirely her cup of tea.'

'I can't quite see her bending the knee to the visiting potentate,' Mortlock said.

'I was looking forward to seeing her,' Bonnie Francis lied.

'Then you'll have to go up to the house,' Charles Winter offered.

'Not yet. I think I'll go and have a look at Mrs Thing, first. What's her name again?'

'Mollie Wilcannia?' Charles Winter said. 'Keith, here, calls her the visiting potentate. I thought it rather good.'

'I'll come with you, Bonnie,' Mortlock said. 'Excuse me, Charles?'

'Sure. I'm going to round up the cooks.'

The group around the visitor had broken up. Now that they were out in the open, it could be seen that they were about half-and-half black and white, half-and-half men and women. The whites were mostly young, jeans and desert boots, T-shirts with slogans, worn and greasy leather jackets with arm-flashes proclaiming foreign travel, actual or imagined. The few earnest, middle-aged people among them commuted from group to group as if looking for something. They appeared to be apprehensive about missing something that might happen while they were somewhere else. Bonnie Francis had worked on enough charitable committees, including those for aborigines, to recognise the type quite readily. They laughed a lot. They smiled a little too readily, and a lot too winningly, at any aborigine they might happen to meet in the no-man's land between groups. Tonight, as always, they were displaying their anthers far too desperately — and tonight, as always, they would go away unfertilised by the contact they yearned for. She pitied them. The blacks were all youngsters, a surprising number of them full-bloods, willowy, shy, withdrawn, seeming unable to credit what was going on, perhaps even that they were mixing so intimately with white people. All wore what might have been a uniform — of pretty, brightly-coloured print dresses for the girls, and brightly-coloured slacks and open-necked shirts for the boys. A few, from their confident bearing, were fairly obviously old-hands at the meet-the-abos kind of party arranged by white fringe-dwellers. They were at pains to establish their veteran status, button-holing white strangers unmercifully, using Christian names like bumper stickers, crying out to whites in other groups: *Hey! Ain't seen you since the night we was at Bill's!*

'It's all so damned depressing,' Bonnie Francis said to Mortlock. 'I suppose young Charlie's heart's in the right place, or whatever it is you say on occasions like this. But I really don't think this's the way to go about it. Just look at that poor little pair over there. They haven't a clue about what they're here for, or what they're supposed to do.' She touched his arm and pursed her lips in a curious, unintentional parody of the aboriginal method of indicating direction. Following her hint, Mortlock saw a young couple standing by themselves at the edge of the firelight. The girl was pregnant. Ordinarily she would have been as slender and as brown as a spear, but the hard, round bulk of the unborn child distended her grotesquely, seeming almost too much for her jabiru legs to support. She was clinging to her companion's arm as her mother, even, might have clung to a buoyant log while crossing a crocodile-infested river — in desperate hope of getting to the other side in one piece. As though wired to a single switch, their eyes moved in a sort of mesmerised wonder from group to group. 'What does he imagine they get out of it?' she demanded, when she was certain Mortlock had identified them. 'A bunrush like this!'

'I wonder more what he gets out of it, himself,' Mortlock said. 'Look at him, for Christ's sake. Future owner of Mullamulla!'

Young Charles Winter and his wife had taken up residence in the old overseer's cottage after their recent marriage. They were sitting crosslegged on the bare boards of the verandah, more-or- less in the lotus position, she strumming softly on a guitar. Both were barefooted, in blue jeans and embroidered cheesecloth shirts, with ropes of blue ceramic beads and dangles of silver coins and charms around their necks. He was bearded, and wore his red-gold Winter hair in a queue on his neck, twined with a leather thong. The lobe of his right ear was pierced to take the heavy gold hoop which he caressed, incessantly, with the thumb and forefinger of his right hand. She wore a small nose-jewel of gold and turquoise in the Indian fashion, although her nostril had not been pierced. Her hair, perfectly straight, long and shiny, fell down either side of her small, pale face, and every few moments she threw back her head in a coltish sort of movement or, forsaking the strings of the guitar, ran one finger down the inner edge of each wing in turn to keep them out of her eyes.

'They're playing pioneer,' Mortlock said. 'I guess it's got its points when it comes with a slow combustion stove and a deep-freeze stocked with turkey and champers. And colour TV in ye olde parlour, and a few thousand bucks of the best colonial antiques in every room. And a flat in town for when you get tired of roughing it out here.'

'Oh — come on! Don't be such a grump!' Bonnie Francis protested. 'I think they're lovely. They're only kids. They're playing cubby-house.'

'Just in passing, they're not kids, you know,' Mortlock said. 'They're voters. They're married. Pretty soon, they might be parents. But it's really the playing that gets me. I suppose this business here, tonight — it's part of the game?'

'Does it do any harm, if it is?'

'That remains to be seen, although, we might find out a damn sight sooner than we expect,' Mortlock said, 'Alright ... you're one of the boongs here tonight. You know that when it's all over, Mr and Mrs Charles Winter, junior, will retire to their old colonial double bed and turn on the air-conditioning. Maybe break out a bottle of bubbly to get them in the mood. *You'll* make your way, somehow, back to some bug-hutch in good old East Perth. Maybe to a sewer-pipe down on the riverbank. What the hell does it do to you?'

'Stop ranting, and listen,' Bonnie Francis said. She was looking intently at the young Mrs Winter, her head tilted in concentration. She turned to Mortlock after a moment or two, and grinned. 'I don't know whether our hostess knows it or not, but she's playing a sort of answer to the whole shebang.'

Mortlock looked at the girl on the verandah, following her drifting white hand through the simple, wandering melody and trying to recognise it. He turned to Bonnie Francis again.

'It's one of Kurt Weil's old songs,' she explained. 'He wrote it about forty years ago, just for tonight.' She paused for a moment, nodding to the tune, and after a while began to sing in a husky whisper. *O, moon of Alabama, we soon must say good-bye. We've lost our good old mama, and we must have whiskey. O, you know why.* 'It's for them,' she said, nodding in the direction of the group under the pine tree. 'It could have been written for them.'

'Whiskey?' Mortlock said. 'They're lucky to get cheap plonk! And I think they prefer it that way!'

'S-s-sh!' Bonnie Francis hushed him. 'It goes on ...' She waited, listening intently to the sad, minor-key air coming from the verandah. *O, show us the way to the next little dollar, she sang eventually. O, don't ask why. For if we don't find that next little dollar, I tell you, we must die.* She stopped singing and looked at Mortlock, her head still on one side, inquiringly. 'Just about wraps it up, doesn't it?' she said. 'They ask for so much. They need so much. And we give them grog and dollars.'

'And the visiting poet,' Mortlock said. The strumming on the verandah had stopped, but the sad air hung in his mind like a strip of tinsel. 'Don't forget the great cultural binge!'

'She's not really a poet,' Bonny Francis said. 'My god, didn't the emperor's clothes get a nice old airing when her opus came out! Nobody was game to slam it for fear of being labelled racist!'

'There were a couple of poems in it,' Mortlock said. 'I heard them on the air.'

'After some editor had a go at them. I was told they had to be polished to the bone, grammar and everything.'

'Hell — that could go for any writer. They all get a final buffing, don't they?'

'Two swallows don't make a summer, whatever,' Bonnie Francis said. 'It's like this bunrush here, tonight. The reviewers tell her she's a poet, and young Charlie tells this lot they can mix it at any level of white society. As it happens — she isn't, and they can't.'

'Well, a while ago *you* asked *me*!' Mortlock said, grinning at her. 'What harm does it do?'

'It's not fair to kid them. It's their shins get barked in the long run. Like you said — they go back to the riverbank. Next Sunday afternoon this lot'll be scoffing bombo somewhere. Like under the bridge, at Guildford.'

'Then — what do you do?'

'What do you do with anybody who's learning a lesson? Insist on them learning before you give them the toffee-apple.'

'Jesus!' Mortlock said. 'How long they got to go on in school?'

Bonnie Francis nodded toward the pines. 'Look. Mrs Thing's coming out of her lair.'

'My god,' Mortlock said. 'She's a big girl!'

Mollie Wilcannia had come out from the shadows of the pine. With three other aborigines, and a skimpy white woman who walked backward in front of her, beaming ecstatically into her face, she was undulating toward the barbecue fires. She was tall, and was made more so by the huge, perfectly globular afro in which she wore her dark, frizzy hair. She was grossly fat, the three mounds of her bust, her belly and her bottom seeming to live lives of their own inside her brightly-flowered muumuu. She and her little entourage were, in a way, directed straight toward Mortlock and Bonnie Francis by a flanking row of massive old agapanthus which trailed their long pennon of soft blue from the pines to the verandah steps. She was, Mortlock noticed, no more than quarter-caste.

'Mrs Wilcannia?' he said, when she had come close enough. 'Mrs Francis and I were just coming over to pay our respects.'

'So the mountain come to Mahomet instead, eh?' Mrs Wilcannia continued to undulate toward them, speaking as she came. She had a deep, velvety voice, and the laugh which followed her words was as deep and as velvety. When she was still several feet away from them they both felt the impact of the personal magnetism which seemed to move ahead of her like some mobile field of force: Mortlock with amusement, Bonnie Francis with a kind of fear.

'I got to take on a lot of fuel to keep me goin',' Mrs Wilcannia laughed again and patted the peplum of solid fat under the waistline of her muumuu. 'I was makin' for where the fuel is.' She held out a large, dark-brown hand to each of them in turn. 'You poets?'

'Well, no,' Bonnie Francis said. She would rather have been able to say yes, and if Mortlock had not been there would have confessed modestly to a bit of random scribbling: it was years since a women's magazine had published several little lyrics evoked in her by the downy innocence of a son and daughter now parents themselves. 'But we've both read your collection.'

'You like it?' Mrs Wilcannia demanded, directly.

'Only some of it,' Mortlock said, just as directly.

The skimpy white woman with Millie Wilcannia had not taken her eyes of that dark face. She now thrust out both her hands, dramatically, palms down and fingers extended and stretched as if sensing the air. To Mortlock's surprise, and then embarrassment, she began to declaim the opening verse of the one poem he had really liked in Mrs Wilcannia's collection.

'When I sit in the hot sand, and the gum-trees speak
With the voice of my people, does my heart break?
No! Not my heart! The sound that comes nearer

Is the tap of the sticks and the drone of the bull-roarer!
It is the voice of my people! Those dark words
Are stored in the hearts of the scattering tribes!'

She turned and looked first into Mortlock's face, and then into Bonnie Francis's. 'Mollie Wilcannia is one of the true, great Australian poets,' she said, earnestly.

'Be a dear,' Mrs Wilcannia said to her. 'Run over and tell whoever's doin' the cookin' I want a nice, big steak with a rim of fat around it, not too well done. An' some kidney, if it's on the me-an'-you?'

The white woman nodded to her, readily, and turned to the dark young man standing alongside her. Obviously not one of those recently arrived in the big smoke from some camp outside Fitzroy Crossing or somewhere, Mortlock thought, following the woman's glance to his face. Rather like an ambitious young first-lieutenant in the presence of the C.O. Intelligent, observant, on-the-ball. The kind, in fact, the C.O. might have to give a Snarler to, one day, to keep his own position. The woman revamped her smile, and made her eyes big and inviting.

'Come with me, Clarrie?'

'Nuh.' The young man shook his head, barely looking at her. He had met her three times recently, on occasions such as the Mullamulla barbecue, and every time she had thrown herself at him with an immodesty that angered him. He had had to take a lot of chi-acking in the crowded cars on the way home, and in the crowded crib he shared with a dozen-or-so other blacks, men and women, in a North Perth slum. In any case, he had access to far more inviting paddocks, and he preferred to sow his seed in them. The woman looked momentarily downcast, and shrugged a sort of little-girl gesture of disappointment. Then she smiled again, brilliantly, at Mrs Wilcannia, and took off alone toward the fire. The two aboriginal girls standing either side of the young man giggled derisively at her retreating back, and Mortlock was surprised to realise that he felt somehow degraded by the trifling incident. He was not permitted to ruminate on it. The young man turned to him, the moment the skimpy white woman departed, as though he had been waiting impatiently to get on with more important business.

'You ever given blood?' he demanded, abruptly.

'I — uh — have, on occasions,' Mortlock said. The question, out of the blue, had taken him by surprise. Why?'

'We're setting up a blood donors' group lunch-time, next Thursday.'

'Where?' Bonnie Francis asked.

'That plaza place, outside the Premier's office.' The young man, beautifully built, black as a stove, spotlessly clean and well-dressed, kept his eyes on Mortlock. He seemed not to regard women as worth talking to. 'We're going to ask him to come along. Some of the other politicians, too.'

'You be careful trying to get blood out of that lot,' Bonnie Francis persisted, smiling at him. Mortlock realised with another shock that, with a small shove, she could easily fit into the same groove as the skimpy woman so unceremoniously given her congé, a moment before, by the same young man. 'You're likely to lose on the deal.'

'We don't want *their* blood — we got more than a hundred Noongahs coming along,' the young man said, impatiently, but still looking at Mortlock. 'We do want a few whites to front up with us, though.'

'Why, then?' Mortlock asked.

'So's we won't get the big arse from the bloody coppers.'

'What's it all about?' Mortlock said. He was becoming interested. 'Sort of community service?'

'Community bullshit!' the young man said, derisively. 'That blood bank mob, they don't give a damn where they get their blood, so long as they get it. But, by Jeez, there's a lot of whites going to feel pretty uneasy about getting a shot of Noongah blood next time they have an accident, or something!'

'Ingenious!' Mortlock said, smiling wryly at Bonnie Francis. 'Sort of mass blood-brotherhood ceremony?'

'Who thought it up?' Bonnie Francis asked. She smiled brightly, looking forward to congratulating him, but he pursed his lips, in the aboriginal way, in the direction of the verandah.

'Charlie,' he said, without looking at her, and still directing his conversation toward Mortlock. 'That's what he called it too. Blood-brotherhood ceremony.'

'Is he giving blood?' Mortlock asked.

'He thought it would be better if none of the regular white organisers took part — like they do a completely black show,' Mrs Wilcannia said. The velvet pile of her voice had taken on an extra depth of nap. 'They reckon the Premier's a great mate of his Dad. Comes out here all the time, shooting and that. Clarrie — take the girls and see if you can give a hand with the cooking and things, will you? There's a mob of us to serve.'

The three aborigines set off obediently toward the fires, and Mortlock found himself once again more surprised. Somehow uneasily, at the alacrity with which people obeyed this woman, and the raw authority in her voice and her manner. *One woman that cheeky young bugger listens to*! he thought, with a grin. And then: *I wonder what I'd do if she told me to do something?*

'That is a bleautiful poem, Mrs Wilcannia,' Bonnie Francis said, sincerely. She had quite forgotten her previous reservations about the black woman's talents. 'The one your friend quoted from.'

'It's the only one I ever wrote, really,' the black woman said, simply. 'Oh, one or two others wasn't that bad. But that one ... it just come. I went for a bit of a pinki in the bush one afternoon. I was workin' at the pub in Wilcannia at the time. This bloke at the pub, he said why didn't I send it to a magazine he used to get up from Sydney. So I did, an' they asked me if I had any more. An' that's how it started. Of course, they fixed up the grammar an' all that. I never had that much schooling.' She laughed, and once again patted the fat around her waist. *In the way some people pat their pockets, Mortlock thought. For reassurance that it's all still there.* 'I'm makin' the most of it. Never know when I'll be out on me ear.' She smiled wryly at Bonnie Francis. 'This year it's boongs and worry-beads. Barbecues, too.' She pouted in the direction of the fires.

'You think, a year or two ago, you'd ever see this Mr Charles Winter dishin' out his own tucker an' grog to a mob of Noongahs like this?' She grinned again at Bonnie Francis. 'Gawd knows what it'll be next year. Niggers gotta hop in for their chop while the hoppin's good!'

While they had been talking, they had been joined by young Charles Winter and his wife, on their way to the barbecue fires. They had been standing, still and silent, watching and listening, like a pair of beautifully moulded and tinted artifacts.

'Come on, Mollie!' the young man said, suddenly, as though a switch had been thrown, somewhere. His tone was petulant, and he made no effort to hide the mild annoyance in his expression. '*You're* not a *nigger*!'

'Bullshit, Charlie,' Mrs Wilcannia replied, although she kept her glance on Bonnie Francis. 'Any part of a nigger's a nigger, Mrs Francis. You got a teaspoon of black blood, you're black.'

'But, if you've got something to offer, what difference does it make?' Bonnie Francis demanded. 'Look at Pastor Wally Mitchell!' She referred to an Anglican parson who, for the past two generations, had acted gladly as a kind of Exhibit A for anyone trying to prove that the aborigine who wanted to overcome discrimination could overcome it. 'He got a decoration!'

'Oh, *Jesus!*' Mollie Wilcannia said. She seemed half-way between derision and anger, with overtones of sorrow and amusement.

'He's just an Uncle Tom,' young Charles Winter said, coldly.

'You know the Sydney mob call him Wally the Warrigal, behind his back?' Mrs Wilcannia stared straight into Mortlock's eyes. 'Mister. Nobody don't call me Mollie the Myall. Anybody does, they go out the window, and I go out the door — straight back to Wilcannia.'

'And give up your work?' Bonnie Francis said.

'I got plenty out of it,' Mrs Wilcannia said. She shrugged, a massive movement of the mounds of fat on her shoulders that drew her huge breasts up beneath the thin stuff of her muumuu like a pair of moles furrowing the earth. 'But not that much, I couldn't give it up tomorrow.'

I got plenty out of it, Mortlock thought, watching her. *Not, I'm accomplishing plenty. Could it be the definitive statement on the glorious black revolution?*

'As a matter of interest, Mrs Wilcannia,' he said, 'what do you get out of it?'

'I get damn well paid,' Mrs Wilcannia said. 'I get to travel around, first class tickets, pretty good pubs. I get to talk to the Minister, occasionally. I get propositioned by all kinds of big-time blokes I'd never'a met before. An' I take some of 'em up on it!' She looked at young Charles Winter, and laughed provocatively. 'Not bad for a boong!'

Young Charles Winter said, without smiling. 'You offer yourself as a boong, Mollie, they'll take you as a boong.'

'They'll take me for a boong, whichever way I offer myself,' Mollie Wilcannia said. 'An' whatever way they offer themselves, I'll take them as a pack of bastards.'

Bonnie Francis had been shocked by the woman's frank run-down of her various emoluments, but she strove to conceal it. She had been at pains to establish herself as a free-thinker in the quasi-intellectual world of the better Perth suburbs, and she was not about to let her guard down in front of Mortlock, of all people. She turned and gestured toward the press around the barbecue fires and benches. It was a scene that would be reproduced on a thousand pearl-tinted evenings that summer, in suburban back gardens, on beaches and at picnic grounds in the hills; for birthdays, for golden anniversaries, to raise funds on behalf of sporting associations of all kinds, and for just no reason at all. The hum that edged out of it to the group on the path was the same scrambled message of good-fellowship, mild intoxication, scandal-mongering and oblique sexual approaches for afterward, all hopefully transmitted and only half-unscrambled, all overlain with the sizzle and reek of charred meat, and body deodorant, and mosquito repellent. *At very few, however, would one find a Charles Winter dispensing the rough red and good, home-raised beef to a crowd of blacks and black stirrers,* Mortlock thought, following with his eyes the direction of Bonnie Francis's gesture.

'What do *they* get out of it?' she asked.

'What's who get out of it?' Mrs Wilcannia said, mildly. 'The blacks or the whites?'

'Well ... all of them, I guess,' Bonnie Francis said. 'But the blacks, mainly. They stand to get most.'

'What does anybody ever want out of any damn thing?' Mollie Wilcannia said. She stared with well-concealed dislike at this small, plump, white skinned blonde, who had never had to keep a drunken hotel manager at bay in a smoky kitchen, or behind a bar after closing. Had never sat in the hot sand of a quiet creek- bed, one Sunday afternoon, and mourned, suddenly, out of nothing, for what had happened to her people. Had come to this Charles Winter's party for the blacks and the near-blacks just to have a look at the animals without the usual cage-bars of distance and social convention to keep her from getting mauled. That was what a lot of them *did* want, a mauling. What did this one want? 'Easy dough an' easy screwin's what most of 'em want!' she said, brutally. She was rewarded, and hugged it to her heart, by the shock the words produced in Bonnie Francis. Young Charles Winter noticed it, too, and turned on her with cold reproof.

'Come off it, Mollie,' he said. 'For Christ's sake!'

'You wouldn't know, Charlie,' Mrs Wilcannia replied, with easy insolence. 'You ain't ever had to hustle for either of 'em.' She turned to Bonnie Francis again. 'You see that little skinny white woman was with me when you come up? All she wants is a length. And she'd like it from that young chap, Clarrie. She gets that, and she goes home satisfied.'

Mortlock felt Bonnie Francis stiffen, involuntarily, at his side. He grinned behind his hand. It was the sort of situation all suburban free souls were bound to get caught up with at some time or other, confrontation with the genie somehow, dangerously, liberated from his bottle. He knew very few who had any idea of how to cope with it, and he was certain that Bonnie Francis hadn't the vaguest idea. He glanced casually at Mrs Wilcannia and intercepted a grin of malicious amusement she had directed at Bonnie.

'I wouldn't mind if she'd just grab the feller by the stalk and drag him off,' the black woman went on. 'But all this damn eye business.' She fluttered her great brown eyes in an appalling parody of sweetie-pie come-hither. 'She's so hot, the poor bugger. If it was to rain now, she'd give off steam.'

'Let's go and get our steaks,' young Charles Winter said. Nobody took any notice of him. He placed an arm around his young wife's shoulder, protectively, obviously in anticipation of further revelations by this dreadful boong from New South Wales. Nothing like it had ever happened before. He made a mental note never to invite Keith Mortlock or Mrs Francis to any future function for aboriginal advancement at Mullamulla. Neither of them had a clue what it was all about. People like that. If they didn't get the blacks off-side, the blacks tended to get cheeky with them.

'What about the blacks, then?' Mortlock said. 'I suppose they come for the white flesh?'

Mrs Wilcannia shrugged again, the same massive displacement of her ponderous shoulders, the same burrowing of her breasts in their colourful sacks. 'If it's offerin', who knocks it back?' She laughed good naturedly at him, and passed it around the little group. 'Most of 'em come to get a good feed and a belly full of liquor. Although I bet they'd rather have something with a bit more kick than this damn vinegar.' She raised her half-emptied glass and looked at the firelight through the claret's ruby glow. 'Mob up in Wilcannia knew I was drinkin' this bull's-blood, they'd laugh me out'a town.'

'I thought it was things like land rights, and sacred places, they came along to talk about,' Mortlock said. 'That sort of thing.'

'Some do,' Mollie Wilcannia said. 'I been around a lot, an' I reckon about one in a thousand's got any idea of what it's all about, that land rights business. They cheer when they get told to cheer, most of 'em.' She glanced at young Charles Winter and his wife, with the same malicious grin she had directed at Bonnie Francis a few moments before. 'It's like when your great-gran'-daddy, or whatever he was, took this bit of country off the Noongahs in the first place, Charlie. There's always a few can see what's to be got, and they bloody-well make certain they get it — for themselves. He was one of 'em. Same's happenin' now, only the boot's on the other foot. Blacks're gettin' ready to take it all back. But don't you think for one little minute it's going back to the black people, to the likes of this lot here. And me. It'll be like it is now, only the blokes on top'll be black, not white.' She pouted her lips in the direction of the fire, somehow singling out for them the broad back of the young man, Clarrie. 'He's goin' to be one of 'em.'

'Well, I don't think they're going to have to take anything,' young Charles Winter said. 'Australians are beginning to wake up to what they've done, and they want to make amends for it.'

'Come off it, Charlie,' Mortlock said. 'We've all been made to feel far too damn guilty for something we didn't do, in my opinion, and I don't know too much about anybody handing anything back without a nulla at his neck. Christ, it's been nearly two hundred years since the bloody balloon went up for the black people in this country. Who's going to unscramble an omelette that size? It's time we stopped beating our breasts about what happened to the noble savage then. The noble savages have all gone. What we should be going to town on is what we're going to do for the urban savage, now. And that doesn't mean all this crap about giving them back the land. Who would you give it back to? And what would they do with it if they got it?'

'What should they do with it?' Charles Winter said, coldly.

'Yes,' Bonnie Francis said, eagerly. Mortlock was amused to see that in some subtle way she had turned entirely against him, and was siding with young Charles, and the give-back-the-land lobby. 'What should they do with it?'

'Work it,' Mortlock said, shortly. 'At least as well as we do, or there's no percentage in giving it back to them.'

'But supposing they just want to live on it?' she demanded. 'Like their people always have? Like they were intended to?'

He recalled that she had put exactly the same question to Charles Winter earlier in the evening. So she hadn't been pulling his leg at all. He gave her the answer she had got earlier, from Winter.

'Intended, by whom?' he said. 'How long do you think the rest of the world's going to let a few hundred thousand aborigines roam around a continent this size, hunting the elusive honey-bag?'

'Yet it will happen,' young Charles Winter said.

'You could start it off by handing over Mullamulla,' Mortlock said.

'I probably will,' the young man said. 'When it's mine to hand over.' He looked toward the fire. 'Dad's waving us over. Our steaks are ready.' He slipped his arm from his wife's shoulders, and took her by the elbow. 'Come on, Jen.'

'Oh — before you go, Mrs Winter?' Mortlock said. 'If you wouldn't mind ... that little tune you were playing a while ago?' He hummed the air, and looked into her face, smiling encouragement. 'You know? O, Moon of Alabama?'

She stared back at him, uncomprehendingly. The firelight twinkled on the nose-jewel she wore, seemed to burn through the almost transparent fair skin of her face. Nervously, she raised a hand and brushed back the smooth wings of her hair, first from one side, and then from the other. She shook her head, and looked for help to her husband.

'She just picks them up from the radio,' he said. 'She has a wonderful ear. Haven't you, love?' He glanced quickly around the group. 'Excuse us? I'd better go and help Dad be host.'

'I'll come with you, Charlie,' Bonnie Francis said.

A nice little bit of polarisation, Mortlock thought. He was rather surprised, in the moment that the thought struck him, to find himself now aligned not with Bonnie Francis, whom he had known practically all his life, but with this curious, coarse, part-aboriginal woman he had met only fifteen minutes before. He glanced sideways at her, backed by the blue trailing cloud of the agapanthus blooms, the dying glow of the barbecue fires touching the greasy texture of her flaring nostrils and the high cheekbones with pink lights. She gave off a warm smell, some strong perfume that did not quite subdue a characteristic body odour she had inherited with the black part of her blood.

They stood unspeaking, looking after the other three, as if in common agreement that there was something yet to be said.

'I wonder what makes him tick?' Mortlock said. *You tend to look no further than the beards and the beads and all the jiggery-pokery,* he thought. *You tend to think there's nothing behind it all. Then, suddenly, you find there is something.* He felt vaguely resentful of young Charles Winter, as if the young man had somehow pulled a fast one. Aloud, he said: 'Could he be dinkum about giving Mullamulla away?'

'Maybe,' Mrs Wilcannia began to walk toward the fires. 'Maybe he does reckon his people stole it from my people. Maybe he does want to give it back.'

'Maybe he can just see the trend of things,' Mortlock said. He laughed, with the residue of the resentment he had felt a moment before giving a spiteful edge to it. 'Maybe he's just getting in good with the future bosses. You said they'd be taking over.'

'If he is, he's wasting his time,' Mollie Wilcannia said. She turned around and looked directly into Mortlock's eyes. 'You can tell him from me, mister. When the crunch comes, you'll all be Whitey.'

'And we'll be chasing the whiskey and the dollars, eh?' he said, laughing again. *O, Moon of Mullamulla!*

She looked at him, uncomprehendingly as young Charles Winter's wife had. 'If you like to put it that way,' she said.

They had reached the fires, and one of the aboriginal men who had been helping with the cooking thrust wooden platters into their hands. On each, he dropped a huge, sizzling slab of Mullamulla steak, with a serve of kidney on Mrs Wilcannia's. For a reason he would not have been able to explain, Mortlock felt a sudden revulsion against it. The availability of it, somehow. The commonplace it had become in the tribal rituals of this overfed world around which the hungry black people were circling, testing the weak places in its defences. Would they do any differently if they were to get in? He looked up from his platter, over the heads of the crush around the fires, to the dark cliff of the paperbarks by the gate. The moon was well up, of frozen silver now, and the shaggy boles gleamed from the shadows with a silent, distant beauty that made his heart ache. For the land. For this land, he was astonished to realise. The great trees seemed inviolate, still, in their immemorial swamp. And yet, he knew, they were not. They could be destroyed. One day, they would be.

'O, moon of Mullamulla,' he murmured.

The visiting poetess glanced at him, her eyes widened in inquiry. He bowed to her, and motioned her toward the bench where they would be served with salads.

BALCONY OF DREAMS

Ever since I first became capable of accepting that there was something outside South Perth, that the whole world didn't consist of that long, narrow, fascinating stretch of Suburban Road which we would see from our front gate — Mr Faddy's grocery at one end and Mr Weir's white weatherboard house at the other, behind its blue plumbago hedge — the strange-sounding names of those faraway places have bloomed in my mind like secretive flowers half-seen in the gloom of a jungle, like unseen hands beckoning around the corners of the buildings infinitely more distant than Mr Faddy's shop.

I suppose I can thank my father for it, partly. If ever I were to ask him the meaning of a word he would propel me in the direction of his huge, coverless, dog-eared dictionary — as often as not with a mild cuff behind the ear to remind me that I'd been told often enough... In the same way he directed me — all of us, I suppose — to his atlas, so that for me, from very early on, the Coromandel Coast became a dream of blue seas and green palm trees, and glittering white sand, or Nijninovgorod a bunch of many-coloured Russian onion-domes like sullen jewels, ghostly in a snow storm.

Macau coalesced as a kind of willow pattern Chinese village of the sort I'd seen in Arthur Mee's Children's Encyclopaedia at school, connected to Hong Kong by a vermilion-painted, zigzag oriental bridge of wood. It stayed like that until, in 1967, for the first time, I made the crossing between the dream and the reality by *fie-iec-sun*, the beautifully named 'flying-wing-boat' which we so grossly call a hydrofoil.

I made that crossing in the wake of brave Gorge Alvares who, in 1557, unconcerned beneath his substantial sails thousands of miles from home, had pushed into that pirate-infested avenue of islands, and claimed for his masters in Portugal a toehold on the mainland of the fabled Flowery Kingdom. A claim which since then has brought to a fine art the use of the looming imponderable of thousands of miles of Chinese land and thousands of years of Chinese history, culture and conquest, poetry and politics, art more gorgeous, etiquette more brittle, tortures more diabolical than anwhere else in the world, to keep firmly in its place the cheeky little foreign enclave protruding like a wart from the Chinese underbelly.

You still feel it there, in Macau. It touches you like a finger drawn insinuatingly across the skin of the senses, as the silt-laden waters of the Pearl River, sifting yellowly among the islands, lacquer the rocks a pale gold with loam from Szechwan.

It says a great deal for the philosophy of getting them young that while I have travelled between Hong Kong and Macau at least fifty times, by ferry and by hydrofoil, that old picture of a higgledy-piggledy vermilion bridge is still the one which takes shape on the celluloid of my mind at the first mention of the little Portuguese entrepôt: although in another way I'll always recall Macau as the place where my first meal consisted of duck-eggs and cake.

For reasons which now seem a little blurred at the edges, I'd decided to spend 1970 living in Macau. I landed there from Hong Kong on a February day of cold and driving rain, with sea-mists tearing themselves to gossamer in the huge dark banyans around the Praia Grande. I spent that first day trying to find somewhere to live, and was lucky, toward the end of it, to meet up with a down-and-out Australian with a Chinese wife and child, who would rent me a room with a bath. It was right on the edge of the Old Inner Harbour which, I'd been warned by the Macau Tourist Agency, was Communist tiger-country where I'd probably be done in and dumped to go out with the tide; but as the same outfit had assured me that I'd have no trouble finding accommodation I took no notice of them — even when I discovered that the premises actually belonged to an absentee Chinese landlord. When, in 1967, the mainland Chinese Communists took over control of Macau (but not government, in their savvy Chinese style!) he feared the kidnap for ransom which many of his class had suffered, and fled to Hong Kong. And was never heard of again.

Before it got dark I furnished my little home from a second-hand furniture dealer — apart from a mattress, which after examining his stock, I insisted on buying brand new. He assured me sincerely that I was getting the pearls of his merchandise, yet for some strange reason, when I tried to flog them back to him on my departure a year-or-so later, he assured me with equal sincerity that there was just no market for such rubbish. As a signal favour, however, he would remove the pieces, and dump them, at very minimal cost. I finished up sharing them between my landlady and the skinny little Chinese woman who was responsible for sweeping my section of the Praia Grande.

When I'd got my room to rights, I walked down town to buy the wherewithal for my tea. Everything was closed, perhaps because of the lateness of the hour but more probably because of the shocking weather. No sane person would have been out, excepting to go to the casinos. Nevertheless I was able to get half-a-dozen eggs from a tiny roadside booth, some tea, sugar and powdered milk from a side-street grocer, and a crusty loaf and some butter from a baker's. Sodden but happy I went home, anticipating a nice tea of boiled eggs, bread and butter, and good, strong, hot tea. I'd not eaten since breakfast in Hong Kong, and was too tired to think of anything but food.

The eggs, I found, when I got them inside, had a curious, opaque look about them, but I put it down to their being Chinese — where I'd grown up everything Chinese had been regarded as a bit quaint. I opened the first of the three I'd cooked, and immediately was assailed by the nauseating fishy odour of their pale yellow, gelatinous yolks. Duck eggs: and I'd been knocking around the New Territories for long enough to know that the main diet of the millions of ducks raised there was the entrails and tiddly-bits of the millions of fish caught there for the same Hong Kong market. Never mind, I told myself. Nice bread-and-butter, and strong, hot, sweet tea. The bread turned out to be a vilely-sweet, brilliantly-yellow, stale cake of the consistency of solid, dried custard, and quite inedible. Still, I had my nice, strong, hot, sweet tea ... and went to bed on my new straw mattress, still smelling faintly of the summertime paddis, with the harbour-side banyans threshing against my balcony and the rain slanting in on my windows from the vast, dark reaches of the South China sea.

... glide up the crowded waters of the Inner Harbour at evening, between the ranks of huge junks and tiny sampans, twinkle of cooking fires and soft shadows of lamplight among thickets of masts and spars hung with nets and washing and drying fish; natter of fire-crackers speeding the day's devils or warning off those of the coming night, tinkle of music and singing, smell of food and wood-smoke and incense, water like a mullet's belly and sky like a dove's breast. At the harbour-mouth, by the old fort of St James-of-the-Bar, long lines of fishermen's junks homing on this haven and the protection of their patroness A-Ma, whose thousand-year-old temple they will pass on the way to their anchorages. Their headlights wink against the dark hills of China, just across the strait ...

Macau was always knee-deep in Japanese tourists. As I came down the hill from the Guia Fort, I used to see groups of them hissing nostalgically among the stunted pines and mossy stones in the obligatory Japanese-style garden outside the Japanese-style Matsuya Hotel.

Arranged in cadres identified by rosettes of different colours, they were chivvied about mercilessly by heart-breakingly jolly group-leaders with megaphones to their faces and flags of the same colour as the rosettes worn by their flock. And strained, automatic smiles.

The tourists enjoyed themselves with touching innocence, snuggling up laughingly for snapshots beside the unlaughing sentry on duty outside the Governor's wedding-cake little palace, laughingly photographing each other laughingly dragging each other around in pedicabs, laughingly cramming the goldsmiths' shops in the Avenida de Almeida Ribeiro: and at word from the man with the megaphone, laughingly quitting the sentry, leaving the shops, boarding the bus and queuing up for the hydrofoil, laughingly flocking to their group flags like the swallows to Capistrano.

In Macau and Hong Kong — of all places! — the gentlemen were talked of in hushed tones as instatiable flesh-hounds...

Typhoon! Several times during each monsoon season, the menacing black-ball final typhoon warning would go up on Penha Hill. Long before things reached that stage, however — the Macau fishermen knowing perhaps more than the Meteorological Bureau about typhoons — the entire fishing fleet out on the estuary would have begun to helter-skelter, under a cloud of diesel fumes even blacker and more menacing than the sky above them, for their haven in the old Inner Harbour.

There the great sea-going junks could ride it out, but not the sampans — literally 'three-boards'. At some juncture I was never able to pinpoint — perhaps when the scream of the wind reached a certain pitch — the entire sampan-village would throw itself into the community chore of dragging the little floating homes up the stone slipway onto the harbourside road. There they were snugged down in the shelter of the shops, literally tied to the ground by ropes thrown over their flimsy canopies and fastened on either side to big stones, baulks of timber, pegs driven into the tarmac — anything which looked as if it might prevent the whole shebang from becoming airborne and finishing up in some distant paddi in Kwantung Province. No panic, no crowding, but plenty of noise ... as always when more than two Chinese get together to do something.

Kids and dogs went wild with excitement; probably not so

much at the typhoon, which they all knew about, anyway, but at the prospect of living on land like other kids and dogs, if even for only a little while.

One stricken evening, in a driving slant of rain and a wind which flattened the flesh on my cheeks, I watched the operation. One of the hardest and noisiest of the workers was a plump, nut- brown, bare-footed, soaked-to-the-skin fish wife who must have been at least eight months, three weeks, six days and twenty- three hours pregnant. *One more heave like that*, I found myself thinking, *and she'll split like a ripe melon!* She was still at it, shouting and spitting and laughing, carting her wonderful great belly around, when I left after rubbernecking for nearly an hour...

In a junk-shop on the Rua do Mercadores I remember seeing a Junoesque Australian lady tourist — with her bearded, haversacked husband and all — who had gone native with her unfortunate baby spreadeagled in a gaudy embroidered Chinese-style sling across her broad back, like a poor little frog against a wall: and boy! what the crossed straps in front did for her impressive facade! And how the passing Chinese goggled and clucked...

I remember my astonishment at discovering that, in Macau, the humble pest-exterminator hides behind the trumpet-call of *Exterminar Radicalamente a Formiga Branca Por Meio de Contaminacao* and that a mere driving-school is an *Escola de Conducao de Vehiculos Automotives* ... I remember seeing a little girl sitting in a sampan beside the floating casino in the Inner Harbour, playing house by herself with some old dishes on an upturned box and a scraggy chicken and a chocolate-coloured dog for family, and a white plastic detergent bottle sleeping soundly in a sling across her skinny little shoulders, just like Mummy ... I remember the wild-looking, crop-headed visionary who at the same time, every day, squatted on the sea-wall of the Praia Grande to work his way fastidiously through a revolting meal of scraps he had gathered from somewhere. At times he would munch dreamily, at times he would unravel old cigarette butts into a tobacco tin, at times he would sit staring at the waves breaking among the rocks below his perch: but one evening as I passed, just at that grey-silk-and-rose-brocade time of day, he was smiling with the joyousness of a child, and singing to himself, softly, a little song about rice. *Fan, fan, fan,* he sang, as lightly and as happily as if he was once more sitting at dusk on the hillside above the village of his childhood, watching the slow buffalo plod home from the paddis.

Macau ... Macau ...!

On the day before I left for home, after nearly a year in Macau, I wandered again through the slums at the heart of the Old City. Quite by chance I took an alleyway I'd not noticed before, and after a couple of turns and twists found myself face-to-face with a Chinese funeral.

Before the entrance to a seething courtyard a coffin on a trestle was wreathed thickly in a haze of incense and cooking-smoke, and inevitably, in the pale-blue miasma of fire-crackers still snarling and spluttering to keep prowling devils from snatching the soul of whoever it was that lay in the box. Alongside it an enormously fat woman, balanced precariously on a tiny wooden stool, was methodically burning in a bronze urn the make-believe paper money the departed would need on his journey to wherever he was going. Beside her another woman, a meagre Buddhist nun about the size, the texture and the cordovan colour of a lacquered duck, was alternately telling her beads and beating a hollow piece of wood with a mallet. All about them, professional mourners in smocks and hoods of coarse, white linen and undyed hessian wailed broken-heartedly ... and just inside the courtyard, in the shelter of the wall, the similarly-clad swing-shift smoked and spat and gossiped and swilled tea as they waited to take their professional turn.

I walked into the courtyard. Beneath the scabby facades of what must have once been beautiful and substantial Portuguese homes, children of all ages swarmed, crawled, shouted and fought, chickens eked out a peck-by-peck living on their way to the pot, cats sneered at the world, dogs snarled and fornicated underfoot. Old men in knitted black skull-caps sat on folding campseats taking it all in, alongside them old ladies in the little black velvet toque of China's millennia, ornamented in the centre of the forehead band with a little jewel of jade — perhaps one of the traditional seven which in God's good time would serve to block the orifices of the owner's dead body. Odd-job-men and hawkers sauntered in and out of the courtyard, baskets across their shoulders, clanking their mournful brass bells and iron rods, and giving vent to the curlew-like cries which I'd already found out meant nothing translatable except that they were selling oranges, or collecting old iron, or mending pots. Itinerant fish and prawn sellers had set up shop at the kerbside to cash in on the funeral crowd, and right at my elbow a young woman with a cluster of children, quite obviously one-a-year for the past five years, was wheedling customers for her bowls of noodles garnished with pickled vegetables and sinister-looking cuts of unrecognisable animals taken from her forever-simmering pot.

Nobody seemed to be outraged that the ceremony of the funeral and the racial privacy of the courtyard had been invaded by one of the nauseating *pak-pei-ei*, the foreign white-skinned pigs. I had long ceased to wonder at this easy-seeming accommodation, and had long forgotten the doleful warnings of the Portuguese officials when I'd arrived at the beginning of the year.

I believed — I still believe — that during nearly half a millennium of Portuguese rule the Chinese of Macau had never been anything but citizens of China, that they were feeling at their toes the magical contact with the ball which for so long had been dribbled the length and breadth of their country by outsiders. They didn't have to manifest their feelings in action. If anything — in my experience — they had never departed from a curious, archaic, impersonal *Chinese* sort of courtesy. What they really felt, and what they could never really hide, was in their eyes, their gestures and their expressions ... the mahogany-hard dignity of people often ragged, often sustaining their faith on watery congee and hope, but indisputably in possession.

As I walked away from my last Macau courtyard, with the din and smoke of those thousand-year-old funeral rites insistent and arrogant in my ears and nostrils, I happened to raise my glance once more to the facades of the houses around it. From a window in one of them, like a bunch of rosy pomegranates, the faces of several Chinese children stared back at me. Directly below them, pegged into the crumbling green plaster of the wall, was one of the blue-and-white ceramic street-markers used by the Portuguese. In faded black letters it bore the legend *Pateo da Illusao.*

Balcony of Dreams...